An Independent Heart

Elizabeth Grant

An Independent Heart

A Novel

Bibliographic information published by the Deutsche Nationalbibliothek: The Deutsche Nationalbibliothek lists this publication in the Deutsche Nationalbibliografie; detailed bibliographic data is available on the Internet at http://dnb.ddb.de

Front cover: Sir Henry Raeburn,
Miss Eleanor Urquhart, *c. 1793, by courtesy of the National Gallery of Art, Washington*

Second, revised edition
© 2022 by the author / Elizabeth Grant
Herstellung und Verlag / Printing and publishing:
BoD – Books on Demand, Norderstedt
ISBN: 9783755748243

List of Characters

Captain Justin Francis Sumners, 95th Foot
    (formerly 15th Hussars)
Pepe Reyes, his batman
Stephen, his late brother
Lord Hawksfield, his father
Matthew (Turtle), Viscount Dallington, his cousin

Claire Lammond
Robert Lyster, her half-brother
Nicola Lyster, née Manvers, her sister-in-law
Alba, Stella, Persephone (Percy), Lucilla (Lucy), her
    sisters

The Earl and Countess of Boughton, Matthew's
    parents

Miss Quinnault, governess
Mrs Stodges, housekeeper
Bootle, butler
Hannah, lady's maid
Planchett, valet
Mr Baillie, factor
Mr Hughes, bailiff
Bob Grimes, groom

Mr Bouverie, Justice of the Peace
Mr Manvers, Nicola's father
Reverend Meynell, parish priest
Farmer Martin, freeholder
Dick Gurney, shepherd
Dr Hurd, physician

Mr Russ, government official

Chapter 1

... Time calls me to relate
My tedious travels and oft-varying fate.
Drayton, *Idea*

SNOW melted on the horses' necks and tangled their manes with glistening icicles. The roads were deserted. Justin waited for Pepe to range up beside him and put a gloved hand on his shoulder. "Not long now," he said in Spanish.

His own weariness and uncertainty stared back at him from Pepe's hollow eyes. Not long now. England felt as alien as the moon. Thinking of nursery tales, Justin began to laugh.

"Now what, Don Justín?" Most of Pepe's face was hidden by the muffler he had wrapped around his neck, but Justin could tell he was grinning.

"English children are told the moon is made of cheese," he explained.

Pepe observed that the food situation had certainly improved since landing, wherever they might be. "Although you did not order cheese for our dinner last night."

"No, and since we had mutton, we must be in England."

Snow turned to sleet when they reached the squalid outskirts of London. Fetlock-deep in slush, they pressed on to Downing Street to lodge the despatches Justin carried.

"And I thought Madrid was big. Or have you lost our way, Don Justín, and we're going around in circles?"

"Don't worry, Pepe, I happen to know this part of the moon rather well."

He had explored these streets with Stephen, but Stephen was dead. It seemed monstrous that the geography of London should be unaffected, yet so it was. Riding on blindly, he had brought them to Hawksfield House.

Golden seams of light in the windows told him that Lord Hawksfield was entertaining. The public rooms were ablaze with candles behind drawn curtains. As he looked up at the house, one of the windows was fully illumined for a moment. Someone must have lifted aside the curtain, dropping it again to shut out the light. A pale blot was visible behind the dark pane, a face, a ghostly figure – a young woman.

The world in which young women customarily wore light-coloured dresses still seemed a long way away. Yet in that world, young women did not customarily hide in window-seats, and this was the window of the library. Perhaps the card tables had been set up there, and she was recovering from her losses. Or Lord Hawksfield's entertainment was not up to much, and she was looking for a book to while away the boredom. From what he remembered of his father's entertainments, this was likely, although it did not explain her presence in the dark window.

"Is this your house, Don Justín?" Pepe asked in an awed voice. Justin shook his head and nudged his horse into a trot. That other world and its mysteries would have to wait; he would try Matthew's lodgings.

"Good evening, Porter. Is my cousin in?"

An uncertain recognition dawned in the porter's eye. "Viscount Dallington is not at home to visitors," he said slowly. "But I believe he would be at home to Captain Sumners," he ended on an interrogative note.

"I'm glad to hear it. Would there be a room in the garrets for my batman?" Justin indicated Pepe, who stood holding the horses.

"Certainly, Captain." More confident now, the porter added, "Do you go up, Captain, and if your servant is inclined to wait just a little, we will find someone to take your mounts to the livery stable, and see the young man housed."

"And fed, if you please."

"Indeed, Captain. Clothed, too, if you permit."

Justin grinned. "I only hope my cousin will do as much for me." A few quick words in Spanish explained the situation to Pepe. "You'll be alright?"

"Of course, Don Justín. And you." His eyes were grave but content, too. They embraced quickly.

The stairs were far too long. When he reached the landing, Justin did not knock but walked straight in, dropped his shako on a chair, crossed the sitting room, and pushed open the folding door to the bedchamber. He found his cousin seated at the dressing table, concentrating on the folds of his neckcloth. Dark-brown eyes very much resembling his own flew to his face; the pupils dilated for a moment, then the eyelids shuttered and a blasé expression overspread the heavy features.

"Good Lord, Justin, where have you sprung from," Matthew drawled, returning his attention to his dress. "Now see what you've made me do." He unwound the neckcloth and regarded the linen with a dissatisfied moue. "It's enough to make one weep."

The peevish tone did not deceive Justin. "Use it to wipe your eyes," he recommended. "So you're not at home, Turtle? Listen, my batman is being fed and housed by your porter, but I want dinner and a bed."

"Dinner! I'm just going out to dinner," Matthew observed. "How typical. Five years in Spain, seven months missing, and for your reappearance you choose the very day and hour that will most inconvenience me." He raised his eyeglass and only now seemed to notice how wet Justin was. "You

3

look terrible, and you're soaked. You'll catch your death, but then I thought you were dead already." Although his voice was indifferent, Matthew's eyes were unnaturally bright.

"I very nearly was," Justin said gently. He came to Matthew's side and slid a hand along his jaw, forcing him to meet his gaze. With a sudden movement, his cousin flung his arms around him and buried his face in the front of his jacket.

"Hey, Turtle," Justin murmured, patting the broad back.

After some minutes, Matthew sat up on an indrawn breath that sounded suspiciously like a sob. "I'll thank you to remember that I'm not a horse," he complained.

"Oh, I do. You don't smell right." Pulling him into the sitting room, Justin found the lacquer tray with decanters and glasses his cousin kept on the sideboard. "Here, have some brandy." He poured two stiff tots. "Sorry to burst in on you like this. We should have gone to an inn. You can hand me to your valet, however, and go and meet your social duties."

Matthew quaffed his drink and set down the glass. "Social duties be damned," he said loftily. "No inn would admit you, either, looking like a tramp. It's a good thing you didn't try Hawksfield House."

"Lord Hawksfield is entertaining; we passed by the house."

"The dinner party I'm meant to attend." With a twisted grin, Matthew added, "At least I'll no longer have to listen to your father animadverting on your dilatoriness, now that you're back. The possibility that you might have been killed doesn't even occur to him. He puts it all down to filial disobedience."

"Why is he so keen on having such a disobedient *filius* back, then?" The only reply to this flippant question was a quick, searching look, so he did not follow it up.

Besides, it all seemed very far away, indifferent, blurred, and shapeless behind curtains of snow – sleet – rain. The silk-hung walls of the familiar room receded, Matthew's bulky figure faded; he was back on a storm-swept hillside, fighting the temptation to creep into the undergrowth and sleep. But he could afford to be weak now. Drawing his greatcoat more closely around him, he sat down heavily on the leather-bound fender and leaned his head in his hands.

"Justin!" At Matthew's horrified exclamation, he pulled himself together, looked up into his cousin's pale, shocked face, and managed a smile. Perhaps it was not the time for weakness after all.

"Sorry. I shouldn't have had that brandy on an empty stomach."

"It shan't remain empty much longer." Shouting for his valet, Matthew issued a flood of instructions. "Now take off those rags," he told Justin. "I'll find you a towel." He strode into his bedchamber.

In front of the fire, Justin let the wet greatcoat slide from his shoulders and stripped off his green-brown uniform jacket, vaguely inspecting the arrangement of knickknacks on the mantelshelf as he undid the buttons. Incongruous among the Dresden shepherdesses was a sketch of his brother by his own hand. *Stephen*. He had done it just before embarking; the drawing caught the moment's wild, effervescent mood. A scrap of printed paper was stuck in the frame. He looked more closely: it was a page from the London Gazette from June 9 to June 15, 1813, which listed among the missing of the general staff one Captain Justin Francis Sumners, 95th Foot.

There was a lump in his throat that had nothing to do with the cold and wet. He dropped his jacket on the floor, considered his shirt for a moment and drew it over his head. Sitting on the fender, he pulled off his boots, the heat warming his back. But in the warmth, his breeches had begun to exude a distinct smell of horse, so he took them off, too, as well as everything else, before he followed his cousin. "Have you some water in that jug? I need a wash. Clean linen, too."

Matthew looked over his shoulder. "Good Lord, Justin," he remarked on a subtly different note of consternation.

Justin had to laugh. "You already said that, Turtle, and that I look terrible, I thank you." He peered into the jug and poured some water into the washbasin. "But at least I've got all my limbs, and you'll notice that all scars are honourably in the front, except for the ones in the back."

Silence; no laughter. While Justin contended with soap and water, the valet brought another jug, warm this time, and offered to pour its contents over his head. Justin leaned over the basin. "That's good. Towel, Turtle!" The soft linen smelled fresh and clean. By the time he tossed it aside, a damp ball now, even his ears were glowing. He ran a hand over his chin. "Ought I to shave?"

"You'll do for tonight." Matthew cleared his throat. "You ought to put some clothes on, however." He met Justin's quizzical look with an angry stare, but when Justin finally tucked in the ends of the borrowed shirt, his cousin picked up his own dressing gown, a voluminous affair of red brocade, and draped it tenderly around his shoulders.

"How splendid. Thank you, Turtle. It's a shame we're not of the same size as well as the same colouring."

"What do you mean, the same colouring?" Matthew said repressively. "I declare you're going white, and you four years my junior."

On a surge of fondness, Justin replied, "Remember how angry Stephen was when you teased him about his first white hairs?"

"Don't I just. He dyed his in the end, did you know? Dyeing, Egypt, dyeing." Matthew threw this out like a good thing at the club, but when Justin caught his eye his gaze fell. "I'm sorry. By God, I've missed you."

"I'm glad you said that, or I might not have noticed." Justin grinned up at his cousin.

Taking him by the neck, Matthew led him into the sitting room. "I hate you, Justin."

"I'm glad you said that, or – *¡Anda la osa!*"

Dishes had appeared on the table, silver and crystal sparkled in the warm glow of candles, and two filled goblets cast red pools of light onto the white damask hanging almost to the floor. The clothes Justin had dropped by the fire had vanished.

"Your batman is partaking of a light dinner in my quarters, Captain," the valet was saying. "Accommodation for him is being prepared in the garrets, and your own wardrobe will be seen to, in course."

"Come and eat," Matthew interrupted. "Not that it's anything but a paltry repast."

"Serves me right for arriving unannounced and uninvited." Justin grinned inwardly at his cousin's idea of misery. Although he ate hungrily, he soon capitulated – the food was too rich, too plentiful – and began to speculate why Lord Hawksfield had wanted him back so urgently. "You say he wasn't worried about me getting killed, and I well believe it, so it can't be concern for the family's perpetuity."

Matthew spared him no attention, concentrating on a cold boiled knuckle of veal, so Justin amused himself by advancing several theories of his own, one more absurd than the other.

"But probably this is all rot and there's no reason at all," he concluded. "I'll just have to trust in providence, as the guerrilla do; or if the outcome is not happy, they call it *el destino*, fate." He refilled his cousin's glass. "Is anything the matter, Turtle?"

Matthew looked down his nose. "Well, you are talking a lot of rot, and it's a dashed bore." He sipped his wine in silence while the covers were removed and a bowl of walnuts set before him.

Collecting his glass, Justin walked around the table, cuffed Matthew's head in passing, and made himself comfortable on the fender. "Toss me some nuts, will you?"

Matthew handed him the bowl. "It's not so much a question of perpetuity as of predominance. You'll sell out, get married, and secure the family a highly favourable connexion; several, in fact. What you need to do first, however, is do something about your appearance. You need a valet and a new coat."

It was a masterpiece of evasion. Lord Hawksfield could not have done better, although his failures to explain himself stemmed from his belief that no explanations were necessary: whatever he said or requested must be right. Justin cracked two nuts in his hands. To his own surprise, he found himself near laughter. Five years was a great distance. "Am I to marry several girls, then?"

His cousin had turned from the table and its bright candles towards the fire. In its flickering light, it was difficult to read his face, but there was an unexpected hilarity in his voice when he replied, "In a way."

Justin handed Matthew the two perfect halves of a nut and threw the shells into the fire. "Perhaps you should marry one of them yourself."

"I couldn't do that," Matthew said heavily.

Justin let the silence hang, wondering if his cousin meant to tell him more or was regretting that he had said this much. "I'm sorry, Turtle," he said at last. He rose to perch on the edge of the table and put his hand on Matthew's shoulder. "You haven't grown out of it?"

"It doesn't seem to work like that." Matthew hunched his shoulder and laid his cheek against the back of Justin's hand in what was surely an involuntary gesture. "I'm not the only fellow afflicted in that way." Then he raised his head and added with a spurt of anger, "You needn't look like that. Of course it's all purely Platonic. No one knows but you. And you should know better than to keep fondling me, damn you!"

Justin did not argue. "I'll keep my caresses for those who want them, then. It's to be hoped the future Mrs Sumners does, 'whoever she be, that not impossible she, that shall command my heart and me'."

"I'll thank you not to speak of her in that style."

"No, I'll raise my glass to her instead," Justin said. "To Mrs Justin Sumners."

They drank. "Damn you, Justin," Matthew said after a while, "Why do I invariably tell you things that I'd rather keep to myself?"

~ ~ ~

Matthew's shell was so easily cracked, if only you knew where to knock. Justin lay staring into the dying fire, sleepless despite his bone-deep fatigue, despite the softly cushioned sofa and his cousin's comfortable snores penetrating through the folding doors. In time, he would know all there was to know, and without wounding Matthew.

Pepe woke immediately when Justin slipped into his room up in the attics, or perhaps he had not slept, either. "What's wrong?" Pepe asked in Spanish.

"Nothing," Justin replied in the same language. "Are you alright?"

"I'm warm, dry, full, and could be asleep if it weren't for you," Pepe claimed outrageously, then added with a lopsided smile that being safe took some getting used to. "I keep waking up, wondering where I am and worse, where you are, Don Justín. However," he said when Justin punched him lightly in the arm, "I can see I need not worry." Fingering the thick brocade swathed around Justin's shoulders, he concluded, "A life of luxury awaits us." He lay back on his folded arms and gazed starry-eyed into space. "A nobleman's personal groom! I wish Mama and Uncle Chicho and Cousin Domingo could see me now."

"Perhaps they can, Pepe." Justin sat down on the edge of the bed and tucked his feet under Pepe's blanket. After a moment he said, "I'm to be married."

"Certainly you are, Don Justín." Pepe beamed upon him. "It's high time you were. You have explained it to me. You are no longer a mere younger son. One day, you will be the head of your family. You are important now to your father." Justin could not recall explaining matters quite in this way, but Pepe continued, "Do not worry. Your family will find you a suitable girl from a family with which an alliance will benefit your family." He nodded enthusiastically.

Justin nudged him with his bare toes. "That's about it. It seems they've already found a girl."

"You do not like an arranged marriage," Pepe summed up his feelings for him. "Well, the family is more important than the feelings of its members." He yawned cavernously. "Go to bed, Don Justín."

As he climbed back under the still-warm covers, Justin thought of a bed warm and soft with a woman's body, a bed he had shared; another bed, which he had not shared, rejecting the invitation of its owner although he loved her for her courage; a bit of straw on hard ground and his greatcoat and a woman who knew what she wanted and what she was about, a comrade in the day and a companion at night – a form of companionship Matthew might never know. He pummelled his pillow as though it were in some way responsible for his cousin's predicament. It was hard to tell what was worse – apart from the dynastic difficulties it would eventually cause – Matthew's inability to feel passion for women, or his being condemned to live a life without passion.

A girl who agreed to an arranged marriage should know what she was about. A companion, a helpmate – the homely word made him smile.

Chapter 2

And seek elsewhere, in turning other books,
Which better may her labour satisfy.
Drayton, *Idea*

THE curtained recess seemed suspended between inside and outside. Inside, all was light and warmth; outside, darkness and howling wind. Claire let the curtain drop behind her. As her eyes adjusted, she was able to make out the street beyond the window, but when two figures emerged from the greyness, she wondered whether her eyes really had adjusted. Huddled in dark greatcoats, one with a stovepipe shako, the other wearing a foraging cap, they could have ridden straight out of the image that Lord Hawksfield's speculations on the whereabouts of his son had conjured up in her mind, of a lone horseman making his way through wild and wintry mountains.

Except that here were two horsemen. They had reined in to gaze up at the house, sleet melting into their greatcoats. With mounting curiosity, she watched them exchange a few words, then the foremost of the two nudged his horse into a trot, and a moment later they had disappeared into the thick night. The cold glass panes rattled in the wind. Hugging her shawl around her shoulders, Claire ducked back through the heavy, musty curtains.

"If that was you, why did you not stop?" The portrait above the mantelpiece was unresponsive, however, unless that half-smile was an answer. Yet there was no saying whether Captain Sumners really looked like that; the lurking amusement might be no more than conventional, devised by the artist to illustrate the two brothers' different roles, with the younger one a foil to the elder and heir. By all she had heard, the accident that had killed the Honourable Stephen Sumners had been the result of a very silly wager.

Even it if was only a device, it made an engaging contrast: the older brother in evening dress, dark and haughty, the younger resplendent in his Hussar uniform, each setting the other off in a way that belied their strong resemblance to each other and to his lordship. One of Lord Hawksfield's griefs was that Captain Sumners had exchanged from the Hussars to the Riflemen. Meeting the captain's painted glance, she said, "Perhaps you will be able to tell me why, one day."

But she had come here to find something to read, not to commune with illusory figures. Claire turned her back on the portrait and gathered up her skirts to step across the carpet. It was badly in want of beating, although it seemed to have been swept not long ago: the brush had made a streaky pattern in its pile. The books were covered by a thin layer of dust, although the edges of the shelves must have been wiped quite recently; they were clean enough.

Claire stood on tiptoe to read the gold-tooled titles and lifted down an ancient folio of Drayton's works. When she laid it on the table, its pages fell open at familiar lines, but as she leafed through it, she discovered poems new and unknown to her:

Love in a humour played the prodigal
And bade my Senses to a solemn feast . . .

She skimmed the next few lines, then read:

And at the banquet in his drunkenness
Slew his dear friend, my Independent Heart.
A gentle warning, friends, thus may you see
What 'tis to keep a drunkard company.

All the breath left her body. Deliberately, she inhaled, closed the book, and slid it back into its place. She had not thought these fanciful sonnets might come so close to home. This must be a more extensive edition than Grandmama's.

Anyhow, it was too heavy and too valuable to borrow. Claire moved on to a shelf with more modern productions. A well-worn copy of *Marmion* – just the thing. Besides, she had better make her choice and return to the drawing room before the last guests arrived.

Slipping inside, she stopped to get her bearings. A small family party, Lord Hawksfield had said, but there were at least twenty people assembled. All the same, it boded well for Robert that he and Nicola and she had been invited. Lord Hawksfield's concept of family must be a generous one if he included his country neighbour's son-in-law, daughter, and son-in-law's sister in such a gathering – or was she better described as his neighbour's daughter's sister-in-law, or his neighbour's daughter's husband's sister?

His lordship's own sister was playing hostess for him. Lady Boughton appeared to be moving casually around the room, welcoming and chatting, but Claire recognized the ritual pattern and admired her skill. Seemingly without effort, she paired off the guests in the correct order of rank. There was something rather satisfying in watching the colourful symmetry alter and form before the light-green walls of the drawing room. Dressed in a violet velvet robe over a white satin slip, Lady Boughton looked very much in place. Now she approached Robert and Nicola, made a remark, and left them laughing.

"A good evening to you." The deep, quiet voice belonged to a tall, large gentleman who must have been watching her ever since she entered the room.

"Forgive my informality," he said. "Do I have the honour of addressing Miss Lammond?" There was a tinge of irony in his voice, and indeed he was so much older than she, and – if he was who she thought he was – of so much higher rank that he could be as informal as he chose. "I'm Boughton," he added.

"I thought you might be." She curtsied. "How do you do, Lord Boughton?"

"Yes," he replied somewhat obscurely, his gaze still upon her. "Dallington told me you had the dark hair, fair complexion, and light eyes of the Celt. But my son said nothing of that lovely, secret smile. Or of the light in those light eyes," he added as she looked up at him in astonishment. "Now what were you smiling at, I wonder?"

She had been appreciating his lady's style and skill as a hostess, but she could hardly tell him that. She swallowed. "I was reflecting upon kinship, my lord, and how limited our vocabulary is."

"Ah." He glanced meaningfully around the room. "In view of the importance we attach even to its remoter forms, it is indeed striking that we have no words for them." Turning over the book in her hand he added, "Walter Scott, eh? Homesick, Miss Lammond?"

She shook her head. "I still find it hard to believe that I am away at all," she said. "And with my brother, and he grown up and married. But I miss my sisters."

Lord Boughton had murmured a corrective "half-brother" as she spoke, but now he said, "Very proper." His next remarks showed his knowledge of her family to extend well into its remoter reaches, too. After the first shock of surprise, Claire told herself that it was only natural. Lord Boughton must be acquainted with all her grander neighbours in Scotland; probably he was related to them. She suppressed a smile. If he had discussed Robert's merits with them, that was an excellent sign.

"So you see, merit also comes into it," Lord Boughton concluded, as if reading her thoughts. "But returning to kinship, we appear to be suffering from a certain lack in the younger generation, judging by the harassed look of my lady." He bowed slightly to his wife as she joined them.

"I'm afraid we'll have to give him up," she told him. And to Claire she added, "You have good cause to look anxious, Miss Lammond. Our silly son has excused himself for tonight, when I was counting on him to escort you to table."

Again Lord Boughton bowed. "May I not have the honour – the very great pleasure?"

"Don't be idiotic," his lady snapped. "You know perfectly well –"

"Ah, I do." He heaved a sigh. "Rank is a great burden, Miss Lammond."

"My heart bleeds for you, Lord Boughton."

His smile was curiously sweet and introspective. "You may laugh at me now, Miss Lammond, but you will learn soon enough." Breaking in on Lady Boughton, who had been murmuring names and shaking her head, he said, "No, my dear. Let your brother take Miss Lammond in."

Her ladyship frowned. "But it will look so very particular!"

"All the better," Lord Boughton replied firmly.

Things did bode well. Claire followed Lady Boughton to where Lord Hawksfield stood chatting to Robert and Nicola.

"Delighted," his lordship said when informed of his duty, and judging by their smiles, Robert and Nicola were equally content. "You have found a book, Miss Lammond? I declare you know your way around those shelves better than I do."

This might well be true. "Thank you, my lord. May I borrow this?" Claire displayed her find.

"That must be one of Captain Sumners's." Lord Hawksfield's expression darkened when he added, half under his breath, "Always has his nose in a book, his head in the clouds."

"My sister, in contrast, has both her feet firmly on the ground," Robert said. "Despite her choice of reading material. Are you intending to corrupt my wife, Claire?"

His lordship recollected himself, beaming genially once more. "And very pretty feet they are, too. Excuse me one moment; Lady Boughton is signalling to me."

"That colour suits you." Robert's eyes twinkled; he was not referring to the pale azure of her gown. "You're blushing to the very toes of those pretty feet of yours. Aren't you pleased to be approved from literate head down to rosy heels?" His gaze narrowed suddenly. "What's the matter?"

"Need you ask, Robert?" Nicola touched a cool hand against Claire's heated cheek. "She's embarrassed! Claire is not used to this sort of badinage, are you, Claire? You must not mind his lordship; it is just his way. Though your feet are very pretty," she added loyally.

"Thank you." Claire slid her arm around Nicola's waist. "From the only person present who has in fact seen my feet, that is indeed a tribute."

"I've seen your feet," Robert protested. "Red and dirty is what they were, but I presume they'll have improved with age, like the rest of you."

Claire shook her head at him. "With regard to cleanliness I have improved, that much is true. Nothing is the matter, really." With a slight laugh she added, "I've had a vision."

He grinned. "As hungry as that? Poor little country mouse. But it won't be much longer before his lordship will guide those pretty feet of yours towards the dining room."

After all these years, Robert still knew her better than anyone. If he turned her remark off as a joke, it was because he understood that she did not wish to say more.

And also because Nicola's wide blue gaze was an invitation to tease. "Didn't you know that Claire has the Sight, like the Highland witches you enjoy reading about?" Laughing at her, he continued, "But come, her prophecies will have to wait. Here is Lord Hawksfield to claim her, as I prophesied, and thankfully you are still bride enough for your husband to squire you to table." He drew her hand under his elbow. As they moved off, he bent to hear some remark she was making. Their fair heads close together, they made a pretty picture.

"It ought to be my son taking you in to dinner, naturally," Lord Hawksfield said. "I really cannot imagine where he is all this time. And now his cousin has absconded! This must give you a very odd notion of our family, but I promise you, Miss Lammond . . ."

It might have given her an odd notion of his lordship, if she had not thought him rather a selfish man as it was. His confidences were not a mark of esteem for her, but of the importance he attached to his own affairs, unable to conceive that they might not be of general interest – or that his son might not relish having them discussed so freely. At least her vision had dispelled the image of a solitary army captain struggling across the Pyrenees. For in contrast to his lordship, she was very well able to imagine where his son might be all this time.

But there had been two horsemen. "Please do not distress yourself, my lord," she said spontaneously. "His batman will be with him. He may be nearer than you think."

Taking his seat next to her, he bent his handsome dark eyes upon her. "I am certain that if he knew with what charming solicitude he is awaited at home, he would have been here long ago."

It was to be hoped that she would get used to his lordship's way, or she would spend her time in London in one continuous blush. While his practised flattery did not seem to indicate any great concern over the thousand possible misadventures that could have overtaken Captain Sumners, it might just as well serve to conceal such concern. Perhaps she was doing Lord Hawksfield an injustice; perhaps he kept his deeper worries to himself. That he had tucked the portrait of his sons away in a room he never used was not necessarily a sign of callousness. "You must be very worried," she said.

"Indeed I am," his lordship agreed. "It makes things so awkward. But Justin always was a selfish, thoughtless boy."

Perhaps not. "Now that Lord Wellington is advancing into France –"

"Yes, with the war as good as over, there is no longer any excuse for him to shirk his duties."

He was referring to his son, of course, not to Lord Wellington. While he talked on, hugging his grievance between spoonfuls of rather tepid soup, Claire's mind returned to the two horsemen. Had they been a vision, were they not Captain Sumners and his batman, they were a symbol of all the soldiers who might soon be coming home. How many would return sound in body and soul? What would peace bring for them all? Snatches of conversation floated along the table, mingling with her own thoughts and Lord Hawksfield's complaints. War formed the main topic – war and the weather.

Neither of these could explain the roguish wink Nicola gave her across the table. The explanation came in an excited whisper when the ladies retired.

"They say the Thames has frozen over." With a rustle of silks and a waft of perfume, she drew close. "And I mean Robert to take us. Shouldn't you adore to see it?"

Chapter 3

Our flood's-queen, Thames,
for ships and swans is crowned . . .
Drayton, *Idea*

NICOLA'S shriek of delight was carried away by an icy gust whipping across the river as they looked down from Blackfriars Bridge. Clinging to Robert's arm, she exclaimed how sublime it was, and how sweetly kind of him to take them there.

The embrasure in the parapet provided a fine vantage point. Claire hugged her muff to herself and buried her chin in its fur. The bridge's gentle curve seemed to stretch endlessly away into a view that was bizarre rather than sublime. In her mind she had pictured a smooth surface of ice, like Duddingston Loch, but what she saw was a crazy landscape of broken floes and jagged slabs heaped one upon another and against the bridge's pillars.

Beneath the tall white sky, the horizon seemed wide and open, the closeness of town falling away. Slowly they walked across to the Surrey side. With something of a flourish, Robert disbursed the thruppence the waterman demanded and ushered Nicola and herself onto the ice.

Strewn ashes marked the path and provided firm footing. Yet for all that Robert pointed out how thick the edges of the piled ice-cliffs were, it was uncanny walking between them, knowing that there was a vast river flowing steadily underneath.

"Don't be scared, Claire," Nicola cried. "Our weight can hardly matter, compared to all this."

It was a full-grown fair. From the bridge it had seemed small, seen from above against the great expanse of sky, river, and town. But within the maze of tents and booths, the bustle and colour were enthralling.

The noise was terrific. What sounded like an enormous rusty gate turned out to be the whooping passengers of a boat-like swing. Fiddles skirled, drums pulsated, boots stomped on the deck of a barge pressed into service as a dance floor. An open fire crackled and roared. Over her shoulder, she saw that a whole sheep was being roasted there, with a large placard advertising Lapland Mutton. Robert gave a wide berth to the entrance of Barley Barge, but drew her attention to a decent-looking place named Father Frost's Coffee-Tent.

Drawing a deep breath, she said, "It's a shame you're not a member of parliament yet, Robert. I think my next letter home will be rather long."

He grinned. "Enjoying yourself? I'm sure Lord Hawksfield will be happy to frank your letter. But perhaps you'll find a picture over there, to spare you the trouble of describing it all in words." With his chin he gestured towards a printing press that became visible when the crowd thinned momentarily. "Will we have a look?"

Broadsheets, booklets, brochures, pamphlets – the diversity was incredible, the quality poor in every way: cheap paper, cheap ink, cheap rhymes. A title set in an almost illegible variety of type caught Claire's eye. "A collection of FROSTIANA, or a History of the River Thames in a Frozen State, with an Account of the Late Severe Frost and the wonderful effects of Frost, Snow, Ice and Cold in England, and in different parts of the world, interspersed with amusing anecdotes, to which is added The Art of Skating, all printed and published on the ICE on the River Thames," she read, picking up the booklet. "Can you believe it?"

"No," Robert said succinctly, while Nicola cried, "Does it have pictures?"

"More than that, the captions rhyme. Listen to this:

Behold the River Thames is frozen o'er,
Which lately ships of mighty burden bore;
Now different arts and past times you see,
But printing claims the superiority."

"Only mangle the words enough and you can call it poetry." Robert shook his head. "You'll not buy it?"

"Of course I will. This is just the thing for the girls."

Under his quizzical gaze, Claire made a selection of four different works. When she inquired the price, she was directed to the other side of the press where, apparently, the cashier might be found. "I won't be long," she told Robert.

"Could you wrap them, please?" Adding another farthing, she handed a few coins across the table, saw her purchases wrapped in rough paper, and tucked the parcel and her purse into her muff.

Her brother and sister-in-law were nowhere to be seen. The crowd was dense, colourful and varied. A ragged child, a dandified shop assistant; that very superior being must be a parlourmaid, those young fellows would be apothecary's apprentices. At the edge of her vision, a Rifleman's stovepipe shako moved into ken. Startled, she turned her head.

His handsome dark eyes expressed as much astonishment as her own probably did. For a moment, they stared at each other, then he bowed, doffing his battered shako to reveal a mop of black hair. "Excuse me, ma'am." He extended his hand; he was holding out her purse. "May I restore your property?" His voice was low and husky, as though he were modulating the tone of command to conversational pitch.

Bereft of speech, she took her purse, half-formed questions jostling in her brain. His gaze held more warmth, his aquiline countenance was thinner, the moustache had gone, and there was a frosting of premature white at his temples, yet the resemblance was striking. And that coat certainly was a Rifle officer's greatcoat. Could it be possible?

A mischievous grin – uncannily familiar – was dawning on his face, and no wonder, she stood there like a gowk. Compressing her lips, she drew a slow breath. Then she said, "I beg your pardon, Captain, for staring. I thought I had seen you before. How on earth did you get hold of my purse?"

"Picked a pickpocket's pocket." He chuckled. "And I believe I was staring, too, although I'm certain that I've never seen you before. 'Blind were mine eyes till they were seen of thine.'"

If she recognized the quotation, it was because the Drayton folio had fallen open at that page when she took it down from its shelf last night.

"May I also restore you to your companions, ma'am?" There was no mischief now in the Rifleman's voice, which was both deprecatory and regretful. Mistaking her hesitance, he added, "Notwithstanding appearances, I am quite respectable," and with a sudden grin, "even if I am trying to force an introduction."

Laughter bubbled up inside her, but she choked it down, replying with barely a tremor in her voice. "Judging by appearances, you are a captain in the Riflemen, and that should vouch for a modicum of respectability. Will you be able to find my brother in this crush?" Taking the arm he offered, she fell into step beside him. His cool assumption that people would make way for their passage turned out to be entirely justified; some even touched their caps. His assurance was agreeable when one happened to be ranged at his side, but possibly extremely galling when one wasn't. "Do you know, I believe I could almost put a name to you, beyond your regiment."

"We can't have met before. I would never forget a face like yours." His voice was so serious that she looked up in surprise.

"Why, what's wrong with my face?"

"Nothing. That's what makes it unforgettable." Matter-of-factly he continued, "But it's not just your face. You have a great deal of poise, too."

"I wish it were sufficient to carry me through this conversation! You are as bad as your father."

"What, is he, too, incurably honest?"

"He, too, indulges in shameless flattery."

"Then you must have mistaken my identity, after all. Sir," he accosted Robert. "May I return this lady to your care?"

"I told you we should not have let her go alone!" Nicola drew Claire to her side.

"Nonsense, my dear, Claire is perfectly able to look after herself." Robert cast a curious glance at her companion. "There has been no unpleasantness, I trust?" What a man of the world Robert was: his question was perfectly non-committal, leaving open whether the Rifleman was to be treated as a rogue or a rescuer.

Claire gave Nicola's hand a reassuring squeeze. "On the contrary, brother, I have been saved from penury."

"Have you, by Jove!" Robert bowed. "May we not know to whom my sister is obliged?"

Again the Rifleman doffed his shako, casting Claire an I-told-you-so glance. "Captain Sumners, at your service."

Claire swallowed a hiccup of laughter. The captain, in turn, showed no such restraint, and laughed out loud when Robert performed the introductions.

~ ~ ~

If Robert Lyster felt any awkwardness in the situation, he did not show it. He certainly had sufficient aplomb for a politician, and Justin readily took his cue when he suggested a cup of something hot for the ladies.

"My cousin is holding a table over there." With a nod of his head, Justin indicated Father Frost's Coffee-Tent. "Unless you object to a public place?"

"A coffeehouse should be respectable enough. Besides, my wife is pining for adventure." Lyster smiled down at the fair girl hanging on his arm. "You won't mind, will you, my dear? With the combined protection of a lawyer and a soldier, I am sure you may dare it."

"Papa would have a fit," Mrs Lyster exclaimed, but it was with a very pretty gravity that she relinquished Miss Lammond's hand. "You have proved yourself worthy enough, Captain Sumners, by returning our sister to us. Pray continue your good care of her."

"Thank you, I will."

Miss Lammond did not immediately turn to follow her brother. In the wintry blue dusk, her light-grey eyes were translucent, absorbing the ephemeral world around her. For a moment – for a small eternity she stood in the shelter Justin's body afforded her. An elbow struck him in the back, someone jostled against his side, but he made no move to hurry her, and instead followed her gaze across the icy expanse. Here at least his view was not cut off by walls. During hours of consultation – at Hawksfield House, at the Foreign Office, at the War Office – he had felt trapped in the close, discreet rooms.

The sun had dipped below the horizon. Flambeaux being lit there and there gave the scene something of an encampment of soldiers at dusk, with campfires glowing yellow against a darkening sky.

"Captain Sumners . . ." She was no longer looking at the scenery but at him. When younger he had often regretted lacking Matthew's impressive height, but now her eyes were only a little below the level of his, her lips well within reach. If he had laughed on hearing who she was, that was the sudden lifting of the regret he had felt only minutes earlier, that he should meet a girl like this on the very day he had learned of his father's plans. Wouldn't Lord Hawksfield be surprised to find him suddenly so compliant!

"Miss Lammond?"

"I am afraid Robert was sadly remiss," she said, hesitating. After a moment she added, very gently, "Please allow me to express our condolences for your recent loss."

The sudden searing pain abated with the pressure of her fingers on his arm. As though she might vanish with the rising of the moon, he tucked her hand more securely in his elbow before he replied. "Recent? I would have thought London had forgotten all about my brother by this time."

"Perhaps London has, but then London has had time to adjust to the knowledge, and you have not. Nor has London lost a brother." After a slight pause, she added, "I hope you do not think me intrusive."

"I think you preternaturally perspicacious."

She shook her head. "I have a brother, and four sisters." An unexpected smile lit up her features. "Our Percy is fascinated with the Riflemen's Corps, that is how I know the uniform. Was it you riding past Hawksfield House last night?"

He lifted aside the flap of the tent. "It was you standing in the window? You who left the Drayton folio open on the library table? Was that why you said you had seen me before, because of the portrait there above the mantelpiece?"

"I wasn't certain." With a direct look she added, "You have changed, but you have a great deal of your father, too. Thank you." She walked past him, leaving him intrigued and somewhat shaken.

Comfortable heat emanated from a cast-iron stove set upon the icy ground, which, apart from a safe radius around the fire, was spread with straw. Its scent, combined with the odour of wet sheep exuded by damp woollen coats, gave the place a rural atmosphere that was strangely at odds with the character of a coffeehouse.

At the best table, Matthew was welcoming the Lysters. Between bowing to Miss Lammond and setting a chair for her, he managed to give Justin an inquisitive stare, at the same time keeping up his conversation with Lyster. "It's quite safe," he said. "My cousin's man inspected the staff and kitchen before letting me taste anything. I must say, Justin, you have trained him well."

"Pepe didn't need training; he's naturally cir-cumspect." In Matthew's ear he added, "You were right, Turtle. I'd happily marry any number of her." His cousin poked him viciously in the ribs while divesting him of his greatcoat, but before he could do more by way of retribution, Pepe came over from the counter to ask for orders.

"Is he a Spaniard?" Mrs Lyster's voice rose to an excited chirp. "Does he address you by your Christian name?"

"My batman, Pepe Reyes. I owe him much." His hand on the lad's shoulder, he felt him straighten as he faced the strangers. Then he added, "He calls me Don Justín. 'Don' is a Spanish honorific, a title of respect, used with one's Christian name."

"That's why we call 'em the dons," Lyster drawled. "Although not as a mark of respect."

Pepe bowed with dignity when Miss Lammond gave him a nod and a smile, but he did not omit to inform Justin, in an undertone, that it would not do to introduce his servant. "Don't be silly, Pepe," Justin said, lapsing into Spanish once more. "This is the girl I'm going to marry; you have to be introduced to her."

Pepe's eyes widened. "*Felicidades*," he said. Then he moved away to collect a tray of steaming cups at the counter.

"Is it to him that you owe your proficiency in dealing with pickpockets, too? I never even noticed that my money had gone. Did I thank you at all, in my surprise? And how did you know I was with my brother and sister?"

He met her gaze but found no words to reply. Nor was it necessary; the others had plenty to say.

"What's this about pickpockets?" Mrs Lyster cried. "What happened? Claire, you have had an adventure!"

"It sounds more like a misadventure," Matthew commented. "Sugar, Mrs Lyster? Miss Lammond?"

In the brief exchange of please and thank you, Justin recovered his wits. "Miss Lammond nearly lost her fortune to a scrawny rascal," he explained. "But it's no wonder you did not notice him, Miss Lammond. These children are trained to their trade."

"But I did!" Her delicate eyebrows sprang together. "I saw a ragged little boy and felt sorry for him. Do you mean to say that he stole my purse?"

"And you saw it, and caught him?" Mrs Lyster leaned forward eagerly.

Lyster had given a great, loud laugh, but now he asked, "Why did you not call the Watch?"

Justin shrugged. "To have that infant transported to Botany Bay? He'll be lucky to survive the winter as it is. I understand the cost of fuel has risen quite steeply."

"You are a philanthropist." Lyster's inflection was that of a professional confronting an idealist. But if he thought he had got Justin's measure, he would find himself mistaken; Spain was no breeding ground for idealists.

"Not at all. I'm sure my opinion of mankind is quite as low as yours." As Lyster drew affronted breath, Justin added peaceably, "But I feel the cold like any man, and like any man appreciate the luxury of flannel and fur."

"I wonder how many of those who enjoy that luxury consider it a luxury?" Miss Lammond said quietly.

Lyster's expression softened. "Not a philanthropist, then, but a philosopher, like my sister." He turned to Matthew. "Is there anything more disarming than the discovery that one's young relation is cleverer and wiser than one's self?"

Justin found himself warming to the man as he talked fondly and amusingly about his sister. She, in turn, appeared quite divorced from his discourse, looking around as if to record every detail – for her sisters, perhaps, wherever they might be at this moment. Lord Hawksfield had mentioned an estate somewhere in the north. That was what made her an heiress, too; the land was entirely her own, and indeed, she looked to be very much her own woman.

Suddenly Justin was weary to the bone. The tent was crowded, the air thick with the fumes of people, the red-hot stove. The conversation dissolved into a meaningless babble, the faces all around merged to form a vague, shifting mass. One set of features alone remained clear and distinct, grey eyes under fine black brows, the still centre of this spinning world.

"You are tired." Her words dropped like three pebbles into his fatigue.

Justin shook his head, not to disagree but to dispel the weary mists. "Forgive me. Why is it so exhausting to sit around and talk? Not here, not with you," he added with a grin, "I mean this morning. And there will be more later, although they call it dining."

"How strange all this must seem to you, return-ing from 'grim-visagèd war'." A slight movement of her head encompassed their table, the tent, the Frost Fair, all of London, England and human civi-lization. "Or perhaps not so strange, the Frost Fair, contingent as it is on an ephemeral, transitory state: the ice that will soon melt and wash away."

There it was again, that uncanny perspicacity. "And now, instead of mounting barbèd steeds, he capers nimbly in a lawyer's chambers?"

Surprised into laughter, she seemed surprised by her own laughter, too, lifting a hand to her lips as if to hide it. The touch of her lips would be warm and soft. Trying to concentrate on what she had said, Justin continued, "What is most strange is that no one seems aware how strange it is. Here I am, with hardly a change of clothes, and yet everyone acts as though I had never been away at all. You are the exception."

A quick frown and shake of her head seemed to indicate that she did not consider herself in any way exceptional. "Perhaps that is because they cannot imagine what it is like, being away." She cast a sidelong glance at her brother, who was still talk-ing expansively. "Never having left this world, they cannot know that entering or re-entering it may not be such a simple matter. They do not doubt its claims."

Did she know what claims were being made upon him, her, the two of them together? "And you?"

"Oh, I do not belong here," she said blithely. "I'm only a visitor."

Then she did not know; he would be allowed to do his own courting. Looking at her, he found the prospect infinitely alluring.

"It is 'lady's chamber', not 'lawyer's', by the way." There was no trace of archness in her face or voice. She was merely imparting information.

"Is it, now?" The unintended irony made him smile. "You may well be right."

It was past six o'clock when they left the tent, and night had fallen. As they picked their way along the rough ice, Justin knew rather than felt the steady, cold flow underneath all the frozen beauty. Though fully appreciative of the arctic vista of ice piled up in mighty blocks and slabs shimmering in the moonlight, with St Paul's looming in the background, he thought he would prefer the live water slapping and gurgling against the quays.

Chapter 4

But when my touching came to play his part
(The king of senses, greater than the rest) . . .
Drayton, *Idea*

THE first-floor vestibule of the Hanover Square
Rooms glittered with light and people. The uncur-
tained windows mirrored the scene against the
night, but when Claire moved closer, her own
shadow fell on the wet ledge of creamy stone outside, and she could see right across the square.

"How bright London is," she said. "I suppose the
ice has melted now that it has started to rain."

Robert had stepped back a pace, gazing at the
panes rather than through them, but now he gave
his reflection an approving nod and turned to her,
blinking with raised eyebrows. "Eh?"

"Do you not mind how bright the snow and ice
were in the moonlight when we left the coffee-tent?
We did not even need a link-boy."

"Not a sennight and yet it's all gone. I passed by
the river on my way to the Temple this morning."
He came to stand next to her. "I'm glad you enjoyed
your little adventure."

"This is my adventure." Claire turned her back
on the window and lifted a hand to indicate the
elegant throng. "The Frost Fair was Nicola's adventure, and this is mine."

Robert looked across the vestibule to where
Nicola formed one of a lively group, the primrose
silk of her gown shimmering like the sun on a June
day. "No, indeed, she would hardly call a concert of
Ancient Music an adventure." He narrowed his eyes
in the curious expression she knew so well. "But
you would? There must be concerts in Edinburgh."
Then a shadow crossed his face and he added, with

sudden vehemence, "And you play, too. Like an angel."

Startled by his low, intense voice, she replied, "Angels play the harp, Robert, not the pianoforte."

He made a strangled sound in his throat. "Like an angel," he repeated. "And it was heaven when Papa brought me to live with you and your mother and the girls. There you were in the drawing room, setting stitches or reading French, singing to the babies or playing Bach, and who was to know that you'd just survived an epidemic and lost two little brothers, that you'd spent the entire morning in housework – that you were waiting for Papa and straining to anticipate what his mood might be that night. And when it happened . . . I still see the music for *The Well-Tempered Clavier* open on the piano, mocking us while the blows fell. Heaven and hell." He reached for her hand, lacing his fingers with hers. "What a strange life we led," he said hoarsely.

A great stillness filled her. They had never yet talked about that time, although she played on Nicola's pianoforte every day. But it was safer here, in public, with the indifferent glitter and hum to steady them. "We did have a maid to help with the dishes and cleaning," she said.

"Oh, Claire." He pressed her hand. "As if that made all right. And things can't have been easy for you when Old Mrs Lammond took you in, either. The way she treated us, one might have thought we were to blame for our father's . . . shortcomings. Making you take her name, too, as if to wipe out his memory."

"I wish she had succeeded," Claire murmured. Matter-of-factly she added, "Is it awkward for you, Robert, us not having the same name? Will people think –"

"No, no! Most people don't think very much at all, you know, and besides, you won't –" He broke off, gave her a quick glance, and lifted her hand to his lips before releasing it.

She thought she knew what he had tactfully left unsaid. "I won't be here much longer. Soon I will go back to the girls and it won't matter anymore."

"Aye, to the girls and the great estate Old Mrs Lammond saw fit to – to saddle you with!" He made a face. "Now I see why the Frost Fair was no adventure for you. You're used to walking on much thinner ice."

"That is how it felt, back then," Claire said. "So much to unlearn and learn. Poor Grandmama. But she taught us how to manage and left us well provided for. And you're doing very well, too, in the career she arranged for you." Opening her fan, she gestured at herself, the crowded room. "Just look at us now, part of all this, so carefree and gay."

Robert's expression when he looked at her was neither carefree nor gay. "That is what I always wanted for you, Claire, the happy life all the other girls seemed to have."

"That is what I have, Robert. And you married one of those other girls!"

Once again his gaze sought his wife. Without interrupting her conversation, Nicola lifted her hand and waved. "You may be right, you know. Perhaps that is what first attracted me to her." Then he added, "God give I don't make mull of it."

It was cruel, not strange, a childhood that led a man to fear himself thus. Claire laid her hand on his arm. "With the example you've had?" she asked gently. "I should think not."

His face was bleak. "That's just the point. I know what I don't want, but . . ." Half turning away from her, he continued, "I don't really know what a good husband is, or how he behaves."

He was standing at the window without really looking out, but now something down in the street seemed to catch his attention. Throwing her a grin, he said, "No, wait, I do know what a good husband is, or at least I can recognize one when I see one."

Relieved at the change of subject, she stepped to his side. A carriage had drawn up in front of the building, its horses steaming gently in the drizzle. The passenger had alighted, and the groom was back on the box, looking down at his master, who stood with his head thrown back to make some laughing remark. It was Captain Sumners.

"Have you no thought of marriage, Claire?" Robert inquired blandly. "You might marry into the peerage."

Not a change of subject, but a complete change of mood. Thrown off balance, Claire took him quite literally, deliberately misunderstanding. "Don't tell me you think Lord Hawksfield is interested."

He nudged her with his elbow, as if they were children still. "Not the present Lord Hawksfield. But the future one. Oh, yes. And you like him, too."

It was true; there was no need for Robert to look so astonished when she admitted it. "He doesn't prate," she explained. "I've seen him decline a number of open invitations to show himself in an advantageous light, and in my experience that is unusual, especially in a man not yet thirty. I wish he would talk more, because Percy will be bombarding me with questions when she learns that we're acquainted with a Rifleman." After a moment she added, "But not even for Percy's sake would I marry him, nor anyone." She faced him squarely. "You know that, Robert."

"I know." He sighed. "It seems rather extreme, however. There's a lot to be said for matrimony."

She could not suppress a shudder, and he saw it. "As bad as that? My dear," he added when, unable to speak, she turned away her face. She took a deep breath, studied the playbill, remarked on the evening's programme.

"My dear," he repeated softly. "Will you be kind to Captain Sumners for my sake, then? It might make a world of difference."

The notion was absurd, but he continued: "These people haven't gathered here to listen to music. This is society, Claire. In this room, you see representatives of all those families who effectively rule the kingdom. Connexions are made, alliances forged here and at similar gatherings – political alliances, family alliances. Often these are one and the same."

It was his world. He saw it from inside, an actor rather than a spectator. "I understand, Robert." She looked up at him. "You're a performer in the social concert, not a mere part of the audience as I am." Lightly she added, "Do you know, Captain Sumners said something quite similar to me that day on the ice. It is fortunate for you that he has no parliamentary ambitions. I expect he will be aiming for the Foreign Office, given his qualifications? There he is." The captain had appeared at the head of the stairs with Lord Dallington at his side.

His return to civilization had progressed by another visible step. The two young men had called twice in the intervening week; on the morning after their first meeting, Captain Sumners had been as shabby and shaggy as the night before, his uniform carefully brushed but worn and faded, his hair kempt and clean but far too long; then he had had his hair cut, and now he had found himself a respectable, even refulgent dress uniform. He swept the space before him with his gaze, like a hawk about to take to his wings, threw a remark to his cousin, grasped his arm, and drew him towards Robert and herself.

There was something derisive in Robert's laugh, and when he said that for someone who called herself a listener she played pretty well, Claire had her doubts whether he meant her performance on the pianoforte.

She paid little attention to the to and fro as the audience took their seats, leaping up to let others pass, to exchange bows, seats, playbills, or gossip while the musicians tuned their instruments. The concert began with a Corelli she knew well in its pianoforte version – a transmogrified version, she decided, pleased with the interplay of instruments and impatient with the hubbub briefly erupting after the applause subsided. For the German dances, the strings were joined by a stately *basso continuo*; craning her neck, she tried to make out how the orchestra communicated with this new member, who sat with his back to them. Then the music swept away conscious thought and all that remained was a sense of utter well-being. It was good to be here, with Robert and Nicola, and with all these people who her brother believed to be more interested in politics than in music. Although his profile was absorbed, she knew that for him at least this was true, but when he turned his head, she knew that he was still her brother, who loved and protected her. Tears rose to her eyes. To hide her emotion, she kept her gaze fixed on the playbill during the short interval that followed.

The next piece began, disconcertingly, with low, intense, abrasive sounds. Then the quintet launched into a sweet melody – almost too sweet, but soon the music changed again, turning grave, stately, with the 'cello booming away. A pause was followed by strumming and pizzicati at once informal and so joyful that Claire's hand as of its own accord sought her brother's. His fingers closed around hers, conveying a message that had nothing to do with politics and everything with music. Their hands remained clasped together even through the reprise of the haunting phrases from the beginning and to the triumphant, sweeping end.

Claire took a deep breath, but when she turned, the words died on her lips. It was not her brother's hand she was holding, nor his faintly amused gaze that met hers. Captain Sumners was regarding her with warm, dark eyes. Quickly she withdrew her hand, but he had already released his grip. Staring down at the playbill, she felt an embarrassed glow flowing up the side of her neck. A touch on her hand made her start violently, then a waft of air cooled her cheeks, and another, and another. He had twisted her fan from her grasp and was slowly waving it.

"La Musica Notturna delle Strade di Madrid." Another wave indicated the playbill. "Someone will have had to pay a thumping great fine. The music played here is meant to be more than twenty-five years old at least, an odd enough definition of 'ancient', and Boccherini only died in the year five. Although, of course, the composition may be of an earlier date."

The nocturnal music of the streets of Madrid: the captain talked, at uncharacteristic length and with a wealth of detail. His low, husky voice enveloped her. Despite the confused sense of shame, gratitude, and resentment that kept her eyes fixed on her hands, the right clasping the treacherous left, she found herself drawn into his narrative – the hushing sound that a thin drizzle made on slated roofs, knocking on a back door, the muted noises of a desperate scuffle, the sounds of flight and pursuit, the silent flow of blood and loud rasping of spent breath.

"So you see, the low screeches that made up the first movement, that is my experience of Madrid."

The way he talked, one might think it had all happened to someone else; yet it was not so long ago. "Was that when you were captured?"

"It was." The fan snapped shut. "Shall we join the Lysters?"

"But ... how did it end?" Arrested by her question, he did not immediately relinquish her fan, although she had already reached for it. Their hands touched. Lifting her chin, she added, "My sisters will never forgive me if I don't tell them the rest of the story."

"I lived to tell the tale." The corners of his eyes crinkled. "I thought Percy alone was interested in the military."

"In the Rifle Corps, yes, but when it comes to the Peninsular War, the others are just as bad, even Stella."

"Well, one day I will tell her the rest, and the others, even Stella."

He was looking at her as though through her he might see her sisters and some future time in which they were all together, and for a moment she felt that it should be so.

This time it was she who made to rise. "Shall we join my sister-in-law?"

"Stay a moment, Miss Lammond," he said, suddenly grave and very much present. "Excuse me if I embarrass you, but ... do you know of your brother's plans?"

So Robert was right, after all, and everything was politics. She had to laugh. "Certainly I do." The captain's expression hardened inexplicably; and inexplicably she was moved to justify her brother. "You must not blame him for his ambition. If he achieves it, and enters parliament, he will do very well, believe me."

~ ~ ~

"They were playing this piece" – Justin whistled softly so as not to disturb the horses – "and she took my hand. I will speak to her brother tomorrow." He had lapsed into Spanish, as he always did when he was talking to Pepe.

"That is a fine tune." Pepe took up the melody. Humming as he worked, he added some melismatic variations of his own, but when Justin reached for a curry-comb, he stopped abruptly. "Leave it, Don Justín." After a silence broken only by the sounds of brushing, Justin's low whistling, and the horses' peaceful breathing, Pepe said, "Do you think she knows of her brother's plans?" As usual he had put his finger on the problem.

"I thought she could not, after what had passed – her embarrassment – so I asked her." The queer satisfaction engendered by her confiding gesture had been banished by one word, one candid look. "She took a most businesslike view, and I cannot say I don't regret it."

The sense of regret was still with Justin when he walked into Lyster's study the next morning. It was just another business call, with an agreement easily reached.

"I will not deny that I have been waiting for this call, Captain Sumners. But leave it to me, do not speak to her yourself." Lyster winked. "A girl does not like to be thought quite so, shall we say, businesslike. Although after what passed at the concert, I wonder how businesslike Claire really is." He regarded Justin with narrowed eyes as though to find the answer in his features.

"Don't be naïve, Lyster. She hadn't noticed our changing seats and took me for you, that's all. I'd be flattering myself if I thought otherwise."

Lyster shrugged. "Anyhow, there is bound to be some awkwardness. Let us go upstairs, but pray do

not mention what has passed. Pretend you're courting her, do you mind?"

"On the contrary." Justin rose as the other man
pushed back his chair and came round the desk.
When they shook hands, Lyster's eyes slid away.

"Miss Lammond tells me that you'll keep your
part of the bargain," Justin said, "and not forget to
whom you owe your advance. I'm not sure what I
think of you, Lyster, but I do like the fondness you
have for your sister."

With a sharp snort, Lyster half turned away,
suddenly very pale. "You will be good to her."

"Nothing could give me greater pleasure."

The conventional remark did not abate Lyster's
solemnity. "I am fond of her, I am," he muttered
fiercely, but when Justin said that he was, too, he
took a grip on himself and led the way upstairs.

Miss Lammond had been an almost palpable
presence during this interview, and when Justin
stepped into the hall, he knew it was not only
because she was its object. The tinkle of the piano,
now clearly audible, must have penetrated to the
study, too: hesitant, inept, although a sudden
confident burst revealed that she was picking out
the melody of the quintettino they had heard at the
concert. When Lyster and he entered the room, she
stopped abruptly.

"How do you do, Miss Lammond?" It was impossible to keep the warmth from his voice. "That was
a fine piece."

"It's too difficult. I'll have to find a score." Her
bosom rose and fell as she took a quick breath. At
the neckline of her dress, an edge of fine lawn
peeped out, and although he knew this was the
fashion, quite commonplace, to be seen on scores of
female bosoms, on her it seemed utterly seductive, a
promise soon to be fulfilled. *That not impossible
she* . . . Yes.

"Was it on the playbill? Well, well." Lyster bent and kissed her cheek. "You must study it and play it to us when we return from Northamptonshire."

She looked up at her brother, then, flushing slightly, at Justin.

"So you are supporting Robert's candidacy? I am glad."

Her confusion was too tempting. If this was a business arrangement, then he had underrated the pleasures of business. "Your brother's arguments proved irresistible," he said. Her flush deepened, and the soft pink spread from her cheeks to the side of her neck. The skin would be warm to the touch. But she held his gaze, as if to prevent him noticing her discomfiture, and he felt a stab of guilt. "I hope to show myself equally persuasive with the electors," he continued. "There are thirty-three of them to be canvassed, and only fourteen are our tenants, another five belonging to your papa." He bowed to Mrs Lyster.

Miss Lammond's attention was caught, as he had known it would be, her confusion forgotten. "And the remaining fourteen?"

"The main thing is the support of their landlord, of course, although some are freeholders. Bouverie is unlikely to go against us, but in any case, I mean to speak to them personally and individually."

"Good heavens, Sumners, you don't intend to call on them all?"

"Certainly I do," Justin said. "It will be a unique opportunity to taste thirty-three different variants of elderberry wine."

Mrs Lyster was horrified. "You will never! It is the nastiest stuff. I had to drink some, once, at Glebe Farm, and it disagreed with me quite violently. Pray do not, Robert. You cannot know if it is safe."

"Why should it not be safe?" Miss Lammond said. "Besides, Nicola, it would never do to offend these people."

"Don't worry, Mrs Lyster. My innards are inured to all sorts of beverage, so if your husband is in any danger, I will endeavour to drink his wine for him."

Although absurd, her gratitude was touching, too, but what affected him far more was Miss Lammond's silent look of approval. It was more than business after all. The pressure of her hand, the feeling of intimacy had been real, and he would have sworn entirely uncalculated.

Chapter 5

How falls it out so strangely you reply?
Drayton, *Idea*

IT had not been all elderberry, Robert assured them: there had been cider and Geneva, too, and a rather muddy port. All this promiscuity had not harmed him, however, nor had the cold journey. He had returned in excellent spirits, satisfied with himself and full of praise for his companion. Even now he was talking away at a great rate. He had good reason to feel pleased and excited, Claire thought with a proud lift of her heart. An honest profession, a rich and happy marriage, and soon, very probably, a seat in parliament: her big brother had achieved a great deal.

By way of celebration, he had asked Nicola and herself to deck themselves out in all their finery, but it was only another dinner party, after all, so Nicola had laughed away his suggestions of velvet, brocade, rubies, emeralds, and diamonds. Instead she chose, for herself, a pink crape with a daring bosom, and lent Claire a necklace of stylized flowers which would go well with her pale green sarsenet.

"Mrs Lyster, your servant." Captain Sumners appeared seemingly out of nowhere. He bowed to Nicola, nodded to Robert, and shouldered Lord Dallington aside. "You look like spring personified, Miss Lammond, Persephone herself. How do you do? It is you who make the flowers grow." Out of nowhere he produced a bunch of daisies and put it into her hands.

"And who do you think you are, to claim Spring for yourself?" Lord Dallington drawled. "Hades?"

"Not I." Captain Sumners laughed up into his cousin's high-nosed stare. "Hermes, if anyone."

Yet for all his fairy-tale tricks, the captain looked tired and preoccupied. Perhaps it was the contrast with Robert's exuberance, or perhaps it was the dark coat – he was no longer in uniform – that gave him such a sombre air: no collar of silver buttons, no crimson sash.

Or perhaps it was because she had something on her mind herself that she thought him worried, too. Claire passed the flowers to Nicola. "Do not the Ancients assure us that Spring is a fair-haired lady? Then these are for you."

Nicola caught up with the conversation. "So it was you, Captain, who made the drawings in Robert's letters?" There had been an impressive amount of correspondence from Robert while he was away, invariably including Captain Sumners's respects, and the margins filled with wildflowers – winter aconites, snowdrops, celandine, daisies – minutely and exactly drawn. "But Persephone is Greek, isn't she? Then she must be dark."

"The only Persephone I know certainly is dark," Claire said, "but she's Scottish, not Greek. I may look like Persephone, but I am not she. If I look like Persephone, it's because she's my sister."

The temptation to send some of those drawings to Percy had been strong, as was the temptation, now, to mention her artistic talent. But it would not do to chatter about her little sisters, and she did not demur when Nicola tucked the daisies into the bandeau Claire wore in her hair that evening.

"No longer so easily flustered, eh?" Robert grinned. "No doubt you had plenty of opportunity to grow accustomed to our London ways while we were away."

In a sense she had. Reluctantly Claire put her hand on the captain's proffered arm. "Are you sure you have the right partner? There are several ladies here who have higher claims than I," she said.

"Impossible." He covered her hand with his in a touch so fleeting that it was over before the impulse to withdraw her hand had even formed. "Besides, I want to talk to you. There's Lord Hawksfield catching my eye. Come along."

"Your father showed us great kindness in your absence," she said carefully as they walked into the dining room, "but I am afraid his preferential treatment has been remarked."

"And not too kindly, I take it. I am sorry; Lord Hawksfield is not always very tactful." His arm rested on the back of the chair he had set for her. Given the nature of some of the remarks made in her hearing, given what Robert had said to her before and again in greater detail after the concert, she ought to have felt uncomfortable with Captain Sumners. She had felt very uncomfortable when they met again after her shameful lapse, but only for about five minutes. Robert's candidacy and their modest electoral campaign were topics that left little room for embarrassment.

Now she felt bereft when he removed his arm to take his seat next to her, and that was curious, for in general she disliked being loomed over. He was smiling softly, but there was a new gravity underneath his smile, and it struck her that she had not been very tactful, either. "I did not mean to suggest that I would object to your talking to me."

"You do like to have things clear, don't you?" He gave her a keen glance. "And yet, at the same time – but never mind that."

"I won't," she promised. With a stern look, he admonished her not to cut jokes over the soup.

Nor was it amusing: it was barely lukewarm. No wonder Captain Sumners was preoccupied. If the state of Hawksfield House was anything to go by, Hawksfield Manor must be in sad shape. Not that he seemed to mind the soup; he would be used to worse fare in the Peninsula. When she inquired about military provisioning arrangements, he gave a crack of laughter.

"You're not impressed with our standard of provisioning here, are you, Miss Lammond? It's true enough, Hawksfield House wants a mistress."

"Or a good housekeeper," she said repressively. Again he laughed, but by the time the soup was removed, the glow in his eyes had faded.

"Whatever the remedy may be, the fact remains that the House is not in good shape, and the Manor is worse." His eyebrows sprang together in a frown. "There is something I cannot lay my finger on," he said slowly. "Some disaffection among our people." A corner of his mouth lifted. "Did I just say 'our people'? That was another surprise: I had no notion how much I care. The land would have been my brother's concern."

"You miss him."

"I've just sold most of his horses."

She saw nothing inconsequential in his reply. "That must have been hard. May I give you some of this poached turbot?" When she finished serving him, she found his gaze upon her, warm and grave, and quickly returned her attention to the fish.

"Thank you. It wasn't hard at all," he said. "Some of Stephen's old cronies had already made noises about buying, but Lord Hawksfield told them that I'd need the animals when I got back. And so he kept them — four hunters, two carriage horses, and two hacks."

That was not what she had meant, but she swallowed the remark.

"That wasn't what you meant, Miss Lammond, was it? But I was too vexed to repine. We could use eight maids or footmen or perhaps a gardener, but eight fine horses no one rides? It's not good for the animals, either."

There was nothing to say; she was in complete agreement. "You don't hunt?"

"I used to; we'll see. Do you?"

"Oh, no." The notion was absurd. "I was too late in learning to ride." He did not ask how that was; all the same, she felt she had said too much. "We lived in Edinburgh when I was a girl," she offered by way of explanation, relying on his tact to keep him from pointing out that this was no explanation at all. "It must be very exhilarating," she added. "I've always enjoyed watching the Buccleuch Hunt."

This remark seemed to please him. "A docile, reliable animal for you, then; not more than fifteen hands. I've traded one of the hacks for such an one and kept the other for myself, a spirited little mare. Stephen's a good judge of horseflesh –" He broke off suddenly.

"I think Lady Boughton would like some of those spiced mushrooms." She directed his attention to the neglected dish.

He thanked her, did his duty, and continued, "The odd thing is that the Stephen I remember isn't the young man I last knew, but the boy, and how we played together. And it's worse in the country. Although considering some of the things I've learned about him, I wonder how well I really did know him."

What a good man he was, after all, despite his unsettling ways. "The ties and memories of child-hood are the strongest. I, too, remember Robert as the boy who – as a boy. How I wept when he was sent away to his apprenticeship! Now I am constantly surprised to see him a grown man. But he is just the same as he ever was. I'm sure your brother hadn't changed much. A prominent family is bound to be the subject of all sorts of gossip, including malicious gossip. I shouldn't lay much store by it."

"What a dear girl you are." His voice was low and husky. "I wish I could have brought you some wood anemones from Nelly's Lea, but it was too early." He glanced at her hair. "Frivolous little daisies aren't really your flower, although they do look pretty."

"They make a good bruise tincture, too." She could hardly object to being called a dear girl when she had just apostrophized him as a good man, if only mentally. But that was the man's prerogative, to say what he thought. "That's common land, isn't it?" she asked instead. "Lord Hawksfield mentioned an enclosing scheme. Could that be the reason for the disaffection you mentioned? You know how folk in the country are opposed to any sort of change."

"And change there will have to be. Fortunately Lord Hawksfield is aware of it, even eager to be doing. But enclosing –" He shot a quick look at his father. "That will bear looking into."

They talked on, only occasionally interrupted by the need to pay some attention to their right- and left-hand neighbours, and continued as though no interruption had occurred when the gentlemen joined the ladies in the drawing room.

"You said 'another surprise'." Claire took the cup of tea he had procured for her. "What other surprising discoveries did you make?"

He drank some coffee, frowned, and handed his cup to a passing footman. "That my knowledge of these matters is wretchedly limited. I hope your tea is drinkable." Lifting an eyebrow when she assured him that it was, he added, "If I don't understand where the trouble lies, how can I know what to do and where to begin? My uncle tells me you've been managing your grandmother's estate these three years," he added. "I'll be glad of your advice."

He was flattering her, of course, but he was going too far. "Even someone with my vast experience cannot advise about land they've never seen, in a country they do not know," she replied coolly. "And I have a good bailiff."

"I thought you might say that." He grinned. "You seem to place a great deal of trust in your employees. And I expect that is why they serve you well," he added.

She had been too harsh. "Whether you manage a company of soldiers, an estate, or a family, the skills required must be similar. You will soon find that you have them."

"Do you think so?" His eyes were dancing. "I was mostly seconded to special duties, you know. Anyhow, I look forward to having you by my side, if not chiefly for that reason. Pray do not destroy Lord Hawksfield's porcelain." In her astonishment, she would have dropped her cup had he not taken it from her.

"Not you, too." Under his inquiring eye, she felt a blush rising. "I told you people have been making remarks, and Lord Hawksfield has fallen into a very strange way of talking."

He had bent his head to hear her over the surrounding noise. Laughter lines fanned out from the corners of his eyes. "Stranger than usual?"

"Yes." She had not thought of it at all during dinner, but something lay between them and it was impossible to laugh it off.

"Miss Lammond." His gaze held hers. "What is it? Tell me."

Although she had thought it all out beforehand, she found herself fumbling for words. "He says – he has said – that I am like a daughter to him. Already. That already I am like a daughter to him."

"Does he, now? I had no notion he could be so sentimental. But very soon you will be the next best thing to a daughter – a daughter-in-law."

His face was the only fixed point in a world that had begun to spin around her. Through the rushing in her ears, she heard him say her name. She was not aware of replying, but she must have, for he threw back his head and laughed.

"You're leaving it rather late, Miss Lammond, if you mean to jilt me."

"Jilt you?" Like a fool she was repeating what he said. Pulling herself together, she said starkly, "Captain Sumners, you seem to believe that there is some sort of engagement between us."

His reply was not in the least reassuring. "So I do; and I'm not the only one." Suddenly his flippancy vanished. "Look at me." When she obeyed, he gave her a long, hard stare, then his expression softened. "Do you remember Moore's retreat on Corunna, Miss Lammond?"

Was this an attempt to set her at her ease, as he had done after the concert, by talking? But this time talking would hardly avail.

"I lost my regiment there," he continued. "I fell asleep on horseback and woke in a ditch under three inches of snow." A wry amusement crept into his voice. "This feels much the same." His head came up. "Damnation! They're handing round the champagne. Excuse me."

She saw him speak to Nicola in passing and almost immediately felt her sister-in-law's plump arm around her waist, heard her voice in her ear, guiding her towards a sofa. Straining back over her shoulder, she saw the captain approach Lord Hawksfield for some urgent words and caught his lordship's clear, sharp reply.

"Nonsense." He turned from his son to the crowded room, the scowl uncannily shifted by a beaming smile. "My lords, ladies and gentlemen, I bid you raise your glasses to –"

"The King!" Captain Sumners reached for a glass of champagne. The loyal shout rang to the ceiling. As Claire sank down on the sofa, she heard him raise his voice to oratorical pitch. He was making a speech.

Through the blur of her confusion, she caught only a few words: something about the war – peace – frost and thaw. His voice carried without strain. Suddenly he seemed to be speaking to her alone. "Not many weeks ago, the ice on the Thames was strong enough to support a man – in fact, a whole microcosm, separated from the cold flow by no more than a thin sheet of congealed water.

"There is no stopping the thaw," he continued, "and do we not prefer the live water, the glitter of waves, and the prosperous ply of boats and barges? I believe the changes facing us in the years ahead will be as fundamental as the melting of the ice. Either we learn to navigate the stream of change, or we drown in its icy waves."

That he should speak publicly about an experience which they had shared – that he should speak thus! Allegorically, poetically, politically, he evoked a chilling image of destruction and yet ended on a confident, patriotic note. At least this was her impression, for his final words escaped her, but they were greeted with such a roar of approbation that they must have been patriotic.

There was a chink of glasses, and Claire, too, found herself sipping champagne. "How beautiful." Nicola squeezed her hand. The room dissolved into the usual hum of voices.

Lord Dallington came over to ask if she were better, making conversation until Nicola's attention was claimed elsewhere, when he suddenly said, "Miss Lammond, I have a very strange message from my cousin, which I beg you will forgive me for repeating as he gave it. Justin says he cannot leave his father at this moment, and asks if there is any possibility of seeing you alone. I am sorry."

The champagne, the toast . . . Claire felt a little sick. Lord Hawksfield had begun a formal announcement, and what he had meant to announce was his son's engagement to herself. If the captain felt he could not leave him, that was because he could not trust him to keep silent now. How swift his reaction had been. She looked into Lord Dallington's concerned face. "Not at all. I am grateful. Please ask the captain to call shortly after nine o'clock tomorrow." Robert left for the Inns of Court ten minutes before the hour, and Nicola never came down until ten o'clock.

~ ~ ~

"But when I asked you, Miss Lammond, you said you knew of your brother's plans. And the way you spoke with me, even last night, about the improvements needed here and at the Manor . . ."

There it was at last, blame and accusations. His behaviour up until then had been impeccable, his punctual, discreet arrival followed by disarmingly frank remarks about the wretched night she must have passed and apologies for the impossibility of leaving Lord Hawksfield to expose his displeasure in front of his guests. And now . . . Claire shivered. Folding her hands in her lap, her head bowed, she braced herself for the storm.

"All this pays no toll, however." His voice was bemused rather than angry. "Since I believed you had agreed to marry me, I would naturally construe anything you said or did as evidence of your commitment." When Claire risked a glance, he was looking ruefully down at her.

"I thought you meant Robert's plan to enter parliament," she ventured. A sudden memory assailed her. "So that was why you didn't like my reply. You thought –"

He nodded. "But what I thought is irrelevant for the moment, Miss Lammond. May I?" At her gesture, he sat down next to her and took her hands, holding them so gently that she felt no urge to pull back.

Her skin felt alive to his touch. Ungloved, she would never have mistaken his hands for Robert's. They were rough and calloused against hers, now as white and soft as a lady's should be, but it had taken many porridge baths and nights with woollen mittens until Grandmama had erased all traces of coarse housework. A Scott of Harden, Grandmama would have been content for Claire to be proposed to by the heir to a peerage, although she might not have approved of all this handholding.

"If this were the day after the concert, what would you reply were I to ask you to marry me?"

The concert at which she had behaved so strangely; and he had spoken to Robert the very next day. "Why did you not speak to me then?" But of course Robert had almost immediately whisked him away into the country; there had been no opportunity.

"I wish I had. But your brother told me that a display of passion would not be acceptable to you, that you were embarrassed about entering into an arranged match." He made a face. "I was rather pleased; I thought it showed –"

She interrupted him. "And he knew you would have too much delicacy not to comply. Oh, Robert!" A sob rose in her throat, but her tears were all wept up. "He knew I would never say yes, if asked. So he simply waived the question, knowing full well that I would stand by him." She had not spent all night weeping. When her hot rage had subsided, when she had stopped imagining what scathing things she might say to Robert, she had thought it all through, and it was then that she had wept. If she cried off now, Lord Hawksfield would withdraw his support for Robert's candidacy.

The captain raised her hands to his lips, then he released them. "Do you mean to marry me to oblige your brother? Surely you don't owe him any loyalty, after this?"

"I do, though." If Robert had betrayed her, he could not have done so if the tie between them were any less close. And the reason it was so close was his stalwart protection of her and the girls all those years ago, the lies he told and the beatings he took, all for their sake. "He is my brother, God help me."

"He is to be envied." The captain straightened his back. "Well, there may be worse reasons for marriage, although I cannot at present think of any, but I suppose I should seize on anything that might persuade you, however absurd."

But he did not. "If that is how you feel," he said instead, "I will naturally do my utmost to ensure Lord Hawksfield's support for your brother. But there is no need for you to immolate yourself upon this particular altar." He rose abruptly and walked over to the fireplace. The proud lift of his head, the defiant set of his shoulders showed plainly that he hated what he was about to do. "There is something else, however."

She knew it only too well. Robert could make life very uncomfortable for the girls and herself. He was her entry to London society. If he broke off the connexion, Alba would never have the London debut that she deserved, and even Edinburgh society might be closed to them. Alba, Stella, Percy, Lucy: they would be condemned to bloom unseen, and all through her obstinacy. "I know," she sighed.

He leaned against the mantelpiece, a sense of urgency hanging about him that sat oddly with his casual stance. His tone gave nothing away, either, only the words themselves, which were entirely unexpected. "Yes, you know how things stand. My uncle, my cousin, my father, your brother, his father-in-law – Boughton, Dallington, Hawksfield, Lyster, Manvers – influence, ability, and money united in a grand scheme to extend that influence even farther. Stephen was always something of a loose cannon, but with Lyster representing the borough, Boughton will control five seats in the House of Commons. Our marriage will provide your brother with sufficient borrowed status to play his role, and flatter his father-in-law into lending any financial support that may be required. Oh, it is a fine web they have woven!" His voice was suddenly rough with disdain, and she must have made some small sound, for looking across at her, he gave a penitent smile and continued quite mildly, "Had I known this only a few weeks ago, I should have said, the back of my hand to them all, and gone back to my regiment. You have observed that Lord Hawksfield is not very discreet, not very wise. But he is my father, God help us. For all that I'm not the ideal son, I hesitate to thwart their schemes and expose him to the ridicule of his peers." His mouth was set, with no trace of laughter.

"I honour you for it," she said.

"Honour!" The word he spat then was foreign but clearly foul, as his quick apology confirmed. The corner of his mouth lifted. "Shall I kneel?" He folded his limbs. At her protest, he merely propped his elbow on the seat by her, leaning his head in his hand as he looked up at her. "Miss Lammond, will you not – what is the phrase – save the fair name of Sumners? Rather than accepting the protection of my name, will you protect my name by accepting it? Honour should come into it somewhere, to be sure. Will you do me the honour of accepting my name? Will you do me the honour of protecting my name? Will you protect my honour by accepting my name? Will you honour my name by accepting it?"

It was too absurd, but she managed to say, with barely a tremor, "Do get up, Captain. These demonstrations are hardly necessary; I have already told you I will."

Suddenly he was very close. "You will?" Her eyes downcast, she sensed his proximity by the clean scent of his linen and something that must be shaving lotion. The animal warmth of his body was almost palpable. When his lips touched hers, they were warm, too. Closing her eyes was a mistake; something dark and powerful seemed to envelop her.

"No." She was on her feet, half across the room before she could control herself. Now he seemed very far away, as if she were seeing him through the wrong end of a telescope. Although he had risen with her, he had made no attempt to hold her back. Nor did he look angry or even annoyed; he simply looked at her with dark, alert eyes.

Resolutely crossing the immense distance, she put her hand in his. "I'm sorry. I don't know what came over me. You see, no one has ever . . . But of course I will marry you."

"They haven't? What a set of cold fish those Scotsmen must be." He spoke lightly, and his clasp was light, but his faintly amused smile did not dispel the intensity, a glow that hung about him, as unsettling as his proximity had been before. "So that was merely a fit of maidenly shyness?" There was irony in his voice, and complicity. He seemed to understand something that she did not. "I don't want you to do anything you'd rather not, you know. I won't expect you to. I don't expect anything at all from you."

The heat rose and ebbed in her cheeks. She opened her mouth, found no words, and closed it again.

With a slight pressure, he dropped her hand. "Don't worry, Miss Lammond. Let things look after themselves. They do, you know."

That was clearly nonsense. Things never looked after themselves. More than that, it had always been her part to look after them. She had a brief, bright glimpse of a life entirely different from anything she had ever known, a life where one could do as one wished, not hedged about by necessity or duty. Carefree and gay ... Her throat tightened. For all Robert's fine words, it was the captain who had (literally) spoken out for her.

"I missed the end of your speech last night. What was it you said?"

The question did not appear to strike him as irrelevant. "I'm surprised you heard any of it, after the shock you had. I hardly know. Something about Wellington's advance across the River Nivelle, His Majesty's armed forces, and the Corsican tyrant." He grinned. "The former would swim and the latter sink, no doubt, and all would be well. I rather rode that river metaphor to death, didn't I, but I didn't really know what I was saying."

Of course he, too, had had a shock. "It was a fine speech," she said.

"It achieved its end." He shrugged. "Not that it makes much of a difference, if you are determined."

But it did make a difference. Thanks to him, the decision was hers, even if the outcome were the same, which it probably would be, despite his veiled promise. He was a man, after all.

"You have a strange, radical view of life, Captain Sumners. All the same, I will marry you."

Suddenly his gravity slipped away, he went down on one knee, kissed both her hands, and said that naturally she was making him the happiest man on earth. Back on his feet, he added, "Or in this room, at least. Now, one thing that will not look after itself is the marriage contract. Your brother told me you had approved it, but somehow that seems unlikely. I'll get you a copy. Have you anyone you trust to examine it for you?"

Laughter bubbled up inside her, contending with sorrow and anger. "I used to trust Robert." Her voice broke. She cleared her throat. "But yes, of course. How much time do we have? I should like to ask Mr Scott."

He was intrigued. "Not Mr Scott, the author of *Marmion*?"

"He's our neighbour, and an advocate."

"Is he! Now there's a man I'd like to meet."

"If things do look after themselves, as you seem to expect, you probably will," she retorted.

He grinned. "I didn't make that up, you know. It was the text of Reverend Meynell's sermon last Sunday: 'Take ye therefore no thought for the morrow: for the morrow shall take thought for the things of itself'."

"Sufficient unto the day is the evil thereof," Claire said half to herself, remembering the few anecdotes Captain Sumners had told her. "That really is your experience, isn't it? What happened after you lost your regiment in the snow?"

"I was saved," he said, "by a noble woman."

Chapter 6

Oh I forbid you, maidens a',
That wear gowd on your hair,
To come or gae by Carterhaugh,
For young Tam Lin is there.
Traditional, *Tam Lin*

THE simple melody of the ancient ballad ran round and round in Claire's head. They might sing it this evening; it was Percy's favourite. The palm of her hand against one of the lichened pillars framing the entrance to the carriage sweep, Claire gazed down the beech avenue that stretched from Hawksfield Manor to the edge of its park. New leaves made a soft green haze above silvery grey trunks among which squirrels quarrelled and chattered. The morning's thin shower had brought out the rich smells of beech mast and fertile earth; the box hedges in the forecourt gave off their pungent reek as they dried in the furtive sun. A woodpecker's sonorous drumming punctuated the soft spring air. Above her, on top of the pillar, a stone hawk indicated the masters of all this dignity. Soon the carriages bringing Alba, Stella, Percy, Lucy, and Miss Quinnault, with Mr Baillie and Lord Dallington to attend them, would come bowling along under the tall trees.

Gravel crunched. Over her shoulder, Claire saw the housekeeper walking briskly towards her.

"They cannot possibly be here yet, ma'am," Mrs Stodges said. "Won't you come inside?"

"Oh, I know." Claire turned to the small, spare woman. "But it's been six weeks, and we've never been separated this long. Forgive my fussing."

The housekeeper shook her head and clucked. They stood contemplating the house for a while, the broad portico set in its creamy limestone façade, with the loom of the stables behind a dense copse on one side, the flower gardens and orchards, bare at this season, rolling down to the lake on the other. Clumps of mature trees dotted the open parkland; an ancient cedar hung dark above the garden wall. Immediately before them, across the gravelled forecourt with its precise box hedges, the tall front door, left ajar by Mrs Stodges, looked friendly and welcoming beneath its stone arch.

"Hawksfield Manor is ready to receive my sisters," Claire said. She extended her hand. "I cannot thank you enough for all you have done, Mrs Stodges. How you managed to find the extra staff!"

The housekeeper clasped it briefly and curtsied. "It looks well, doesn't it, ma'am, with the windows washed and fresh gravel in the sweep. Nor are the rooms anything to be ashamed of, for the present, although much remains to be done that's been neglected too long." Again she shook her head. "Staff is one thing, ma'am, but knowing when they're wanted and what to do with them, that is another. The house has been wanting a mistress." Again she curtsied. "Begging your pardon, ma'am."

Claire had raised her eyebrows, but now she smiled. "Captain Sumners said that, too. Isn't it astonishing how helpless men can be? It seems he never even thought of ordering a load of gravel."

Stepping onto the bright new pebbles, she led the way into the house. The entrance hall was redolent with the scent of hyacinths in a bowl on a side table. A hum of male voices filtered through from the library.

"There's nothing left to do upstairs, is there? Have you anything to keep me busy, Mrs Stodges, until my sisters arrive?"

"You have not tried the pianoforte, ma'am, which the young master gave orders to have tuned." The housekeeper opened the door to the drawing room for her to pass through. "I hope it's been done as it should, ma'am. Let me send some refreshments."

"Yes, please!" Nicola said. Ensconced in a wing chair in front of the fireplace, she had a book open on her knees. "I hope you haven't been ravished or abducted, Claire? As a chaperone I'm a complete failure, I know, but I simply couldn't put this down. Such villainy!"

Claire drew a long breath. "Since I introduced you to Lord Marmion, I suppose I can hardly blame you now." She turned to thank the housekeeper. "You won't forget the gentlemen, Mrs Stodges?"

The pianoforte stood in a part of the room separated from the rest by a screen of Grecian columns and looking out onto the forecourt. She could not possibly miss her sisters' arrival if she sat here. Claire struck a few keys and, pleased with the sound, played a few bars. *Oh I forbid you, maidens a'.* She stopped. Whoever had tuned the instrument knew his business, and the revolving bookcase next to it offered a good selection of music: well-worn copies of *The Tea-Table Miscellany*, Gluck, Handel, but the Corelli was new, and *The Well-Tempered Clavier*. This might take her mind off Tam Lin.

Opening its pages at the prelude in F minor, she began to play, but the piece was too familiar and her thoughts wandered. Captain Sumners must have given orders for the pianoforte to be tuned when he was here last, campaigning with Robert – getting the house ready for his bride, arranging for banns to be called. Her fingers lost their way among the keys; she tried again. Hawksfield Manor had been ready for her inspection when she arrived. Although Mrs Stodges was competent enough – the principal rooms were in good order, the kitchen flags well scrubbed – there had been much to do yet. Claire had stayed with Robert and Nicola and Nicola's papa at Manvers Park, but spent most of her time at Hawksfield Manor, with Nicola as her charming – if inefficient – chaperone and assistant. This day they had driven over with Robert and Mr Manvers, who had business to discuss with Captain Sumners and Lord Hawksfield.

Claire struck the final, melancholy chord. The captain had kept out of her way, and had kept her brother out of her way, too. If the few hours she had been in Robert's company this past fortnight were anything to go by, Captain Sumners must be having an uncomfortable time, but perhaps he did not mind it – he would get what he wanted, after all. Swiftly turning back a few pages, she began on the prelude in C minor. Its vile repeating motif could be relied upon to claim her full attention.

~ ~ ~

They were there! Carriages in the sweep; crumpled travellers staggering down the folding steps and across the gravel, shedding shawls, tears, and caps into the box hedges; a promiscuity of embraces; a confusion of bundles and bandboxes tripping up the footmen summoned to unload the trunks; and now Mr Manvers's groom drove his chaise into the fore-court, the horse shying at all the activity there.

"Are you a noblewoman now, Claire?" Percy's voice pierced through the melee of arrival.

"No, my love." Claire shook her head. "Nobility depends upon birth, not marriage, and I'm not even married yet."

"What nonsense you talk, Miss Lammond," Lord Dallington said over the hubbub. "Certainly you are a noble specimen of womanhood. Justin can't make you any more or less so."

"Thank you, Lord Dallington." Seizing her little sister by the neck, Claire added, "But noble or not, Percy, I will always be your elder sister, and in that capacity beg you to wipe your nose." Having performed this office for her, she planted a swift kiss on the now clean and rather pink nose.

She felt the girl stiffen in the same moment that she, too, heard a noise unrelated to the commotion in the hall. Angry voices approached from inside the house. The footmen continued to weave back and forth among the parterres, but the new arrivals all stopped still. Only Lucilla was unaffected, not interrupting her skipping game until the quarrel had reached the hall.

Mr Manvers was throwing the peroration of his harangue over his shoulder, his voice rising to a squeak in what was clearly intended as a rhetorical question which, however, Captain Sumners chose to take up.

"No, sir," he cried, no trace of huskiness remaining as he raised his voice to commanding pitch. He was looking taller and darker than Claire remembered him. "No, sir, I do not agree. If you object to ragged labourers crossing your precious view, I suggest you increase their wages, rather than depriving them of their right of way."

Claire had never seen him angry, and although – knowing Mr Manvers – he probably had reason, her insides felt cold. As for the others, Alba, Stella, Miss Quinnault, and Mr Baillie were staring at him in silent consternation. Percy had buried her head in Claire's breast. Only Lucilla and Lord Dallington regarded him coolly, like some strange animal.

He stopped so suddenly that Robert, following behind, blundered into him. Putting out a steadying arm, Captain Sumners took in the situation at a single glance.

"Mr Manvers, we are offending the ladies," he said. "Let us behave." His companions remained on the threshold, looking glum, but he walked into the hall, briefly put his hand on Lord Dallington's arm, and bowed to them all. "Forgive the sad spectacle. Usually we are quite amiable."

Lucy giggled. He winked at her, then looked at Claire, but at this moment, Alba cried, "Robert!", and Nicola admonished, "Papa!"

Alba's delight and Nicola's laughter dispelled the tension. Suddenly everyone was bowing, curtsying, shaking hands, or embracing, with Robert, Nicola, and Mr Manvers making their farewells at the same time. Claire was pleased with Lucilla's bob and clear how-do-you-do, but Percy could hardly be made to raise her head.

"Is he always like that?" she whispered as they trod up the stairs, and shrank into Claire's skirts when the captain addressed her and Lucy after the end of an early dinner.

As a social event, this was not a success. Claire had named the new arrivals to Lord Hawksfield, but he had little to say to Mr Baillie or Miss Quinnault. He clearly felt that the factor, the governess, and her younger charges were beneath his notice.

The travellers were tired. Lucy stared dreamily at the tall windows and the garden beyond, glittering with raindrops. Every now and then, she took a few mouthfuls of soup, which Percy was spooning up with the rapidity born of real hunger. Carriages made her sick; she would have eaten little during the journey. Claire gave them an encouraging nod. Lucy waved. Next to them, Miss Quinnault and Captain Sumners, by their gestures, were discussing the layout of the park and gardens.

Alba was looking across the table at Stella, who chatted amiably if desultorily to a silent Mr Baillie, interrupting herself every now and then to remind Lucy to eat and Percy not to wolf her food. Alba had a new dress, and her hair was different. She could not possibly have grown in six weeks, but she looked much more grown up than Claire remembered her. Perhaps seeing her every day, she had not noticed it, or perhaps Alba had matured in her new role as oldest sister.

Lord Hawksfield, seated between them at the head of the table, consumed soup, baked carp, and roast beef in a silence suggesting that he was by no means reconciled to all these additions to his household. By the time Claire put a baked apple and some spoonfuls of custard on his plate, however, he had mellowed enough to address her. "A strange start, this," he said. "The bride and all her family staying under the same roof as the bridegroom! And no honeymoon, everyone to stay put as though he had no establishment of his own to go to. What's the sense of marrying an estate if not to live there?"

Alba's eyes widened. Claire caught her gaze and made a small grimace. Lord Dallington, wrapped in a fatigue not unlike melancholia, gave a guilty start and cleared his throat. Lord Hawksfield seemed to feel the infelicity of his remarks, for he suddenly changed tack.

"Not that you are not welcome, child, on the contrary." Patting Alba's hand he turned back to Claire. "But what a beginning to your married life, my dear, away from familiar haunts and familiar faces, and keeping house for someone who is little better than a stranger!"

Claire smiled politely. "Is that not the fate of a bride, to leave her home and start afresh among strangers? And I am lucky enough to have my sisters with me. Thank you for your hospitality towards them."

Complacently his lordship replied, "Hawksfield Manor is a very well-kept house, to be sure, with room enough for any number of guests. Perhaps a little grander than what you are used to, my dear. Remind me to give you a tour some day. The ladies usually admire the portrait gallery, and the parterres and flower garden."

Making a suitable comment, Claire reflected that she should know him better by this time than to be surprised. Prompted by his son, he had rather airily granted her authority over all household matters, so she had been given a tour of the house, but by the housekeeper. The head gardener had shown her the grounds.

His lordship sighed. "It ought to be my son teaching you about the house and its history, of course, but Sumners has always been a perverse fellow. No pride, no sense of family."

Were it not for his son's pride, Lord Hawksfield would now be a laughing-stock, scorned by his allies, foremost among them his own brother-in-law. Claire swallowed several cutting remarks. "And yet the family have reason to take pride in Captain Sumners," she said instead, "not least in his professional achievement." Her voice was sharper than she had intended. Alba gave her a shy, wondering look. The conversation between the captain and Miss Quinnault ceased. But Lord Hawksfield had raised his eyebrows, so she continued, "Was he not mentioned specially in Lord Wellington's despatches?"

Lord Hawksfield snorted. "He would have done better had he stayed with the Hussars."

"Our Percy is quite fascinated by the Riflemen," Alba made an heroic attempt to change the current of the conversation. "Because they are so different – such a highly trained, expert body."

"Maybe they are, maybe they ain't, but what has my son to do with training? Is he not a nobleman? He might as soon train as a surgeon . . ."

"Some surgical knowledge would have been quite useful in the field," Captain Sumners began, but he was too late.

". . . or for the bar!" His lordship's disgust was all too patent. Claire suppressed a strong urge to laugh.

The captain exhaled audibly. "Nor is legal knowledge to be despised," he added.

"Especially when getting married," Claire murmured, more to herself, but by the captain's swift glance she thought he had heard. Soon she rose. The girls had finished dinner. "If you will excuse us, my lords, gentlemen, we will leave you to your port. Come, girls."

Lord Hawksfield made half a motion and dropped back into his seat. The other men stood; Captain Sumners opened the door and strode across the hall. "Allow me, ma'am."

With breathless thanks, Miss Quinnault ushered the older girls past him into the drawing room. Lucilla and Percy lagged behind, carefully hopping from white tile to white tile.

Claire stopped on the threshold to wait. "It can only be a matter of hours," she said.

He was watching the little ones with unhurried interest, but his smile when he spoke was a perfunctory one. "Miss Lammond, I –" His features relaxed. "You're laughing."

"Yes, I am. It was too absurd. I'm sorry."

"There is no call for *you* to apologize." He shook his head. "After all you have done, too. This must have been the first warm meal I have had in this house. What was that green soup, tasting like spring? And the silver is positively shining."

"Some small repairs sufficed to set the warming room in order." With an effort, Claire managed to keep a straight face. "And the soup was winterweed, but don't tell his lordship."

He gave a crack of laughter. "Well, there are enough weeds of any kind in the park. Listen, my dear, we will leave you and your sisters to take tea *en famille*. They must be tired, and you have some catching up to do." With a nod towards the little ones, he added, "Are they always this quiet?"

"Alas, no. Do you object to their presence at table? Grandmama was used to say it's the best way of teaching them how to behave in polite company."

"You are the one who decides what is right for your sisters. There is only one thing." He waited until the little ones had reached the door, Percy shrinking into Claire's skirts.

"Thank you for waiting," Lucilla piped up. "You see, we are not allowed to step on the black tiles."

"Of course not. Speaking of prohibitions . . ." He looked from one to the other.

"Yes, Captain?" Lucilla balanced one-legged on a white tile, but Claire could feel Percy's hand clutching at hers.

"You have not yet explored the grounds. You recall the irate gentleman here in the hall when you arrived – Mr Manvers, the father of your brother's wife? His land marches with ours on the north, but he does not like trespassers. So if you ever cross the boundary to his land, you will be in trouble with me personally. Is that understood?"

Claire's heart sank as Percy nodded, stiff with terror, but Lucilla only repeated, "Yes, Captain," and tripped away into the drawing room. There she stood stock-still for a moment, then threw a delighted grin over her shoulder and ran to hide behind one of the Grecian columns.

"I used to do that, too." The captain's swift smile faded. "You were right, Claire, it is enclosure that's worrying people. More than that, Manvers wants to abolish the old rights of way. Hence the row. I'm sorry."

Shaking her head, she reminded him that he had apologized at the time. With a quick thank you, he shut the door on himself.

The sun had dipped under the low bank of cloud hanging in the west and slanted long rays into the drawing room. Percy was curled up on the sofa where Claire's workbasket waited; Alba and Stella were by the pianoforte; Lucilla was walking round and round the columns. In the golden light, it made a harmonious, homelike scene. It was almost too quiet.

Miss Quinnault seemed to read her thoughts. "Let us enjoy the quiet while we may," she said with an ironic lift of her brows. "Think of the uncommon activity the new people and surroundings are likely to stimulate – at the latest by sunrise tomorrow."

With a laugh, Claire sat down on the sofa and reached for her whitework. "But I cannot work with your head in my lap, sweetheart," she told Percy.

"Must you work?"

"Indeed I must, or we won't have enough pillow-cases to go round next time we change the sheets."

"Let me mend that bit linen," the governess said, "and you sing for us a while. We do so rarely hear you sing."

"If we sing, you must join us, Miss Quinnault. Perhaps you're right, Percy-love. What would you like to hear?"

Percy did not hesitate. Briefly lifting her head from Claire's lap, she said, "Tam Lin. I want Tam Lin."

~ ~ ~

"Listen." Justin cocked his head. His hands rested on the back of the chair he had pulled out for Mr Baillie. Matthew had already moved up to fill the seat vacated by Claire.

"They are singing," Mr Baillie said. "They often sing of an evening."

In the hall, the music was clearly audible. At his father's protest, Justin closed the door to the dining room, motioning to Baillie, who had followed him, to join him as he sat down on the bottom step of the great staircase. "Do you know the song?" he asked in a low voice.

"It's an old ballad," Baillie whispered, "about an elfin knight and a young lady. Listen; Miss Alba is singing the narrator's part."

Next came a voice he did not recognize, absurdly deepened for the part of the elf, followed by Claire, well-modulated and confident, before the narrator took over again. The story unfolded in its intricate structure, question and answer, repetition, reprise, until at last the knight was saved.

"I'm glad it was a happy ending," Justin said when they returned to the dining room. "Strange how children like the most harrowing tales best."

"They like to have their sense of order affirmed. To them, even the cruel order of the ballads is better than no order at all." An interesting thought, but Baillie did not continue, looking uncomfortable at having advanced an opinion at all. The other two men's silent presence was no help to conversation. There was no breaking through Lord Hawksfield's icy determination to deny Baillie the attention due to a guest, and Matthew – "I'm going upstairs," Matthew said abruptly. The rising flame when

Justin lit his candle briefly illumined a face streaked with tears.

"Hey, Turtle." Justin gripped his shoulder.

Matthew drew a rasping breath. "Have a care, Justin. Can't you see you're making me spill wax all over my hands?" He stalked from the room.

"He's jealous," Lord Hawksfield observed. Justin swung round. His lordship's face bore a triumphant sneer. "Smitten with your bride, Dallington is. No doubt he'd rather be bridegroom than best man."

Light-headed with relief, Justin said, "Well, he could marry one of her sisters instead." He caught Baillie's horrified stare and silently agreed with him on the infelicity of his remark.

It was no use prolonging an evening that no one enjoyed. "If you'll excuse me, my lord, I'll take a turn in the garden." With a grin at Baillie, he added, "I'm a tobacco-smoker. Do you care to come, or would you prefer to retire?"

~ ~ ~

Faint clouds illumined the night sky with their soft shimmer, and the wind whispered in the massive cedar that made a black blur to his left. The scent of box hedges was pungent in his nostrils before the aroma of tobacco covered it. Slats of yellow light fell from chinks in the drawing-room curtains.

Now the pianoforte was to be heard again, and the opening bars of a hymn floated across the cool air. Voices joined the pianoforte. Justin thought he did not recognize the text, but after a few draughts of tobacco, he found the words "Keep me, O Lord, from the hands of the wicked, preserve me from the violent man" revolving in his mind. A telling choice; a chilling one.

Slowly he exhaled the smoke. It had given him a queer sense of satisfaction to hear the banns read at

St Edmund's when he was here last, with Lyster. The banns had been read, and Claire had not had the least idea. On Friday, Reverend Meynell was to instruct the bride on her duties.

The lights were extinguished in the drawing room, then reappeared in the staircase, on the upper floor. Walking around the house, Justin made his way towards the stables.

Pepe hardly stirred when he entered the gable room, only snorting a little and burying his head deeper in his pillow. There had been times when the slightest noise would have ripped him from sleep to dangerous alertness, and Justin felt pleased to see him so secure and unperturbed. He sat down in the only chair and looked around the dim room. It was furnished sparsely with a chest of drawers topped by a basin and ewer, a small mirror, and some shaving tackle; clothes and a cap hung from hooks at the back of the door. That was all, apart from the bed, and only last year would have seemed luxury to both of them – and still did, for what more did a man need than a roof over his head and bread to eat? Justin knew a pang of envy.

He was roused from his thoughts by Pepe's sudden inquiry whether he was intending to sit there all night, or was anything the matter?

"You're awake?" But of course Pepe had been awake all the time, having heard his steps on the stairs and on the flagstones outside.

"Besides, you've been smoking." Pepe yawned cavernously. "So are you going to tell me what's wrong?"

Justin considered for a while, but it would not do. This was something even Pepe must not know. "No, I don't think I will," he said at last, adding with a laugh, "I'm jealous of the bailiff."

"Fine." In the uncertain light, Pepe's face was unreadable, but he folded his arms so elaborately that Justin knew he was shamming it. "That's the way to treat a friend. Next time you wake me up at dead of night, consider beforehand whether I'm worthy of your confidence, will you, instead of fobbing me off with some tale about the bailiff. I need my sleep." He tossed his head. "I might have known. The same thing happened to my cousin Domingo." Suddenly dropping the offended pose, Pepe continued, "After his best friend married, Domingo saw that something was amiss. It's a long story. In the end, it turned out right, only Domingo felt his friend should have told him straight away. 'What could I do?' his friend said. 'You are my best friend, but she is my wife.'"

"I do perceive here a divided duty." Thoughtfully Justin rubbed his chin. "We have a similar tale, only it's about a woman's duty to her husband and her father. Thank you, best of friends."

Pepe made a deprecatory gesture. "Actually, I think Domingo was a bit of an ass. What kind of a friend is that, who thinks in terms of duty? Besides, your duty is divided enough as it is."

"So you've seen that, have you?" After a silence, Justin added, "But it's true about the bailiff. I wasn't fobbing you off."

"I know." Pepe weighed his head. "But you aren't jealous of her brother, who has known her longer."

"He has no idea. No. He doesn't value her as he ought." He felt Pepe's eyes on him as he sought for words. "Baillie knows full well what it means to be attached to a family like that, even as a dependent. And I am beginning to learn it, God help me."

Chapter 7

I hear some say, "This man is not in love."
Drayton, *Idea*

THE parcel lay on the breakfast tray brought to
Justin's bedchamber, where he shared the meal with
Matthew. By its shape and weight it was a book.

With gentle fingers, Justin withdrew the pale
primrose tucked under the ribbon and slid it into
his buttonhole. A few deft movements and he had
undone the bow, pushed aside the silk paper. Turning to the flyleaf, he read the inscription. His heart
must have been beating steadily all the time, but
until now he had not been aware of it. "A noble
woman," he said half to himself.

"What is it?" Matthew set down the coffeepot.

"The bride's gift to the bridegroom."

"Yes, but what is it?"

"An inscribed copy of *Marmion*." Justin came to
the other side of the table and showed him the calf-
bound quarto.

Matthew peered at the open page. "'To Claire
Lammond, may she come to be a lady, but never
suffer the fate of her namesake.' And in a different
hand, 'To the fulfiller of that wish'." He raised his
eyebrows. "And that means?"

"Scott's heroine is named Claire, too: Lady Clara
de Clare." Justin touched the inscription with his
fingertips. "He must have given her this when it
first came out. By the gods, the girl has courage.
Courage and a sense of humour."

"Come, come, Justin, what is there courageous in
marrying you?" Matthew pushed a cup of coffee towards him and added a dash of cream to his own.

"She is entrusting her person to a man she barely
knows, and that without the excuse of her loving

him or him loving her. Does that not strike you as courageous?"

"Not to mention her property." Matthew inclined his head. "I concede her courage. But is that a reason to go all dewy-eyed about a hand-me-down book?"

"Not her property." Justin grinned. "That would not be courage, it would be madness. We've had the settlements redrafted. Did you know that Scott is an advocate as well as a poet? He acted as her advisor, and it's all securely tied up." Scott had also written him a curiously personal letter, which he now removed from his inner pocket to fold into the book before he laid it aside. Perhaps at a later time he might puzzle it out. He picked up his cup.

"That is madness, Justin." Matthew dipped a piece of bread in his coffee and began to eat, daintily and noiselessly. Surely Matthew was the only man in the world who could eat bread dipped in coffee without slurping or spoiling his clothes.

"My father will agree with you, I make no doubt. Granted, bringing the estate into order needs some investment, but that is not where it's going to come from, not unless she agrees. If the investment is worthwhile, she probably will." He drank some coffee. It was strong, and still hot. "Bless her. If she does agree, I'll know the investment is worthwhile."

Matthew swallowed and patted his mouth with a napkin. "But you were pleased to find your father eager to be doing, to be making the estate profitable, rather than merely replenishing the family funds through a rich alliance and going on the same as before."

"I am, and I'm going to help him all I can. But not like that."

"You are mad," Matthew said starkly. "Will you stop fidgeting, Justin, and sit down to breakfast like a Christian?" But the elegant drawl was back in his voice when he added, "Raving mad. I thought so when you stopped Lord Hawksfield announcing the engagement and asked me whether it were possible to end it, and now I know. It's time you made up your mind, little cousin. Do you or do you not wish to marry Miss Lammond?"

"Yes," Justin said through a mouthful of bread. When Matthew threw him a black look, he added sharply, "You said ending it would be her ruin."

"Have some more coffee." Matthew poured. "Are you sure you don't want cream? No wonder you're so thin." He leaned back in his chair. "A lady may draw back from an engagement. In your case, however, the thing had gone too far, and with her knowledge."

Justin swore quietly, but did not enlighten him.

"It's a fine, tight net they've woven," Matthew continued. "We'd all have looked extremely foolish, but she would have been the jilt of the century." He looked down at his hands. The corners of his mouth curled. "And having met her family, I'm rather glad those girls aren't to be consigned forever to some Scottish backwater." He raised his eyes. "And you . . ." In a hoarse croak he concluded, "She may not be conventionally beautiful, but you were slavering like a bloodhound when we chose your morning gift for her."

"Damn your conventions, Matthew! She's beautiful, desirable, clever, and courageous." And scared, he added mentally.

"Are you quite sure you're not in love with her?"

Setting down his coffee-cup, Justin withdrew to the window. "I've been in love, and it was nothing like this." Nor had he ever misjudged a girl's reactions as badly as Claire's. When she flinched away from him that morning in Lyster's drawing room, he had hardly noticed the blow, so intent had he been on persuading her. Her courage had strengthened his resolve when her patent fear ought to have undermined it. It was only later that he started to feel it: that she did not care for him in the way he had grown used to thinking of her – as a spouse.

Yet he remembered her lips as warm and yielding, her cheek soft against his hand. His memory was a most treacherous organ; a moment later, she had been on the brink of hysteria.

The sharp rattle of crockery brought him back to the present. Matthew was stacking plates, cups, and saucers. He, too, was on the brink of some strong emotion. God alone knew what all this must cost him. "Turtle," Justin said softly, "I want to thank you for all you have done – your advice, your many services. You have been a true –"

"Another word and I'll strangle you." Matthew's own voice sounded as if someone or something were slowly strangling him. When Justin made to rise, he checked him with an outflung hand. "If you dare to touch me –" He inhaled sharply. "Don't look at me like that!"

"Turtle . . ." But Justin did as he was bade and turned back to the window. A movement down in the garden caught his attention. Over his shoulder, he said, "I think the bride is making an eleventh-hour escape."

This brought Matthew to his side. "What?" Together they watched Miss Lammond crossing the parterres with a quick step. "You don't really think –"

"No, I don't. But I had better go and make sure, hadn't I?" Fetching up his gloves and silk hat, Justin walked out, ignoring his cousin's protests. The last that came to his ears was that he could not possibly marry with a primrose in his buttonhole.

~ ~ ~

The orchard was a soothing place after the tensions of the breakfast parlour. The grass had been carefully scythed, with little islands around the early primroses flowering there and there. The bark of the cherry trees shone darkly red in the sunlight, buds clustering along their branches. The apples were more backward, but all the same Claire was beginning to feel hungry among all this promise of fruit. Perhaps she should have breakfasted after all.

"Would you like an apple?" Captain Sumners suddenly appeared at her side, producing out of nowhere a wrinkled specimen from last year's harvest, like a conjurer. She had not heard him approach.

"Thank you." It was sweet and juicy. In preparation for the wedding breakfast, she had inspected the stores of fruit and preserves, shocked to find so little when the yield must be enormous. A thin-lipped Mrs Stodges had been unable to throw much light on the matter. The housekeeper, the cook, and the head gardener would have to learn to talk to one another before this year's strawberries ripened. Fortunately it was a while yet, and there had been enough raspberry preserve to make a cream crowdie. Wiping her fingers on the handkerchief the captain gave her, Claire said, "I am not making an eleventh-hour escape."

"I should hope not. It would be a shame to miss the wedding feast when you've been so busy about it." Despite his words, he looked grave. Perhaps he had felt his cousin's presence as something of a strain, too. The girls were certainly overexcited this morning, but it was Robert with his significant looks who had led her to escape.

"Shall we run away together?" Captain Sumners reached out his hand. "Will you walk to church with me?"

Before she knew it, she had put her hand in his, withdrawing it rather self-consciously to pick up her skirts. He waved up to where Lord Dallington's bulky form loomed behind a window, then led her through the kitchen gardens and onto the well-trodden path skirting the garden walls. "This is the right of way Manvers means to abolish," he said. "Would you mind very much if I came to your room tonight, just to let your maid see me?"

She nearly laughed at the way he sprang the question on her, but the question itself startled her, too. It was odd that he should return to what she had taken for a mere piece of rhetoric, for he could not possibly have meant it as a promise, however oblique. He was a man, after all.

"Not at all," she said politely, stepping onto the path. When she looked over her shoulder, he was standing quite still, regarding her with alert eyes. "What is it?"

He shook his head. "Nothing. I admire courage, that's all."

Perhaps he was right in thinking her coura-geous. But she knew what she might be letting herself in for, and he could not know that. "Is there anything to be afraid of?" He was a man, but so far she had found him to be considerate, clean, and sober – although the latter might not last very long on this day, his wedding day.

"No, there isn't. But – forgive me for mentioning it – there have been occasions when I had the im-pression that you were afraid."

So he had seen it: that it had not been maidenly shyness. He was far too perceptive. She lifted her chin. "You are strangely inconsistent, Captain. Are you now calling me a coward?"

"Never." The warmth in his gaze was almost palpable. "You have all my admiration – no, let me say it just this once – and my gratitude."

This had to be stopped. "Oh, I know that," she said airily. "You are forever thanking me, for every little thing. But you know, there are benefits for me, too. Such scope for my housewifely fervour! And then I mean his lordship to host Alba's debut next year."

His laughter was a little shaky, but he said no more and helped her across a stile where several paths met.

A fair number of people were going in the same direction. Curtsies were dropped and forelocks were tugged, the captain responding with calm friendliness, but there was a certain reserve, too, sidelong stares, and few smiles. The small ironstone church would be filled to bursting; their union was, after all, a matter of great local and perhaps even wider import. With no less a personage than Viscount Dallington acting as best man, the people would expect to see Lord Hawksfield's elder sister and her spouse at the wedding. It was not every day that a countess and an earl came to Hardingstone.

A cluster of villagers blocked the porch, but as once before, the captain's assumption that people would make way for him proved justified. When they entered St Edmund's hushed dim space, a sea of faces turned towards them. Apart from the family stalls, every pew was filled. People even stood at the back and in the aisles. The Honourable Captain Sumners's wedding was a good opportunity to have a long look at him, too, not only at his exalted relatives. After his years of absence, after all that was said about his brother, the rumours about Lord Hawksfield's plans, they might well feel the need to do so. Hazarding a glimpse of her own, Claire saw him sweep the crowd with his gaze. Finally his eyes alighted on her. No matter why one might choose to look, she thought dispassionately, he was well worth looking at.

"Meet the yeomanry," he said. "Are you certain, Miss Lammond?"

Her perplexity must have shown, for he added, "Are you certain you want to be the woman these people think they are looking at: Mrs Sumners, the future Lady Hawksfield?"

She had not considered it in that light. "I am not going to draw back now." A twinge of bitter amusement stung her. "Wouldn't that be leaving it rather late?"

"Not at all." He grinned. "We could walk up the nave, walk into the sacristy, talk to the reverend, and walk out the back door."

The idea seemed to appeal to him, and she could see its attraction. "If only to see their faces . . . But we wouldn't, you know. We wouldn't be here."

"No," he agreed. "A shame." He continued to look at her, however, apparently awaiting her decision. She put her hand in his. He raised it briefly to his lips. "Then come and meet the yeomanry," he repeated. "There is Farmer Martin."

The name rang a bell. Snowdrops, that was it; the captain had embellished one of Robert's letters with a drawing of the snowdrops in Mr Martin's window-box. "How do you do? Was it your snowdrops that the captain drew for me?"

"Aye, ma'am, that they were. Drew them from my mother's parlour. It seems he likes wildflowers best." He gestured at the pale primrose in Captain Sumners's buttonhole.

Next were Mr Martin's mother, more farmers, the huntsman of the local hunt, the innkeeper. The old schoolmistress and the young schoolmistress she had already met, but not the physician, nor the apothecary. It might have gone on indefinitely had not the carriages from Hawksfield Manor arrived.

"This is all very irregular," Lady Boughton complained. "Your brother is waiting for you outside, Miss Lammond."

"We've been impatient." Captain Sumners looked towards the porch. "There's the party from Delapré Abbey, too. Come and meet Bouverie, Claire, or do you wish to join your brother?" She shook her head. She had no desire for Robert to give her away.

The girls ran up the nave; Alba and Dallington followed at a more dignified pace, the one scolding gently, the other pale and haggard. Mr Manvers and Nicola climbed into their pew, Miss Quinnault motioned the girls to their places, Robert came in. At some point in all this to and fro, Claire found herself in the front pew. Reverend Meynell made his appearance. The ceremony began.

~ ~ ~

To have and to hold, from this day forward. That would have to wait, and if he had abjured tobacco for the evening, washed all over with warm water, vigorously cleaned his teeth, and had Planchett shave him a second time, it was only to keep up appearances. The lavender scent of shaving lotion mingled with the silken scent of his dressing gown as it warmed against his skin. Rising with a quick acknowledgement, Justin barely waited for the valet to retire before he picked up Claire's gift from the bedside table and unfolded Scott's letter yet again.

You have to take your ground in a new family, he read, *whom I know you will find all you can wish but they must be above humanity if they have not prejudices and fears of one kind or other – to these my dear Captain Sumners you will accommodate yourself as far as it is possible because in doing so you will best show your affection to your lady.* It was good advice, if a trifle obscure. Fighting down the urge to laugh he read on. *I trust and hope you will excuse this presumption because I am on this occasion a Papa sort of person to Miss Lammond and determined to exercise my full right*

84

to be dull and dogmatical. This sobered him. At least there was someone looking out for her. No, he had better not attempt to hold or have her.

If she looked uncommonly beautiful with her dark hair cascading over her shoulders, it was not by design; that was simply the way she looked with her hair down. Nor was the dressing gown of pure white lawn that seemed to cling to her out of sheer affection a sign of anything but a determination, matching his own, to keep up appearances. Probably a gift from Mrs Lyster, it must have done Claire's sense of propriety considerable violence to don it. Tied snugly around her waist, it revealed rather than concealed her figure, its high ruffled collar plunging deep over the bosom of the equally scandalous nightdress underneath.

The maid had greeted his entrance with a curtsey. Claire's expression was impenetrable, but the child on her knee – Persephone, or Percy – who had regarded him with hostility all day seemed to see no reason to stop doing so now. Their hold on each other tightened for a moment.

"It's like Tam Lin," a small voice from the bed announced: the youngest girl was playing among the bed-curtains.

"Will the Sassenach vanish at Hallowe'en, then?" Persephone's whisper was devastatingly audible.

Claire chuckled softly, rocking the girl in her arms. "It is unlikely, love, for he is quite real."

"But he's dressed in green, like the fairy folk."

"Unlike Tam Lin, however, he is not 'fair and full of flesh'."

"And he took Holy Communion in church to-day." The little one hopped down from the bed.

Justin found himself subjected to the scrutiny of three pairs of eyes – one light grey, the other two bright blue – seeking to establish whether he were quite human.

"Now, Miss Persephone, Miss Lucilla, will Hannah put you to bed?" The maid extended her hands, but the older girl shook her head.

"I don't want to sleep with Alba, I want to sleep with Claire." Suddenly she slipped from Claire's knee and confronted Justin, tilting back her head to look him in the face. "Why should you want to sleep with Claire? You're a grown man, you don't need her. I have nightmares," she concluded in a tone that suggested she was rather proud of that affliction.

Justin reached for a chair and sat down. Now he was nearly at eye-level with the child. "Your claim is perhaps older than mine, but you have had some time to accustom yourself to Miss Alba, and she to you. I do not believe she would readily consent to solace my midnights rather than yours."

"Do you have nightmares, too?" Lucilla came to stand next to her sister.

"No. My need for Claire is a different one, but just as great."

They stared at him for a moment. "I told you it wouldn't work," Lucilla informed her sister. "Not with Claire wearing a special nightgown." Turning back to Justin, she said unexpectedly, "Will you put us to bed, then?"

She stepped forward into the crook of the arm he extended, one hand gripping the collar of his dressing gown, and he lifted her up easily. "Can you carry the candle?" he asked her, and with a nod she took it. "Come on, Percy," she commanded, and indeed the other girl tagged after them, if only after Claire had given her a gentle push.

Holding the candle aloft, Lucy lit them through the hall. Justin stopped by Miss Alba's dressing room to open the door for Percy; she slipped through with a muttered goodnight. As he mounted the stairs to the nursery, the little one leaned her head against his shoulder, talking sleepily.

"What's that?" Gently removing the candle from her grasp, he bent his ear towards her.

"I said if there are ghosts." A touch of petulance did not conceal the underlying anxiety.

"No," he replied firmly. "What makes you think there are?"

"Percy and I looked at the picture gallery. All those people – so ancient, and so many, some of them are bound to walk. Why are there so many?"

Justin denied that the probability of ghosts increased with the age of portraits. "My family is rather old, that's why we have so many pictures. Which ones did you like best?"

"I liked the dogs. Percy liked the big ones with rivers and trees, but she says how it's done is more important than what's in it. She tried it, too, but she said it was no good."

Justin was impressed, and said so. "I could show her how. Do you think she'll go on disliking me?"

The little girl raised her head and gave him a sceptical look. "You know about painting?"

"Drawing mountains and rivers was part of my duties in Spain." Her black eyebrows drew together in a doubtful frown. "So the army would know where to go. You know, like a map, but like a painting, too. Here we are," he added, about to set her down, but she protested.

"Won't you put me to bed?" She leaned down and pressed the handle, so Justin walked in.

"And where have you – oh." Miss Stella was sitting up in bed, her candle still burning. "Well, I can see where you've been all this while. Didn't I tell you to say goodnight and then come back? It serves you right if you got in trouble." Turning to Justin she added, "I am so sorry, Captain. I ought to have gone with her."

"I didn't get in trouble," Lucy announced. "He doesn't mind. Do you?"

"Not at all. Don't worry, Miss Stella." Justin set down the candle and tumbled the child onto the bed. Snuggling under the covers, she directed him to tuck her up, to make a cross on her forehead, to give her a kiss.

"Perhaps you'd like the captain to bring you a glass of hot milk, too?" Miss Stella inquired with scathing irony. "I told you that it's a special night. You weren't to bother Claire, and you're not to bother the captain, either."

"But I'm not bothering him," the little one contended. "Besides, it's far too early for him and Claire to go to bed."

"That's right," Justin said. The older girl had suddenly lost her assurance and was silent. "If it hadn't been for you and Percy, we'd be sitting around yawning at each other for sheer boredom," he added.

Lucilla giggled. "Alright, I'll stay in bed now. You're sure about the ghosts?"

"I was a boy in this house, so I should know."

This seemed to satisfy her, and she promised to sleep well and dream sweet dreams. "And you, too, Miss Stella."

On his way back, he stopped by a window for a moment – Venus low over the roof – and allowed himself a sweet dream of his own, of a soft, pliant Claire waiting for him, her loose hair dark and enveloping as the night. But she had enough duties and demands plucking at her; he would not even mention Venus.

~ ~ ~

Robert had caught up with her in the end, remarking with a detestably superior smile that he would spare his breath. "For it's plain enough that my advice isn't needed. You are your mother's daughter, after all, and judging by the way you look at him, the captain is welcome to his new command. How well things have fallen into place."

She had turned her back on him. He had no right to speak to her like that – even if it were true, which it most decidedly wasn't. Things falling into place, forsooth! Yet the phrase evoked a memory, and suddenly she remembered Captain Sumners talking about things that looked after themselves. Was this what he had meant, too? The confidence that had impressed her at the time, was it nothing but an odious reliance on his indisputable charm? Well, he would see. She might submit, but she would never succumb.

A sound at the door did not herald his entrance, however, but Hannah's, carrying a tray with an ashet full of delicacies left over from the wedding breakfast, two cut glasses, and an ice-filled silver bucket holding a bottle of champagne. Apparently he did not mean to rely entirely on his charm.

"Set it down on the table there," he said, coming in after the maid. "Thank you, Hannah."

By his quick nod and smile, it appeared that he had perceived Claire in the window-seat, but he did not approach her. Hannah had moved the candles from the dressing table to the side of the bed, where they cast a pool of light on the elegant curve of its head, the hangings bunched in shimmering folds of dark blue, and the immaculate white linen of lace-edged pillows. In passing he now lifted the candelabrum to the mantelpiece. Reflected in the wide mirror above it, the flames illuminated the two easy chairs that faced each other across the hearth and the loaded tray on the low table between them.

There was a scrunch of ice as he lifted the bottle from the bucket. He freed the cork of its wire cage and, gently rubbing the bottle's neck, eased it out of the opening without so much as a pop, the only sound the froth of champagne as he poured. "Your very good health." He brought her a glass, but did not remain by her. "Are you warm enough?"

She wasn't, but if he thought she wanted anything but the warmth of the fire, he would find himself mistaken. "It's this dressing gown." Raising her shoulders, she indicated the garment, which immediately fell open at the front. "Nicola gave it to me for a wedding gift." He did not seem to notice, however, so she tucked the collar back into a more seemly position. "It's not very practical." Still he made no comment. "Are you trying to make me drunk?" It struck her then that he was entirely sober. Had there been the slightest sign of inebriation, Percy would never have gone with him, nor would she herself have permitted him a moment alone with the two little girls.

"No, only to keep up appearances. And we might as well be comfortable. Did you manage to eat anything at all at the reception?" He indicated the ashet with its artless arrangement of cold ham, pickled asparagus, some herb pies, a small heap of salmagundy, and a slice of veal cake. "Come to the fire, won't you?" He talked on, maddeningly, as she watched and listened and waited for him to come to the point, but he never did come to any point at all. Instead his talk drew her in, as it always did, distracting her, and suddenly she found herself opposite him at the low table, warmed by the fire, smiling at his remarks. A pleasant smell of lavender hung in the air, and indeed his chin was as smooth as in the morning. His hair was a little ruffled, but innocent of pomade, as if he had washed his head that night. "At least my relations weren't the only ones to disgrace themselves," he was saying.

"Poor Percy." The cream crowdie had proved too much for the little girl, but the captain had recognized the symptoms and alerted Miss Quinnault. There seemed to be no ill effects apart from a tendency to whine. "You reacted very well, Captain, and you can't have much experience with little girls and their stomachs."

"The symptoms of drink are similar – that glassy look, which as an army man I know only too well. I suppose that's what enabled you to recognize Matthew's trouble in your turn."

Let him think that; she would not enlighten him.

"I'm glad your sister's mishap hasn't spoiled your appetite." Somehow she had eaten her way through to dessert, the cream crowdie on which Percy had gorged so shamelessly.

"It's very good. Have you had any?" When he shook his head, she leaned forward, offering her spoon, only to withdraw it again when he opened his mouth.

After a little of this, he grabbed her wrist. Her blood rushed through her veins in an ice-cold flow. So here it was, after all, as she had expected.

He took the mouthful she had been offering and licked the spoon clean. "Delicious." Their eyes met. For a small eternity his gaze held hers. "Now that I've got you alone, Claire . . ."

"Yes?" Her throat felt raw.

He leaned back, turned to the table, busied himself about the champagne. "I'd like to ask you about this enclosing scheme."

She suppressed a crazy desire to laugh and assumed an interested expression.

~ ~ ~

He had seen it too often to be taken in. She led me on, she wanted it, she was asking for it – he had heard it often enough, too, and had had men hanged for the crimes these words belied. He could only thank his stars that when it had first happened to him, he had been too young, too shocked himself to believe that anyone could possibly want to make love under these circumstances: his men dragging the last of the corpses strewn across the yard away to a common grave, the corner of the stable block still smoking from fire laid by retreating Frenchmen, himself smeared with dust, sweat, soot, and blood that was not his own. And suddenly this handsome young gentlewoman had appeared at his elbow, apologizing for the state of the house and offering the great hall as accommodation for his men. The roof leaked, she said, rendering the upstairs rooms uninhabitable, and would he do her the pleasure of dining with her and her aged parent?

She must have had a dreadful time with him; dazed and exhausted as he was, and disbelieving, too, when he finally became aware of the lures she was casting out. "*Señora,*" he had said firmly, "I sleep downstairs with my men." But his curiosity had been roused and before he went down, he had looked into the (allegedly) leaking rooms: so many scared white faces looking back at him. He had slept across the foot of the stairs.

He had seen it too often, a woman's determination to bring on what she thought inevitable in a desperate bid at least to control when it happened, and to whom. He had not expected to see it at home, however, and he was very nearly taken in. It was only when he raised his eyes from that elusive spoonful of raspberries and cream and saw the look in hers, half hostile, half triumphant, that recognition came upon him.

And so he refilled their glasses and talked about enclosing and rights of way as if it were the most natural thing in the world to sit with a lightly clad young woman and talk about these things between sips of champagne. Her unselfconsciousness was one of Claire's most endearing traits: present her with a problem and she forgot her own immediate concerns; tell her a story and her reality remained suspended until the ending was achieved.

Now she said, "Isn't enclosing a thing of the past? I should have thought it would have been done decades ago." She flicked back the sleeve of her dressing gown and picked up her glass. His gaze slid from her delicate wrist to her feet, but her ankles were neatly tucked away under the hem of that shocking nightdress.

"It was, too. My grandfather did a great deal, clearing, hedging, ditching, draining, all that was necessary to make wilderness into pasture and some arable, too. No, these are odd bits and pieces left over at the time, and Nelly's Lea, of course." He drank some champagne. "Manvers simply wants to consolidate his estate, establish a herd of deer, and raise ring-necked pheasants, but my father talks about turning his share into arable. Labour will be cheap when the war ends."

She raised her eyebrows. "Soldiers to plough-shares?" How white her forehead was against her black, black hair. A strand of it had fallen across her cheek. Without conscious volition, he reached out to smooth it back.

Her arm flew up, the palm of her hand turned outwards, her fingers spread. The wedding-ring flashed in the candlelight.

"*Qué demonios...*" He drew back, and when he looked again, her hands were demurely folded in her lap, and she was facing him with an expression of friendly inquiry.

Deliberately he lowered his eyes, eased his tense shoulders, and kept himself quite still, impassive – harmless. "Shoemakers to shovels," he said. "With no more army boots to be made, Northampton's shoe industry is very likely to decline, so there'll be plenty of men looking for work, and men who are used to work and regular hours, too."

"All the same, will it be worth the investment? Mr Baillie and Grandmama discussed the possibilities of grain when the war pushed the prices up, but our land isn't suited, so we never made the change. It's nearly all pasture. If the war ends, the grain price will go down, too, however. You believe that it'll be over soon, don't you?" He nodded. She tilted her head. "What sort of land is it? Some of it might make good grain or root land, and pasture, now, pasture is always worth having." A faint smile hung about her lips; she must have been quoting someone of whom she was fond.

Her lips were red; they would feel warm and soft. Justin dug a handful of ice from the bucket holding the champagne bottle and watched it melt in his palm. "That's the trouble. I'm not farmer enough to tell, and Hughes won't give me a straight answer. He is my father's man, after all."

"What a mess you are making." She gave him a napkin.

"All I can tell you is that I found a nightjar's nest there when I was boy. Perhaps it is mere sentiment that makes me not want to give up Nelly's Lea."

"Then it is a good thing that I cannot wax sentimental about nightjars – their horrible noise." At her shudder the dressing gown fell open yet again, yet again revealing the soft swell of her breasts under the thin nightdress. Quite unselfconsciously she tucked it back. "Another good thing is that Mr Baillie is very much my man and understands a good deal about land. I should like to see for myself, too. Will you let Hughes show us, one morning, before Baillie returns to Scotland?" She gave him a direct look. "I understand that all this is at quite an early stage and no petition has been got up?"

He remembered how her eyes had first struck him; how he had heard her voice, low-pitched and calm, her accent soft and lilting, almost French; how he had seen her hair, black as a raven's wing, and expected an olive complexion and dark eyes. Instead, her light-grey gaze had seemed to pierce right through him, although that was probably an illusion, that those unusual eyes showed her things differently. But it was clever of her to see that the degree of forwardness and publicity of the project would make a great difference if it came to dissuading his lordship from taking it further.

"To think that I should one day be grateful for my father's lack of efficiency! They haven't even measured and charted the land."

And what else had she seen? What in her life could have led her to act the way she had? Taunting him, tempting him, but it had been cold fear, not coquetry. *My dear young friend has seen enough of the wretched consequences of family dissention to make her for her whole life regard it as the service of domestic unhappiness. I do most sincerely rejoice that she is out of the reach of all this tracasserie*, Scott had written. But what could she – poised, beautiful, well-bred, and rich – know of trouble and fear?

To look at her now, one would think, very little, for she was laughing at him. "I should have remembered that you find it exhausting to sit around and talk. But I'm tired, too." The dressing gown slipped again as she rose, and this time she left it. "Besides, we won't get any further until we've inspected the land. Good night, Captain Sumners."

He did not call her Mrs Sumners. "Good night."

When he looked back, she was extinguishing the candles, one by one, her arms raised. The wide lace ruffs had fallen back, revealing her lower arms; her bare neck was milk-white against the dark mass of her hair. He pulled away his gaze, quickly, to prevent it finding more bareness and whiteness. His eyes hurt.

Chapter 8

Nor thinks, nor dreams, my noble lord,
By slightest look, or act, or word,
To harass Lady Clare.
Scott, *Marmion*

"EYEBRIGHT, coltsfoot, cowslips, stinging nettles, daisies." In the cold, oblique light bathing the still-room, Claire contemplated the shelves with dismay. At the end of a harsh winter, stores were bound to run low, the remedies for colds and sore throats all used up, but comfrey salve was essential, and there was none here. "There's no comfrey salve."

Stella looked up from her list. "There isn't? Oh, dear. And it's only March."

Too early in the year for comfrey, but perhaps the arnica would tide them over. Claire lifted the pot from the shelf and opened the lid. "The arnica is running low, too."

"Well, we're not likely to contract any bruises, are we?" Stella's dark sense of humour never failed to alarm Claire, but it also made her laugh, if somewhat shakily.

Stella wrinkled her nose. "Unless we fall down the stairs, or walk into a door in the dark." Leaving her list on the table, she came and stood next to Claire, her head on her shoulder. "Lucy did trip over the edge of carpet the other day," she said thoughtfully, "but the captain saved her and consoled her."

For a moment they stood holding each other. A pale sunbeam penetrated the tall window. "Daisies," Claire said softly, puzzling over a memory. "The captain brought me some, weeks ago, as a gift, and I said they make a good bruise tincture."

She felt Stella's head move against her shoulder. "Does he know?" Stella's voice was very low.

"No." Claire smoothed a straying curl behind her sister's ear. "At least I told him nothing. But he's not stupid."

Stella straightened, breaking their embrace, her face alight with rare, infectious laughter. "No, he isn't, is he?"

Claire kissed her cheek, then turned around and shut the cupboard. "We'd better stock up on tonics for coughs and colds, too. It's promising to be a fine afternoon, and surely we'll find some warm nooks with coltsfoot, creeping charlie, daisies, or stinging nettles. Let's get the girls together –"

As if on cue, Percy stole into the stillroom. She never said a word, but sidled over to Claire and caught hold of her skirts.

"Why, there you are, Percy, we were just going to look for you. Have you seen Alba and Lucilla?"

The girl shook her head, but this seemed to indicate an inability to speak rather than a reply to Claire's question, for there were swift steps and a rustle of skirts, and a moment later, Alba put her head round the door.

"Is Percy –? There she is. Really, Percy, you oughtn't to run off like that. It's terribly rude and quite unnecessary."

"They were shouting." The words came out in a thin whisper. "He's always shouting."

"Who is, Percy?"

But it was Alba who replied. "Our brother and Mr Manvers, your husband, and Lord Hawksfield are closeted together, and we could hear their voices raised. But it was not shouting, Percy, and it's quite unreasonable to say he's always shouting. I don't even know who you mean. Nor is it any reason to run away without a word to anyone."

"I was scared." Percy's voice was a mere thread.

Catching Alba's eye, Claire gave a small shrug. "There's no need, Percy. Anyway," she continued brightly, "we were just going to look for you, and Lucy and Alba, because it's a fine day and we want to go a-herbalising. Come, let's find your bonnet and your boots."

It would be no use trying to persuade the little one to fetch her own bonnet, since that would mean passing the study, so Claire left the three of them to put on their boots while she went upstairs to speak to Miss Quinnault and collect Lucy, bonnets, wraps.

She suppressed a craven impulse to use the back stairs and walked into the great hall that was like a hinge between the two wings of the house. A murmur of male voices, no more, an oaken tread sighing under her feet – no need to be frightened, no need to hold her breath – here was the gallery. Even if the door of the study had been wide open, which it was not, she would have been out of range of vision now. There was no need to hurry. There never had been any need to hurry.

She had reached the next half-landing when an explosion of voices sent her up the last flight in unseemly haste.

~ ~ ~

"He's always shouting." Percy beheaded some nettles with a hazel switch. "And sleeping with Claire. Will he sleep with you every night, Claire?"

"You're meant to be collecting those nettles, Percy, not destroying them," Alba intervened. "Here, put on your gloves. Besides, if you mean Captain Sumners, he does not always shout. And I take it very unkindly that you keep fussing about where you sleep when you're allowed to sleep in my dressing room." Her cheeks flushed, Alba shot Claire a quick glance.

She shook her head. Percy would not be argued out of her crotchets, and Alba should know better than to engage in fruitless argument. Another look at that flushed countenance told her that Alba was trying to spare her embarrassment. "Never mind, Alba," she said softly.

Percy looked mulish. "I don't like him."

"I do," Lucilla piped up. "He doesn't shout. When I tripped over the edge of the carpet, he didn't shout. He picked me up and asked me whether I was hurt. And I'd come near to smashing that big blue vase. But he didn't shout. He didn't even tell me to watch where I was going. He blew on my hands, just like you do, Claire, to blow away the pain."

"You always like everyone," Percy said.

"You never like anyone," Lucilla replied.

Their squabble would continue for the rest of the day. They might keep it down within Claire's ear-shot, but whenever their cutting and picking took them away from the older girls, it flared up again. They kept it down, too, while helping to sort and process their harvest, only to re-erupt when Alba took them upstairs to wash and change. Claire found herself hoping that Percy's fear of Captain Sumners would keep her subdued during dinner.

"This is nearly finished." Stella had been layering daisies into a full-bellied glass jar. Claire unlocked the cabinet and measured out the spirits to pour on the flowers, trying not to breathe as the alcoholic fumes rose to her nostrils. By the time she had replaced the bottle and turned the key, Stella had corked and sealed the jar.

"We'll put it up there." The empty shelf across the top part of the window must have been installed with tinctures in mind. Stella climbed on the step-ladder, Claire handed her the jar. They were done.

"This is much more like it." Stella looked with satisfaction at the bundles of nettle hung up to dry, the green leaves and yellow flowers spread out on racks, the tincture glowing from its sunlit shelf.

"Prepared for the worst, that's what we are." When Claire turned to hang up her apron, she perceived her sister-in-law standing in the doorway. "Why, Nicola! I didn't hear you come in. Is it that late already?" The party from Manvers Park were to dine with them. "You'd better run and get changed, Stella."

"Why would you want to prepare for the worst?" Nicola's frown sat uneasily on her usually cheerful countenance. "There's nothing wrong, is there?"

"Of course not." Nearly everything was wrong; nothing was wrong that herbal remedies could set right. But Nicola believed in a bright and sunny world where everyone was kind and good, and it would be cruel to shake that faith. "Except that I will be desperately late; I promised Cook to look in before dressing."

"No, you won't. I came early." With wondering eyes, Nicola looked around the stillroom. "But what are you doing, Claire? It's not four days since your wedding. You cannot begin householding four days after your wedding. Even if you're not going away, you ought to have a honeymoon, not mix medicines and haunt the kitchen."

"I couldn't bear it," Claire said. "I started holding house before the wedding, and I'm not going to stop now. This household needs it." Locking the stillroom behind them, she steered Nicola towards the hall. "But Cook only wants a reassuring word. Will you join the gentlemen?"

"I will not." Nicola gave a tinkling laugh, twisted away from her, and began to mount the stairs. "I'll choose a gown for you and help you dress."

When Claire entered her bedchamber, her dinner dress lay ready across the foot of the bed. Her sister-in-law was rummaging about in the jewellery box. "I'll wear the new necklace, Nicola." The slim string of silver with its pendant of grey topazes had been Captain Sumners's morning gift.

"Of course you will, darling. But I want a comb to go with it. Ah, this will do." She laid her find on the dressing table and turned to Claire with a saucy smile. "I take it you did not find the dinner burnt and the cook in hysterics? I have to admit that I was not too enthusiastic about dining here until Robert reminded me that with you in charge, the food on the table would be fresh, hot, and plentiful. Turn around." She undid the hooks on Claire's gown. "He also said that Papa and he needed to discuss all sorts of dreary matters with Captain Sumners and his papa. There now." Claire felt Nicola's hands on her shoulders as she pushed down the dress for her to step out of. Glancing up with a quick thank you as she gathered it up, she saw Nicola's pretty mouth turned down in a worried pout. "But that's not why you married him, is it? You do love him, don't you?"

Claire laid her walking dress on the bed. "I'm sure the gentlemen are quite capable of having dreary discussions independently of whether I'm married or single. But how can you talk so, Nicola? Surely Robert's entering parliament is not dreary? Or your father's plans for the estate?"

As Claire discarded her underclothes, Nicola's frown was banished by a look of frank appraisal. "What a lovely figure you have, Claire. Almost too thin, perhaps, but then the captain will hardly cavil at that. For myself, of course, I like a man to be a little higher in flesh; Sumners looks to be all bone and sinew."

Fortunately the exigencies of dressing made a reply unnecessary. At last, Claire sat at the mirror, smoothing her long white lace-and-satin sleeves. "Will you do my hair?"

Nicola planted a quick kiss on her cheek. "How I've missed this! We both miss you terribly; Robert hasn't been the same." She heaved a short sigh. "I did want to talk to you before the wedding, but Robert said there was no need. He said the captain would know what he was doing."

In the mirror, she saw Nicola smiling. With an effort, Claire concentrated on her own reflection, touched her hair, turned her head this way and that. "You certainly know what you're doing, Nicola. It's charming."

"Thank you." But Nicola was not so easily distracted. "I was so happy to think we'd be neighbours, and Robert a member of parliament, and Papa... and Lord Hawksfield... I never considered how things might be the other way around." She seemed to feel that her statement was a little obscure. "You were very well together, right from the start," she added by way of explanation.

A shadow of doubt had fallen on her sunny world, and she wanted to be reassured. Not that the world was at all like that, but somehow Nicola's belief made it a little more so.

And it wasn't even a lie. Things would have been easier had it been a lie. "We were, weren't we?" Something twisted painfully inside her. If Robert had not betrayed her so, they might still be well together, Captain Sumners and she; but it was he who had offered her an honourable way out of her dilemma. For some reason, the memory brought a smile to her lips – of course, his whimsical marriage proposal, with honour coming into it. How well he had done it. *The family are highly spoken of as a race of honourable men who adorn their rank and country*, Mr

Scott had written. Captain Sumners certainly was an adornment to society; and he really did appear to expect nothing at all from her. The last four nights had all followed the same pattern.

She tilted back her head to look up at Nicola. "And the captain does know what he's doing." Yet his behaviour was too perfect to be rationally planned. "Or perhaps it is all intuition, or instinct," she added, momentarily forgetting to whom she was talking and how such a statement must strike her sister-in-law.

Nicola blushed. "Well!" Before she could comment further, a knock fell on the door. She went to answer. "The man himself," she said archly, going out as he came in.

He did not come in. He made no move until Claire beckoned. And since Nicola might still be within earshot, she added cheerfully, "Do come in, Justin."

He shut the door. She could stop pretending. All at once her limbs were heavy with fatigue. Closing her eyes, she leaned her head in her hands.

"Did you tell her what an ogre I am?" His voice was hard. "I merely ask for information; if I am to be an ogre, I'd like to act the part."

He was angry. She looked up, saw her alarmed eyes in the dressing-table mirror, collected herself, and turned to him.

He had not advanced far into the room, but stood just inside the door. He did not look like an ogre. Nor did he look very angry; nevertheless she said, contritely, "You're angry. I am sorry."

He did not take this as a cue to vent his anger on her, however; instead he said, "Thank you, Claire." He added something in Spanish and offered a paraphrase: "A shared trouble is less cruel. I feel much better." His attitude relaxing, he walked to the fireplace, then to the window, twitching aside the curtain to look out into the gathering dusk. "So what did you tell Mrs Lyster? Your brother could do with a little scarifying; he seems a stranger to guilt."

She had told Nicola that Captain Sumners was a wonderful lover. She could not possibly tell him that, no more than she could have let Nicola have an inkling of the truth. Lost for words, she simply gazed at him.

"I know." He rubbed his chin. "Any attempt at wiping Lyster's eye is invariably thwarted by consideration for that kind-hearted, affectionate girl."

That was putting it in a nutshell. He was still on his feet, but when Claire gestured towards a chair, he shook his head. "Sorry to be so restless, but I've been sitting around all day." He grimaced. "That's what I came to talk to you about – the outcome of our meeting." A corner of his mouth lifted. "And to apologize for the din. Lord Hawksfield is none too pleased about our changes to the marriage contract. Manvers is not pleased about my attitude towards rights of way. Your brother is not pleased, either, but he was quick to smoke that they'd have to humour me if I'm to continue my support for his candidacy."

The pressure must have been enormous. "How very . . . unpleasant for you. I am sorry."

"Not at all." He seemed amused rather than crushed. "Isn't it odd that my father, who always deplored my disobedience, should have convinced himself and conveyed to these two the impression that I would simply go along with their plans? But we've all swallowed our various spleens and will sit down to dinner together like civilized men. Or so I hope. And if you're still of the same mind, I'd be grateful for your opinion – about the land, I mean."

"You are welcome." It must have been a terrific row – what she had heard on the stairs would only have been the first distant rumbles – but it did not appear to have touched him at all. "Don't you mind being shouted at?"

"Not really." He shrugged. "I can always shout back, can't I?"

Of course he was not invariably gentle; he could not be. "Percy hates it."

"Do you shout at her a lot? You surprise me." She opened her mouth to protest, realized that he was making game of her, and shut it again. His lips twitched. "I beg your pardon. Percy doesn't like me much, does she?"

"Percy is being daft about you, and so I have told her. But her daftness is its own punishment, since it prevents her asking you about the Riflemen and hearing all your stories. Did you do any drawings while in Spain? That might make her change her mind; she's a fine artist herself. And I told her how good you are at telling stories."

His eyebrows shot up. "Am I?"

"You know it, too, or you wouldn't use it so cleverly. If you can set me at my ease by talking, you should be able to do the same by Percy." He was uncannily good at making her give herself away, too. To prevent his following up this line, she turned abruptly to the mirror, fixed her earrings, fumbled with the clasp of her necklace.

"Here, let me help you." Three strides brought him to her side. "Matthew said you ought to have diamonds and sapphires, but I wanted something you could wear every day, and he helped me choose this." She felt his hands over hers, briefly, as the story span out. He was doing it again. Then the chain lay cool against her neck. "Matthew has excellent taste, I will say that. The stones are like your eyes, as clear as water."

Chapter 9

There is a spirit in the woods.
Wordsworth, *Nutting*

THE rain-saturated meadows glittered with puddles. The furrows in the freshly ploughed fields resembled miniature canals. Claire narrowed her eyes against the dazzle. In the distance, the river made a silver ribbon bordered by the greyish green of willows. The low green hills were dotted with sheep and criss-crossed with blackthorn hedges faintly frosted over with buds. A procession of fair-weather clouds marched along the horizon, their smooth bellies tickled by St Edmund's battlemented tower. So bright, so wide – the rolling landscape under its open horizon gave her a strange sense of safety. One might ride into the distance and never be seen again. Her mare tossed its head, the bridle tinkling. Nervously Claire shortened the rein.

Captain Sumners made an unintelligible murmur that seemed to soothe the animal. "Let her stretch her neck a little," he added. Reaching across he moved Claire's hands on the rein. "There."

Oddly enough, she felt reassured rather than censured. She leaned forward and patted the horse's neck. Its sweet, warm smell mingled with the damp scents of cold air and wet earth.

"Will you tell us what we see, Captain?"

He began to explain the view. The low ground – a chequered handkerchief of dark brown and bright green – consisted of wheatfields and moist grass-lands, interspersed with solid blocks of human and animal habitation: Glebe Farm, Park Farm, Church Farm, Rookery Farm; Mr Manvers's land over to the west. This severe geometry was relieved by the curving lines of willows straggling along streams and by the irregular patches of fallow that were the remainders of the common land.

"The village was only slightly diminished when my grandfather enclosed Hardingstone Common, and he didn't enclose it completely. You can see what was left of it over there." He pointed. "That's not the land we're concerned with, however. My father's interest is in Nelly's Lea, beginning down here and extending right up to the Eleanor Cross from which its name derives."

The untidy tract of land lay between Delapré Abbey, Hawksfield Manor, and Manvers Park. By cutting it up, each of them could very prettily round off their holdings, or at least that was what it must look like on paper. Even from a distance, however, those shapes and colours seemed to call for closer inspection. She looked at Baillie.

"Would it be possible to examine the ground itself, ma'am?" he said.

"It looks uneven, does it not, Mr Baillie?"

"Aye, ma'am, that it does."

"Let's ride over, then." Captain Sumners led the way. Seeing him, it was impossible to believe that he had lost his horse all those years ago at Corunna; he seemed one with the animal. Following more slowly, Claire kept her eyes on the slippery ground, reassured by Pepe bringing up the rear.

She only noticed the small group on the other side of the gate when the captain hailed them. This must be the common: against the winter-grey straggle of brambles and coppice willows, the men in their worn homespun were barely visible. One was sitting on a recently cut willow stool, another had a bundle of brushwood next to him – a casual group of chance-met neighbours. Too casual; even as she willed herself to expect a friendly response to the captain's hail, she knew that this was not a friendly group. There were no direct looks or even words, but no one stepped forward to open the gate, either.

The surest horseman, Justin had drawn ahead and now took his mount across the gate in what seemed a mere lengthening of stride, landing neatly despite the mud. He was abreast; heads turned abruptly; one rough voice cut through the silence. "Good fences make good neighbours."

Wheeling his horse, reining in, and dismounting were all one swift movement, then he was advancing towards the fellow who had called out. "Speaking to me?" His voice was mild, but clearly audible in the still air. Although a head taller and twice as broad, the man hung his head, struck dumb.

"If you have anything to say to me, you may come up to the house and say it to my face, instead of murmuring behind my back."

With a vague notion of easing the tension, Claire let her mare sidle up to the gate. One of the men – an old man – left the group and came towards her, apparently with the same idea, for he touched his cap and opened the gate for her.

"Thank you . . ." Claire looked down at him.

Lines fanned out from his eyes as he smiled, revealing few and crooked teeth. "Gurney's the name, ma'am, Dick Gurney."

"Thank you, Gurney."

Although no one paid any attention to this interchange, the mood altered subtly. "We did, Captain," another man said. "We spoke to Farmer Martin and 'e said to speak to 'is lordship and 'is lordship sent us off with a flea in our ear."

Baillie and Hughes had passed the gate in her wake. Hughes made to press forward, but was arrested by a single look Captain Sumners cast over his shoulder.

Head held high, Justin stood among what to Claire seemed a crowd of huge, hulking fellows, all talking loud, barely intelligible dialect. Pepe seemed to be fiddling with the gate.

Claire glanced at Gurney's hands "You are a shepherd, Gurney," she ventured.

"How d'ye know that, ma'am?" He looked at once surprised and pleased.

"It's your hands: a combination of strength and softness peculiar to shepherds." As he turned over his hands, regarding them with mild astonishment, she added, "How does the lambing go?"

She understood him to say that it was well enough, although too cold, but neither of them was paying full attention to their conversation; each had one ear cocked for the group of men surrounding Justin.

Raising his voice to the carrying tone she had heard before, he cut through the rumble of voices. "You were too previous, men. Nothing is decided. That's why I'm here today. I cannot stay now, but I will come and drink my ale at the Bird-in-Hand Saturday week, on St Joseph's Day, my batman's Saint's Day." Ignoring the murmur of approval, he led his horse clear of the group and remounted. "Tell your friends," he added.

No, he was not always gentle. For a moment, when he turned, it seemed inconceivable that he was ever gentle: he looked tough and arrogant. Then his expression changed.

"If it isn't Dick Gurney," he exclaimed, leaning down to shake the old man by the hand. "I thought you'd be dead and in your grave, my man."

"Gurney has been so kind as to hold Cloud," Claire said. "She was a little fidgety."

Justin gave her a swift smile when Gurney observed that the filly did not like loud voices. "Death 'as forgot me," he added gravely, "and the worse, I'd 'ave been glad to take the place of some younger folks. May they rest in peace."

"Amen." Justin removed his hat. "And here you are looking as strong and healthy as ever. How does the lambing go?"

"And thee'st the same smooth tongue in thy head. Meanin' no disrespect, Captain." He added that Mrs Sumners had asked about the lambing, too.

Justin raised his eyebrows. "Then she may tell me all about it. Will I see you at the Bird-in-Hand, Gurney? You'll help me keep the men steady?"

The old man nodded slowly. "Thee knowst the sayin', Master Justin. A smooth tongue and a sharp knife." Stealing another glance at his hands, he touched his cap and, instead of a farewell, told Claire that the young master had a good hand with a ewe as well.

Unfamiliar with the people and their speech, she could not tell if Gurney had intended any innuendo, but all the same the heat rose wildly to her cheeks. Claire averted her face, hoping that the captain might not see and draw his own conclusions about so unladylike an ear for bawdy.

But he only said, "Stephen and I used to follow the shepherds around like two orphaned lambs when we were boys, and claimed that we were helping." He turned in the saddle and called to Hughes and Baillie. "Shall we ride on?" Pepe waved in acknowledgement.

Her embarrassment faded. "We looked after one of the little creatures in our first spring at Sunderland Hall, all milky softness. Grandmama always kept a fire going in the servants' hall for the shepherds to warm themselves at night, and a large ham on the table."

"Our farmers do that, too." A frown sprang to his brow. "We used to contribute a keg of ale for each farm. I wonder if Lord Hawksfield keeps up the tradition; I should have inquired."

"Don't worry, Stodges mentioned it, and the tradition is being kept up."

The frown was still there when he looked at her, his eyes curious and full of approval. Without waiting for him to comment, she urged her mount into a canter; the broad ride looked safe enough.

The common land was far more varied than one might expect from looking at it from above. The name was misleading, too. Although Nelly's Lea did include extensive tracts of heath and grassland – they were hailed by an old woman leading two goats, a boy tending a flock of geese – it was criss-crossed by steep gullies running with water, some of which widened into small valleys filled with shrub willow, ash, and oak where pigs rooted in the undergrowth. A sudden drop in the land and Justin reined in on the tangled brink of a large pond.

Somewhere behind them, Hughes was holding forth, his monotonous drone punctuated by a wood-pecker's sonorous drumming. A nuthatch called. A pair of whooper swans sifted the water by a fallen tree. The bare branches dappled and dimmed the light. An invisible stream trickled through the grass with a satisfied gurgle. This was a fairy-tale, folksong world, the greenwood of the ballad, where Tam Lin was . . .

Except that he had disappeared, including his steed, as effectively as if he had been spirited away by the Fairy Queen. There was a muffled thud of hooves, twigs broke with dry little snaps, and as Claire followed the sound, a steep bank rose before her. The call of the nuthatch came again and, from the top of the bank, Justin's voice. "Go round in a circle and set her straight at it; she'll take it."

She did, too. The horse seemed as pleased as Claire was herself at the short, hard scramble, and it was hard to tell which of them Justin meant when he said, "Good girl." Both, probably.

They had come out in a clearing dominated by an ancient oak. Wood anemones had pushed up through the dead leaves covering the ground around its trunk, hundreds of small white stars turned towards the pale sun. Now she saw the bird, two, three, blue-grey and rose-pink, flitting among the bare branches.

Her horse stood still, and she, too, felt stilled, quieted in the oak's embrace. From its massive trunk the branches spread sideways, strong and sure, and in her mind's eye she saw the same shape reflected underground, its roots reaching deep into the earth. A rustle of leaves revealed Justin moving slowly under the tree's compass, stooping now and then to add a flower to the bunch in his hands.

She was not sure that she would have dared to pick flowers here, so enchanted was the place, but no more would she have challenged his right to do so. For how many generations had his kind gathered flowers underneath this tree? It was his birthright; he looked as rooted as the oak itself.

Perhaps this was why Robert had not scrupled to trick him: he stood for everything that Robert envied and resented. An aristocrat, a landowner, he belonged to the land as much as the land belonged to him. Not that Robert rebelled against the principle of the thing, as they had done in France. But for a moment, she felt she could rebel against all those who made the rules and asserted them: landowners, lawmakers, men.

Slowly Justin came to her side, his hands full of flowers. "You look very grave."

"I was reflecting upon the French Revolution."

He looked up at the tree. "It does suggest itself." With a soft laugh he added, "Yet those coppice willows are equally ancient, and far more useful."

If the French aristocracy had conceived of themselves as coppice willows, there might never have been any revolution. Claire had been about to suggest that he relay the idea to Robert for his maiden speech, but the nuthatches were calling again and she decided that she did not want her brother mentioned. Not here.

Justin reached up with the flowers. "I'd forgotten what this place is like." His eyes reflected her own enchantment. She did not dare to let go of the reins, however, and seeing her at a loss, he tucked the bouquet into the breast of his riding coat. "Let me carry them for you. They'll revive when you put them in water."

She smiled her thanks. "One doesn't expect a place such as this to exist outside of one's imaginings. Those flowers won't revive; they'll vanish."

Chapter 10

O young Lochinvar is come out of the west,
Through all the wide Border his steed was the best:
And save his good broadsword he weapons had none.
Scott, *Marmion*

THE bunch of wood anemones revived and adorned the drawing-room table. When Claire thought they would soon need to be replaced, they were replaced, as if by magic, with a fresh bunch. She was hardly surprised.

The surprising thing was that, for all his fairy-tale sleights of hand, Justin was not sentimental about Nelly's Lea. He did not contest the fact that it was an uneven, wet, and sour desert which would take countless hours of hard work to ditch and drain; he merely inquired whether, given the political and economic situation, pasture might not make more sense. "If it is to be enclosed at all," he had added. "But I see now that before anything can be decided, the land needs to be properly surveyed. I'd forgotten how varied it is. A morning's ride isn't sufficient to chart the different types of soil, flora, and function around the seasons."

"Perhaps a lifetime's experience is, however," she had said. "Yours, and that of your people. I wonder what they will have to say."

Yet when the evening of his rendezvous at the alehouse came, she not only wondered, she was anxious, too. That the men had shown him respect, that he had handled them well, that Pepe went with him to the Bird-in-Hand should have allayed her fears. But she looked up from her work more than once, thinking she had heard a door slam.

Lucilla interrupted her reading and nudged her with her foot. She was ensconced within easy reach at the other end of the small sofa.

"Have I been fidgeting? I'm sorry, Lucy, dear. Do go on."

"I'm not surprised," Lord Hawksfield said from behind his newspaper. "The captain's odd behaviour could give anyone the fidgets. To be frequenting a public alehouse! And in the company of his groom! Fine behaviour for a Sumners; fine behaviour for a newly wed husband." He looked across at Claire, shaking his white head.

Considerably taken aback, Claire murmured that it was Pepe's Saint's Day, after all. "I do not mind it, my lord. I do not know why I am so nervous."

"A young wife may well have reasons of her own for being nervous," Lord Hawksfield said tolerantly. "And you, my dear Mrs Sumners, are not usually so. You have remarkable sense for a woman."

"Thank you." Claire cast a quelling look at Lucy who, she was certain, had been about to question how sense was dependent on sex. Coming from his lordship, even so limited a commendation was high praise, and she wondered what had prompted it.

"I'm very pleased with your entertaining the tenants' wives to tea," he said. So that was it. "Precisely the thing. Gracious invitation – affability and condescension – the children there – just the right note of informality."

Claire was silent, somewhat overpowered by his lordship's approval, but Alba observed that Mrs Martin was very agreeable. Encouraged by Alba's example, Stella chimed in: "Captain Sumners has been calling on the tenants, too."

But Lord Hawksfield was not going to discuss his views with a bevy of girls. He disappeared once more behind his paper.

"I think it's time for bed, Percy." Claire stroked the dark head leaning against her knee.

"But I haven't finished," Lucilla pointed out. "We stopped in mid-sentence."

His lordship lowered his newspaper. "Aren't we to have any music? I shouldn't want to miss my music only because Captain Sumners isn't here."

With hot cheeks, Claire bade the little one finish the chapter, countering Stella's faint ironic smile with the information that she would be the one to play – the Handel sonata should be ready for performance. But Stella was not so easily flustered and his lordship was satisfied, although Miss Quinnault knit her brows over some passages.

~ ~ ~

At last the house was quiet, the only sound the rush of wind outside. "Thank you, Hannah. That will be all." It was the first time since the wedding that Justin had not come in before she dismissed her maid. Clad in his dressing gown and slippers, he would prowl about the room until Hannah had gone, then drop into an armchair for half an hour's talk. Only yesterday he had remarked, looking at the clock before he left, that he was a terrible husband. She did not know what he meant. He did not terrify her; he talked with her, she now noted with surprise, as with an equal. She wondered briefly how long it would last, but while it lasted, the experience was as pleasant as it was novel.

The tenant farmers, when he had called on them, had confirmed what their wives had hinted to Claire. Dark looks had been following the electors, and they were worried about possible discontent among the poor, whom enclosing Nelly's Lea would rob of the last resort that the common land had always provided: wild fruit, firewood, grazing for a cow or two, and acorns for the pig. Mr Baillie, in turn, had confirmed her impression that the land would need to be very thoroughly drained, and even then it might not be sweet enough for wheat. And if the war ended ... when the war ended ... Justin said it was a question of how much responsibility one meant to take. If the landowners brought under their control and management the land previously accessible to the poor, then they made themselves responsible for relieving the poor, too.

"Manvers says it would make the land more like an army camp, orderly and well-laid out. His words, not mine, and I don't think he's ever seen an army encamped." Justin had grinned. "But in a way his comparison hits the nail on the head. It's impossible to control men to the extent he'd like." Then he had looked at the clock and taken himself off.

Tomorrow it would be a fortnight; a likely interval for newly wed passion to wane. *Love swells like the Solway, but ebbs like its tide.* How late it was. But surely that was a good sign? He would be standing the men a couple of pints, forgetting how anxious they were at home about the outcome of his meeting. Obviously it was the outcome about which she was concerned. Again she looked at the clock. Perhaps it had come to words – to blows.

Perhaps he was badly mauled, unconscious, or even dead, she mocked herself. He could not know that she might be anxious, or waiting for him. "I'll be off then," had been his parting words, and all she had said was, "Alright."

The Bird-in-Hand reputedly served good ale and cider, why should he not enjoy it among his people? She smiled, thinking how naturally the expression had come to him: his people. Would there be strong liquor? A fierce, choleric-looking fellow, the innkeeper no doubt drank and served gin. Justin would be rather well to live. Her insides clenched. He might be drunk. He might be dead drunk, lying in a ditch somewhere.

"And serve him right," she muttered.

Shutting a drawer with more force than necessary, she had barely registered the quick steps in the hall before Hannah burst into the room. "The captain needs your help, ma'am!"

For a moment time stood still, rolled back, stood still once more.

Not that again. How often had she been wakened with those very words? "Miss – Miss – yer da' needs yer 'elp, Miss." The urgent whisper would pull her out of her sleep in the wee hours, and together with the maid she would tackle the drunken wreck that was her father, grateful even when drink had rendered him completely incapable. Any vestige of sobriety led to far worse than squalor. The predominant feeling when he did not make it home one night, drowning, ridiculously, in a ditch, was relief. No longer the broken nights, the abuse, and the filth.

Not that again, was her first thought upon perceiving man and master. If they were hatless, it was not out of courtesy but because they had lost these articles; their torn clothes showed ominous dark stains. Pepe was disfigured by an encrusted purple swelling on his upper lip. A smell of cider and smoke mingled with the cool scent of night air that hung about them.

Claire braced herself when the captain turned round. At least he was able to stand.

A dark bruise marked his left temple. "I'm glad you're still up, *cariño*," he said quite distinctly. "Have you got some sort of ointment for Pepe here? This cut lip is swelling rather badly."

She stared at him in disbelief. He was not drunk. Nor was Pepe; but Pepe was hurt. "Hannah, fetch hot water. Come along, you two." Preceding them to the stillroom, she snatched her apron from the peg by the door and tied it over her dressing gown, swiftly making preparations. How fortunate that they had made the tincture when they did! Meanwhile the captain used the lantern he had been carrying to light all the candles. Then he divested Pepe of his coat.

"Take off your own coat, too, Captain, if that's blood. It must be soaked in plenty of cold water. Now, sit here, Pepe. Captain, if you could hold the light to his face. Very good. Oh, thank you, Hannah. Pour it onto the leaves, please, and the rest into this bowl, and then take these coats to soak. You will have to be brave now, Pepe, this may hurt."

She bathed his wound in warm water tinged with tincture. He drew his breath in sharply when the spirituous liquid penetrated the wound. "I'm sorry, Pepe. And on your Saint's Day, too." A compress of daisies, a pad. "Hold that to your lip." She dipped a fresh piece of linen into the bowl to clean his face and neck, then she inspected his scalp. "Does this hurt? No? Breathe in. Cough. Does it hurt when you laugh?" Apparently no ribs were cracked, but Pepe indicated some trouble with the collarbone.

"He says he felt a heavy blow there, a cosh perhaps," the captain explained.

Claire pulled down the shirt and felt the bone. "I think it's alright." She bathed and bound up Pepe's right hand, which was cut open at the knuckles. "Oh dear. Are your hands as bad, Captain? I don't want you dripping all over the floor."

"No, I was wearing gloves." His voice quivered.

"There, Pepe, that's better, isn't it? Now breathe deeply and slowly, and tell me if it hurts you inside. No, take your time."

The Spaniard closed his eyes for a moment, then looked up at her. "*No, Doña Clara.* All is good."

"Then off to bed with you. Hold the compress to your lip until you fall asleep, and come and see me tomorrow. I want to renew those bandages."

"Now let us see that black eye, Captain Sumners. Sit down," she added with a twinge of amusement when he hesitated, claiming that the innkeeper had applied fresh steak. "It won't hurt, at least not very much." Just as Percy would have, he bridled at having his courage suspected and so complied. The steak had a ring of truth about it; there was very little swelling. Cautiously she felt the bones of his face, tapped some of the infusion into the bruised skin, inspected his scalp. "What happened?"

"We were set upon on our way to the Bird-in-Hand, but we weren't much hurt, so we decided to go on regardless and have a wash at the alehouse. Pepe's lip only really began to swell on the way back. It must have been the gin they made him drink for a birthday gift."

"That's terrible, Justin," she said automatically, her mind on his wounds. "Who would do such a thing?" The skin at the back of his neck was raw and discoloured. The bruise seemed to reach down past his shoulder. "Take off your shirt."

He did not reply, but pulled the garment over his head and tossed it on the narrow bed in the corner. Then he said, "We'll know more when Bouverie has questioned the prisoner."

"You captured him?"

"One of them. We sent him round to Delapré Abbey with an escort of stout men. Bouverie is Justice of the Peace."

At least the blood was not his own. There were no open wounds.

"Anyhow, we've marked them well. That must be their blood on my coat, because I'm not bleeding, am I?" He looked over his shoulder, trying to peer down his back.

"No, but there's a hideous bruise all over this side. Can you move your shoulder? Does it hurt?" As he lifted his arm, she felt the muscle slide under her hands.

"I was thrown against the bank where the path dips down in that little copse we passed the other day. Good place for an ambush, I will say that."

"This will sting a little." She tilted his head forward and to one side to expose the bruised skin. "Keep still!"

For he had begun to laugh, his body shaking with it. "Are those daisies in that jar there? Are you anointing me with tincture of daisies?"

"I am." She dipped the linen into the diluted infusion and began to tap it into his skin. He fell quiet, so to distract him from the inevitable discomfort, she asked, "What did your people say?" His frame hummed quietly under her hands as he replied. Nicola had been right. There was not an ounce of fat on him. Every bone, every strand of muscle was clearly palpable, and a good thing, too, since this made it much easier to ascertain whether he had dislodged anything.

Everything seemed to be in the right place, however, the long white scar running down his back clearly of an older date. She had swallowed the exclamation that rose to her lips when she saw it, but when she had finished with his shoulder and shifted the light to inspect the ribs, a horrified gasp escaped her.

He gave her a quick, tight smile. "Pretty, isn't it? A souvenir of Madrid." He rose to his feet, reaching for his shirt. "Are we finished?"

Small wonder that he could talk of bruises and a black eye as no grave hurt, and keep his rendezvous as though nothing had happened. He had known far worse. His ribcage was criss-crossed by a web of scars running together in a mass of puckered tissue on his belly.

"Never be so distressed, *amor*, it wasn't as bad as it looks." All the same his voice was strained. "The knife glanced off the ribs, coming from above. That is why there are so many scars. I'd wrapped my cloak around my neck for freedom of movement, and that protected the parts they meant to hit." His throat and shoulders; his heart.

His heart beat visibly against his chest. When she put her hand there, the pulse was strong and even. Sliding her other hand to the back of his neck, she pulled down his head and kissed him.

~ ~ ~

The touch of her fingers on the bruised skin was exquisite. The touch of her lips was soft and hesitant, softer by far than the sisterly kisses by which the girls bade each other goodnight, and more hesitant, too. She had no notion how to kiss anyone who was not her sister.

He tasted her mouth, slid his arms around her, kept his hands from straying. She had completely forgotten about his bruises, yet the satisfaction was far greater than the pain. She melted into his embrace.

Then her back tensed. Her hands came to his shoulders, and she pushed herself away. Without her in his arms, he felt more bruised and naked than ever, but her eyes were wide and terrified, and he did not try to hold her except by his voice. "Claire."

"No." She took a few backward steps. "No." And she ran from the room.

"Claire!" Not even a pause in her retreating footsteps; if anything, the quick patter accelerated. He remained on the threshold, taut with unspent emotion. A door clapped upstairs.

Taking a deep breath, he went back into the stillroom. *"Me deja con la miel en los labios,"* he muttered angrily, but the sound of his own voice startled him out of his anger. How odd that it should vent itself in Spanish; or perhaps not, given that the blessedly few times a girl had left him with a bare taste of honey on his lips had been in Spain. He picked up the discarded shirt, pulled it over his head, and tucked in the shirt-tails.

But it had been sweet, and in all probability Claire's first taste of lips and honey. The first time she held a man in her arms; and it had been he.

And the sensation had made her run away without so much as untying her apron or putting away her remedies. With a dry laugh, he replaced the lid on the tincture and lifted it back to its shelf. The bits of linen she had used were already gathered in a wide bowl; she was a tidy worker. He collected his cigar case from the day-bed on which he had dropped it when he gave Hannah his coat. That bed could have been put to better uses, but a No was a No, and two Nos were not a Yes, whatever the logicians might say.

Claire had run off with the keys, so all he could do was blow out the candles and shut the door, taking the lantern with him. Hopefully no one would raid her store of medical spirits by tomorrow. He considered taking something spirituous himself, in a medicinal manner, but decided against it. Brandy would numb his senses but dull his mind as well. Tobacco and night air might cool him. He turned into the morning room and, picking up a rug as he passed the sofa, let himself out into the garden.

A blustery wind was chasing thin clouds across the inky sky, allowing brief glimpses of the moon's waning feather. The moist air, mild for mid-March, was welcome on his heated body, and it was not until he had reached the orchard that Justin set aside the lantern and wrapped the rug around his torso.

She was here – she couldn't be. The sense of Claire's presence was so strong that his hands were shaking. He had placed the lantern in a niche in the entrance to the orchard, where it illumined the cut limestone of its arch, no more, and the night was very dark; in two days there would be a new moon. All the same, he must have known if anyone but himself were there, his alertness heightened by the events of the night. He listened. "Claire?" Nothing.

Nothing but the rush of wind in the ancient cedar. No one but himself. What he had picked up in the morning room, however, was not a rug but Claire's fine woollen shawl. Imbued with her scent – that elusive combination of apples and beeswax and marigolds – it held him in her disembodied embrace. *Mil diablos.* Bunching its folds in his hands, he buried his face in the soft fabric for a deep, tantalising breath, then he dropped his arms and threw back his head. He swore.

The tobacco would cover her scent but taint her shawl with its reek. Well, she would have to bear it. He reached inside his shirt and drew out his cigar case. Stepping back under the arch, he lit a cigarillo on the lantern's flame. For a long time, he walked beneath the bare branches of the plum trees, exultation and depression contending in his breast. What a night! And tomorrow – tomorrow would be awkward in many respects; first thing tomorrow a visit to Mr Bouverie was in order.

Chapter 11

So faithful in love, and so dauntless in war,
There never was knight like the young Lochinvar.
Scott, *Marmion*

IT was more than awkward. It was the damnedest thing. Justin stopped to exchange a few words with Pepe, perched on a mounting block with a bemused look on his face because, he informed his master, Doña Clara had made him another compress and told him to take it easy.

"You'd better do as she says, *guapo*, and keep that wound clean."

"She wants to see you, too, Don Justín. I am to remind you."

"*Vale.*" Justin did not immediately go, however, but stood tapping his riding whip against his boots. "It's just as we thought, Pepe."

"*Puta mierda.*" Pepe pursed his mouth to whistle, gave a painful grunt, and abandoned the attempt. "*Qué asco.*"

A sickening business, indeed, but by the time he walked into the drawing room, Justin had again forgotten the bruises that had moved Planchett to tut-tut and exclaim while shifting him out of his mud-spattered riding clothes.

"It's the damnedest thing, Claire."

He was met by a resounding silence. Five pairs of eyes were fixed on him in unnerving scrutiny. He should have known they would all be here; it was Sunday, after all, with no lessons, no business in offices, stillroom, or linen room. "I beg your pardon," he said stiffly. Her sisters all seemed to draw closer to Claire, Alba inhaling with an audible hiss. The others continued to stare at him.

Let them look. He stood with his hat and gloves in his hand, facing the light from the tall windows. They were unlikely ever to have seen a face disfigured by blows. The longer they looked, the less awful it would appear to them.

Little Lucilla's stare was one of curiosity, however, her question one of sympathy and concern. "What happened to your face, Captain?"

He winked at her. "You have three guesses." It was up to Claire to decide how much of his adventure was suitable for her sisters' ears. "Perhaps I fell down the stairs?"

There was another absolute silence, suddenly broken by a hysterical giggle. Miss Alba was pressing the back of one hand to her lips.

At last Claire spoke. "It's alright, love." She touched her sister's cheek. "It's alright." Looking across at Justin she added, "I think you had better tell my sisters what happened." She made a gesture. "Do sit down."

~ ~ ~

He gave them only the bare bones of the incident, telling a sombre little story. Gone was last night's reckless captain. He was grave, contained; even his clothes were formal. A weight seemed to have settled on his shoulders. The notion that he presented himself thus in order to impress her with his sobriety occurred only to be dismissed. Whatever he did, he did it for the thing itself.

Yet the contrast was disconcerting. The girls did not seem to notice it, although Alba's eyes were swimming with sympathy, but of course they had not seen him last night. As Claire watched his mouth form the words of his tale, she could no longer hear what he said. She could only see – the now clean-shaven upper lip that had rasped so roughly against hers, the mouth that was so surprisingly soft, the lean, gentle, open hands – she had forgotten to examine his hands. Now they lay loosely on his knees, and indeed the right showed signs of bruising. When he had finished, Lucilla took it and blew softly.

"Children's magic," Stella said. "That will do more than our tinctures."

"I hope so," Claire heard herself say. "You were meant to come and have those bruises seen to before you changed, Captain."

His dark eyes crinkled at the corners. "Give your tinctures to Planchett and he'll look after me. Careful," he added to Lucilla, who had climbed up next to him and was about to lean on his shoulder to blow on his temple. "There's a big black bruise all down that side." He gave her his hand to steady her as she bent forward.

"You are such a bleeding heart, Lucy." Percy's voice was small, gruff, and shockingly audible. "Two soldiers against one scallag, it's not even fair, and they on horseback."

"Percy!" Claire and Alba exclaimed in one breath, but Lucy had already rounded on her sister.

"You never listen! He said they captured one of them, so there must have been more than one."

With a sniff, Percy conceded that there might have been two. Stella rolled her eyes. "You had better tell us the exact number, age, and size of your attackers, Captain, or we will never have peace."

"Four; and we weren't riding. But your sister has reason, and I'm not proud of the exploit. They were no match for two soldiers trained and experienced in close combat."

"Four!" Claire felt goose-bumps rise on the back of her neck "How many people know this?"

"Just Pepe and Bouverie . . . and the fellows who attacked us, obviously. Why do you ask?"

"Oh, no reason." This could not be discussed in front of the girls; she was not sure it should be discussed at all.

He gave her a keen look. "Well, I must go," he said at length. "I mean to attend Evening Prayer." He drew on his gloves, picked up his hat. "I suppose you wouldn't . . . would you care to come, Claire?"

A period of quiet reflection was exactly what she needed. Giving her an hour's quiet was unlikely to be his object, but what she suspected to be his object would have to be got out of the way sooner or later, and the sooner it was over, the better. "I should like that."

~ ~ ~

In the mellow afternoon sun, the pastures glittered with innumerable puddles. The blackthorn hedges, burst into bloom, formed ribbons of brilliant white. Above the white clouds banked on the horizon, a buzzard soared, a tiny speck against the soft blue sky. The only sounds were its piercing cries and the bleat of lambs calling to their mothers.

The captain walked in silence. Perhaps he was waiting for her to speak. It was only reasonable. She owed him an apology.

Slipping a hand under his arm, she said, "There has been no opportunity so far, Captain, but I do wish to apologize."

His other hand covered hers, but the gesture must have been instinctive, for he only made an interrogative sound in his throat. This was more difficult than she had thought. "I don't know what you're talking about," he said.

Worse and worse. "I'm talking about my behaviour last night." She had not meant to speak so sharply. The rest came out in an embarrassed whisper: "I don't know what came over me."

But he only laughed. "Don't give it a thought, *amor*. I like being kissed." Another chuckle, and he added, "I just wish it hadn't ended there."

Suppressing the impulse to withdraw her hand, she gripped his arm tightly. He had a right to tease her, after all.

"Forgive me, I couldn't resist that. Don't refine too much upon it, Claire. It could happen to anyone, and if you ever find yourself overcome again, why, I am entirely at your service."

She kept her eyes on the path. "Your restraint was admirable, Captain, but I have no ambition to discover its limits."

"So that wasn't another attempt to provoke me? Angels fear to tread where sheep may safely graze." He led her around a patch full of sheep's droppings. "But you said 'no'."

And that, it appeared, was enough for him. She stood stock-still. "What a woman says is usually seen to be less important than what she is." Her voice was bitter in her own ears. "And what a man does, inevitable."

He had stopped, too, half turning to look at her. "Inevitable!" He gave a low hoot. "Trust me, Claire, if ever a man tells you he cannot control his desire for you, that's because he doesn't want to." He snorted. "Did you think it was that on which I was brooding? No, my mind has been less pleasantly occupied."

She fell into step beside him once more. All at once she felt selfish. He had been ambushed, he had confronted a discontented mob, and all she could think of was one fleeting kiss.

"I didn't want to mention it with the children there," he continued, "but it really is the damnedest thing. I rode over to the Abbey this morning to see the prisoner. He's a stranger to these parts, that's why no one recognized him last night. He wouldn't

130

say anything, but Bouverie and I set out to track the others and found two, both locals, day-labourers who live with their families in those tumbledown cottages over by Quinton." He held a gate open for her. "Damnation!"

Involuntarily she winced. In a more moderate tone, he continued, "I'm sorry, Claire. But these two claim that they wanted to keep me from attending the meeting at the Bird-in-Hand, since they're in favour of his lordship's enclosing scheme. I knew there was some opposition to it; I hadn't realized that there was support, too, nor this kind of support. God help us if that's a portent of things to come. Civil unrest, even on so small a scale . . ." The lines around his eyes sprang into relief as he frowned. He would be thinking of Spain and the effects of civil strife he had seen there. "They think it'll mean better employment. But what it could mean, the way they've gone about it, is the gallows. The only light in the affair is that they put the blame on two strangers – one of whom we captured last night – who egged them on when they were shooting their mouths off at the Crown. Of course they would say that, but if there's any truth in it, they may get away with transportation. I do hate sending a man to the gallows."

His distress was as unexpected as it was touching, but all she said was, "How did you identify them? Did you see them well enough to know them?"

"No, it was too dark. But we marked them. I almost wish we hadn't, but then you can't let people go around beating up their betters and getting away with it. As Bouverie put it, this ain't France, you know. Good evening." His grim smile suddenly gained real warmth as he returned an old man's hail and stopped to exchange a few words, taking his leave when the call of bells began to sound from the village.

"You know what I like about you?" It slipped out before she could stop herself.

The question was purely rhetorical, but he grinned and said, "My nose?"

She could not help laughing. If there was one thing one might criticize about his looks, it was his nose, which not only tended to the aquiline, it was aquiline. "That, too," she conceded. But it was his way with people that had struck her – how he recognized and acknowledged every man, be he ever so humble, and even women and children.

"Is that so unusual?" he replied when she tried to explain this. "How else would one meet people?"

"As representatives of their class – their nation – their profession – their sex."

"But surely that's a very limited way of looking at people? When you consider the complexity of the human soul?"

"It is, Justin," she said. "And a limited way of looking at people narrows their compass, too, not only yours. And you don't do that. That's what I like about you."

"Hm." He rubbed his chin. "I have a feeling that from what you say, there is a good argument to be built for you to come to bed with me, but it eludes me at the moment." Over her shocked gasp, he continued, "A pity, although it does perhaps indicate a certain high-mindedness on my part."

And she had felt selfish because her thoughts revolved around a single kiss rather than questions of wider import. Her cheeks burned. But he could say – and do – whatever he pleased; she had given him every right, by her own choice, in the very church they were about to enter. Except that he did nothing of the kind. "I'm sure it does," she said.

They had reached the edge of the village and, skirting the little cluster of houses around the green, began to climb the path beneath the horse-chestnuts that paced up the gentle slope in giant strides.

"There's one thing I would like to know, Claire." His voice was serious, but a guarded look showed her that he was smiling. "Tell me, why do you smell of apples, beeswax, and marigolds?"

She exhaled slowly. "That will be the green apples we put among our clothes to keep the moth away. And my hand balm, made with beeswax and marigolds." Taking courage from these irrelevancies, she brought him back to the matter at hand. "But, Captain, surely bruises and black eyes are not evidence? Your attackers might have got those anywhere."

"Yes . . ." He hesitated, then seemed to make up his mind. "Two of them had a knife, but not for long. They each have a slash on their forehead."

Standing there beneath the chestnuts, his gloved hand on the low gate to the churchyard, he looked utterly civilized and not in the least like a man recently engaged in a bloody brawl, but then a gesture of his head brought the livid bruise into view. He was a soldier, after all. Violence had been his trade. It was surprising that he should feel in need of spiritual consolation at all.

"And save his good broadsword he weapons had none," she said faintly. Walking past him, she made her way among the tombstones to the porch, where Reverend Meynell was talking to Mr Bouverie. As he exclaimed at Captain Sumners's face, deplored its cause, commended the captain's generosity in going to see the families of his attackers, her surprise faded into something she did not care to examine too closely. The captain had not mentioned this part of his day's activities.

O Lord, make haste to help us. Her responses came automatically, leaving the greater part of her mind free, but still there were things to push aside before she could puzzle over the question nagging at its back: how did Robert know?

They had talked after church that morning, and she had told him of the attack in a rapid undertone while the girls put a bunch wildflowers on Lady Hawksfield's tomb.

"He fought them off?" Robert had exclaimed. "All four of them?"

And that was the first time she had heard the number of attackers mentioned. Neither Captain Sumners nor Pepe had said anything last night. She had managed to swallow her surprise, but it had stayed with her, much as she tried to explain it away. Robert would have heard about the attack from . . . from whom? And he had not betrayed any prior knowledge, had not asked her about it, had seemed completely unconcerned until she brought it up. And there had indeed been four attackers. And surely it was very odd that two strangers should thus involve themselves in Hardingstone affairs.

For ye suffer, if a man bring you into bondage, if a man devour you, if a man take of you, if a man exalt himself, if a man smite you on the face. The text of the Second Lesson brought her back to the surface of reality. The reverend's voice had taken on a harder tone. In the silence that followed, Claire felt the congregation's presence at her back as a solid wall of tension; they must have stirred a little during the reading, for surely tension was not palpable. As she fought the urge to look over her shoulder, she slanted a glance at Captain Sumners and found it difficult to withdraw her gaze.

He was wholly absorbed. Responding firmly in his husky speaking voice, for the Magnificat he raised it to fuller and rather beautiful pitch. Small wonder he had suggested church. The service did for him what it never could for her, preoccupied as she invariably was with worries saved for that precious period of inaccessibility to ponder. It must be wonderful to be able to concentrate one's entire being like that, to escape from the present to some place far removed from things, or was he wholly immersed in the present, or did it come to the same? She found herself thinking of music – Stella's Handel sonata – her own playing in a stolen half-hour – the Boccherini they had heard at the Academy of Ancient Music – but her mind had not strayed, it was providing an answer she had not consciously sought. Here was the similarity: the familiar ritual of the church service gave him what she got from music.

"You have done great things, O God, and holy is your name," he said confidently. With bowed head, he followed intercessions and prayer, but during the Lord's Prayer, the set of his shoulders changed as with a weight falling away. "Thanks be to God."

The service ended. He turned to her, his countenance serene. "Would you mind if I look in on the Sumners chapel, or will you come, too?"

Wordlessly she preceded him. In the side chapel, he touched the marble of his brother's memorial plaque, as if in greeting, and the foot of his mother's tomb. "Someone's brought Mama flowers."

"The girls have taken a liking to her." Without thinking why she should tell him, she added, "Even Percy, although she has taken a violent dislike to your brother."

He grimaced. "And to myself."

"Don't take it to heart. She's a wary creature." Again she did not know why she had said it. The childish bunch of wildflowers looked absurdly small against the expanse of crafted masonry.

"Thank you." Looking down at the flowers, he added, "Mama would have liked that."

About his brother he said nothing, but he stood for a long while gazing down at the inscription, still fresh and raw compared to the worn marks that reached back into the centuries. His only brother, his elder brother – it was a terrible loss, although somehow she felt that death was not the cause but time, the years the brothers had spent apart, experiences not shared, in different places, among different people.

"*Non sum qualis eram.*" Justin turned away. "And nor was he. The Stephen I miss had ceased to exist by the time he got himself killed. Percy may have a point, you know."

Though she knew the answer, she had to ask. "Have you spoken to Robert about the attack?"

"Ah, I'm not the only one disappointed in a brother." He shook his head. "I haven't seen him all day. Did you?"

The church was nearly empty by this time, with only a few parishioners clustered around the door to the porch.

"This morning." But it would not do to raise his suspicion, not before she had spoken to Robert herself. "They'll be at Hawksfield Manor now, Nicola hoping for you to give her all the gory details." She hesitated. "Do you think I could beg them off?"

He stopped dead in the middle of the nave. "You could what? Whom?"

"Beg them off," she repeated. "Your attackers, from hanging. Mr Scott once told me there is a tradition in England that accords brides special rights. Perhaps I could ask Mr Bouverie to convert the punishment to transportation."

He looked gravely into her eyes. "I'd be grateful, Claire, I cannot tell you how much. We'll have to ask Reverend Meynell." With a grin he added, "And if the tradition doesn't exist, he'll have to discover it." He propelled her towards the porch. "Come, my bride, let us catch Bouverie before he goes home."

His bride; Robert's sister. It was too absurd. If she had married him, it was to ensure his and his father's support for Robert, and now she was suspecting her brother of ensuring this support by all manner of insidious means. More than suspecting, for was not her marriage itself ample proof of what Robert was capable? If he did not scruple to trade his sister for a place in parliament, he would hardly baulk at a little intimidation where his brother-in-law was concerned.

"There are precedents, although not in Hardingstone," the reverend was saying.

"All the same, I would hesitate to apply them." Mr Bouverie frowned, looking towards the road, where his carriage waited in solitary state. "Surely you haven't come on foot, Sumners, after what happened last night?" He thrust out his chin and glared. "And with Mrs Sumners, too! Let me take you up. It'll be dusk soon."

"No, this kind of thing may do in France," he observed when the carriage had rattled out of the village and was bowling along the country road, "but not here."

Claire compressed her lips. Not that he would have seen her smile in the carriage's dim interior, nor would he notice Justin's foot nudging hers under cover of that same dimness. At least she hoped the foot was Justin's. She gave the shin attached to it a sharp kick. The indrawn breath could have been anyone's, but the chuckle that followed it was his.

"And I would not ask it of you, Mr Bouverie," she said, "if Captain Sumners had not come out of it so well. They wanted to show him up as vulnerable and weak; instead, they have proved his strength. And it's not just that their plan has failed; it would also be good, in the present situation, to demonstrate the Sumnerses' magnanimity."

"In the present situation . . . My dear madam, you flatter me, but my support for the Sumnerses is by no means as wholesale as you seem to believe – as they know."

"So we do," the captain said. "But Mrs Sumners is referring to the election, while you, Mr Bouverie, are thinking of my father's enclosing scheme; two very different things, just as the Sumnerses you are considering in a lump are in fact two very different men, or three, if you count Lyster, given that he is the Sumners candidate."

"Ah!" Mr Bouverie exclaimed. The wheels of the carriage crunched on the gravel as it passed beneath the stone hawks peering arrogantly down from the gateposts. The groom let down the steps. The captain jumped out. Across the forecourt, the lit windows gave a clear view of the dining room.

"Look, there's a cold dinner on the table," Claire said. "Please come in and join us, Mr Bouverie, and you will be able to speak at your leisure to all three gentlemen."

"And sample some fine claret," Captain Sumners added from the forecourt. Reaching up he assisted first Claire, then Mr Bouverie. "Your groom knows where the stableyard is?"

"I'm afraid he knows only too well where the kitchen is."

"Don't worry. Now that Mrs Sumners holds sway, the standards of hospitality above and below stairs have reached a very satisfactory balance – that is, higher above and not quite so lavish below."

Mr Bouverie's renewed "Ah!" as they entered the dining room showed him fully alive to the improvement. The little girls had already started on their dinner, monitored by Miss Quinnault. The rest of the family was scattered in loose groups around the room, Stella looking rather doubtfully at a glass of ratafia in her hand.

"You don't have to finish it," Claire said quietly.

"Thank goodness," Stella whispered in reply. "It tastes like poison."

"Now, when was the last time you drank poison? But I know what you mean." Moving on to greet Nicola, she declined an offer of ratafia for herself and nodded and smiled in what she felt to be a singularly false manner when Robert explained that she preferred claret.

"Allow me." With a bow to Lord Hawksfield, he poured and handed her the glass: the perfect opportunity for them to detach themselves from the group gathered around Captain Sumners. Nicola had uttered a horrified shriek when she saw his bruise. Now she was besieging him with questions.

"I suppose you have no need to hear the story," Claire told her brother in a low voice. The door to the library stood open. She moved unobtrusively through, and he followed her.

In creating an oval room, the architect had shaved off its corners, which now formed four triangular nooks framed by columns and entablature. It was into one of these that she now turned. "You know all about it, don't you?"

But if she suspected Robert, he seemed to have suspicions of his own. He planted himself squarely between the fluted columns and regarded her from narrowed eyes. "I should have known this would happen." He drank some wine. "Damn you, Claire, I'm your brother! Don't you think you owe me some loyalty?"

Pretending ignorance would only waste time. "Don't you think you have forfeited any claim to my loyalty? You manoeuvred me into marriage, and it was for you that I went along with your scheme. Is that not enough?"

"For me, eh?" He took a step towards her; she sat down in the window-seat. "Are you not deceiving yourself just a wee bit? You liked Sumners from the start, I know you did, and don't tell me he's not a braw husband," his lips curled, "if momentarily a hideous one. I hear he comes to your room every night, with not a stitch beneath his robe."

"There never was knight like the young Lochinvar," she said. "You're very well informed." But that was precisely what Justin had intended by letting her maid see him in that garb, the collar of his dressing gown snug against his neck, with no edge of linen showing. She had never taken notice, but of course there wasn't any linen: the dark-green brocade had been his only garment. Her throat felt dry. She took a sip of wine. Then, lifting her chin, she said, "And what if he does? Wouldn't you say a wife's first duty is to her husband?"

"Duty?" Robert put his empty glass on a side table and, taking hers, drained it and set it aside as well. "Come, come, my dear, you know it's not duty you feel towards him. You're but a woman, after all." He gave a scornful laugh. "And I thought he'd be too busy taming you to meddle in my affairs."

"Your affairs? Yours?" She was on her feet. "This is not about me, Robert. But you have no right . . ." It occurred to her that neither of them had mentioned the attack, although they both appeared to assume that Robert had arranged it. A moment of piercing clarity showed her what this meant; her anger ebbed, and what surged back was a great sense of loss. "Oh, Robert!" But he remained silent, a mulish look about his mouth.

Half turning towards the window, she gazed out into the garden, already shrouded in dusk. "Not that I agree with Desdemona," she said sadly. "Duty is neither here nor there. It's the thing itself that matters. If I do not believe in enclosing Nelly's Lea, my duty is to prevent its being enclosed."

He snorted. She swung round. "Or to prevent you from making a great mistake, brother. If I still owed you any loyalty – if I still cared for you."

A slow grin spread across his face. "You do, you know, or you wouldn't argue quite so passionately. Have you told him of your suspicions?" She did not reply but walked past him into the oval body of the library. He gave a sudden laugh. "What a joke! If that is your philosophy, it's a dashed uncomfortable wife I've given Captain Sumners."

Then he added, his voice suddenly low and vicious, "If not loyalty, then what about gratitude?" She stopped in the middle of the room. "Or has your fine inherited property in the Borders quite wiped out the memory of what it was like, three rooms on the fifth floor in Edinburgh's Old Town? All this," he raised an arm in a sweeping gesture which encompassed the harmonious oval with its tall bookcases, the classical mouldings on pastel walls, the whole suite of elegant rooms, the house, the park, the land. "All this is nothing to you, is it? A title for you, a peerage for your son?"

From where she stood, she could see Justin by the dining table. He was setting a chair for Mr Bouverie, helping him to various dishes: eggs with sorrel, dandelion fritters. Straightening, he looked towards her, his eyebrows raised. She was tired and hungry. "Better is a dinner of herbs where love is than hatred therewith," she told Robert, leaving him speechless.

Chapter 12

So light to the croupe the fair lady he swung,
So light to the saddle before her he sprung!
Scott, *Marmion*

"I COULD envy Lyster," Justin told Pepe. As usual
they were speaking Spanish, although Pepe had begun to lace his discourse with the English he was
picking up.

"For his ruthlessness? You may well envy him
that, Don Justín. It is a quality you lack entirely."

They were riding back from Northampton,
whither they had been summoned to identify the
fourth attacker. Tomorrow he would be confronted
with his accomplices, locked up at Delapré Abbey.
Bouverie had not been happy to hear the news. It
was an ugly story, and Bouverie did not know the
half of it. Nor did Justin see fit to point out how odd
it was for a couple of strangers passing through
Hardingstone to treat two day-labourers to gin and
revolutionary talk before setting out with them to
take revolutionary action. He could only hope that
Claire would not draw her own conclusions, either.

"For his sister's loyalty. You should have heard
her speak up for him with Bouverie last night, and
seen her draw him apart from the company. They
had some very serious talk – about the enclosing
scheme, I make no doubt."

Mildly Pepe observed that he was not making
much sense. "You said she is against it."

"That's just it. She believes her brother is in
error, and that acting upon that error would detract
from his character – would diminish him. So by
opposing him, she is defending his chance of doing
what is good and right."

"And you would like that, too, for yourself?" Pepe weighed his head. "You are a strange man, Don Justín, but a good one. What would happen to her loyalty if she found out that Lyster arranged for the beating, do you think?"

"I don't know, but it would hurt her damnably," Justin replied. "I hope she'll never know, that's all."

"Keep her in ignorance to spare her pain? You don't believe in that, Don Justín. Come on," he added, half to Justin, half to his horse, which sprang forward.

Before they had embarked for England – only two months since! – Justin had learned that Pepe's native village had been destroyed, and he had elected to tell him.

When they reined in at the edge of the field, Pepe gave him a ghostly grin. "No, you don't believe in blissful ignorance. And you're right."

They trotted along the Hardingstone road in silence, both lost in memories. "We'll take the shortcut." With hardly a thought, Justin set the mare at the stile and took her across, Pepe following in his wake. The ground was soft from the intermittent showers of the past few days, and blue-black clouds massing in the west threatened more rain. They had reached the stableyard when, from the tail of his eye, Justin saw one of the little girls running towards the house.

Pepe had seen her, too. Watching her, he said to Justin, "Does it not occur to you that Doña Clara spoke up for you and your family? Because that is what it sounds like in your telling."

"What? No. Wishful thinking, that's all."

Probably she was trying to reach shelter before the rain set in. Justin looked up at the darkening sky, then once more at the girl. She was tearing across the lawn as if all furies were behind her. Something was wrong.

"Percy!" he called. She turned her head, swerved, but did not change direction. "Come here!" Now she slowed. He dismounted and strode towards her. She was utterly spent, her breath coming in great, painful gulps. He sat back on his heels to face her. "What's the matter?"

"Claire, I need Claire," she gasped, darting frightened glances all around her.

"She's not here. Tell me. Look at me."

Her eyes were wide and scared. He held them with his gaze, willing her to talk, and she did.

"It's Lucy. She's –" The girl uttered an agonized cry. "I need Claire!"

"Is Lucy hurt?"

A vigorous nod. If one of the girls was hurt, she would indeed need Claire, and perhaps – "How bad is it?"

A great sob was the only reply. A physician, then, and Claire would need to be prepared. Swiftly instructing Pepe with a message, he turned back to the girl.

"Where?"

Speechless, she pointed in the direction she had come from.

"On Mr Manvers's land?"

Another nod, and in a horrified burst she added, "She's trapped! Like a badger!"

"*Diablos.*" Straightening himself, Justin looked over his shoulder. Bob Grimes was holding the mare by the head. "Hold these," Justin said to the little girl, handing her the reins, and walked a few paces with the groom, "Get me a few stout iron bars. Have you any bandages here? Then get me those, too, and be quick about it."

He took the reins from Percy, who was standing transfixed by the horse, and lifted her into the saddle. "Up you go." Then he swung himself up behind her.

She was shivering. It was raining. He had not taken notice, but the girl's hair and the shoulders of her pelisse were wet. Where was her bonnet?

"I'm sorry, child, but you'll have to brave the weather and show me where Lucy is. Thank you," he added as Grimes attached a roll of implements to the saddle.

"*¡Arre!*" He urged the mare into her easy canter, supporting Percy with one arm. At the boundary of Mr Manvers's land, he abandoned the horse. "Come on," he said, and now the girl grasped his hand and drew him along with her, following a narrow path through rank grass and bushes.

"There," she whispered hoarsely, pointing. Not a sound to be heard, nothing to be seen until they were right next to the injured child, cowering in the undergrowth. She was fully conscious.

Percy made a move towards her. "You stay on the path," Justin said. "We don't want another injury. Start back to the house. Tell Claire I'll bring her the little one in thirty minutes. Get out of those wet clothes. I'll speak to you later."

Lucy's voice was a mere thread. "Go, Percy. I'll be alright."

No more attention to spare for the older girl, Justin tapped the ground with the cudgels provided by Grimes. Then he stepped across to where the little one lay hunched over her leg. "Bravely now. We'll have you out of here before you can say Jack Robinson." He shrugged off his coat and wrapped it around her.

"Yes." She slipped an arm around his neck.

Thirty minutes later, he was striding towards the house with the child in his arms. How quiet she was. "Hey, are you alive?" he asked the wet head at his shoulder, but the only reply he got was a tightening of her grip upon his neck. He felt a painful throb in his chest, probably because one of her fists was digging into the bruise on his torso. "*Boba, bobita*," he murmured, soothing her as Pepe might soothe a nervous horse. Claire was waiting at a side door.

"It's not as bad as it could be," he said quickly. "The trap had smooth jaws and a large offset. And she was wearing strong boots. Anything I can do?"

Claire shook her head, but the little one would not let go of his neck, so he knelt by the bed in the stillroom, holding her while Claire cleaned and bandaged the purple, swollen mess that was the child's lower leg.

Lucilla's eyes were tightly closed, and she was biting her hand, letting only an occasional whimper escape her. He undid the strings of her bonnet and pulled it aside, then he reached for a towel and began to dry her face. "*Hola, guapa*, look at me." Holding her gaze, he continued to talk as he dabbed the rain from her cheeks. By infinitesimal stages, she relaxed, breathing more evenly.

Neither she nor Claire took notice of Miss Alba arriving with an agitated rustle of skirts, although Claire responded with an occasional "Yes, dear" to her sister's exculpatory speech. Not that anyone was blaming the girl, and surely this was not the time for explanations. Claire's patience was admirable, or was it abstraction?

He turned his head. "Miss Alba." She fell abruptly silent. "Go and get some dry clothes for Lucilla. A flannel nightgown. A woollen stocking and a woollen sock."

"Oh! Of course." She ran from the room.

Claire was regarding him with an arrested expression. It was only a moment, then her attention was with the child again. But she said softly, "Thank Heaven you got the boot off before the swelling started."

"I had to cut the laces," he replied. "The jaws of the trap did not penetrate the boot, did they?"

"It's hard to tell. The skin is broken and the flesh mangled terribly." He thought there was hysteria in the rising tone of her voice, but glancing at her, he found her calm and self-possessed. "There is Alba coming back, and you must change your clothes, too." Reaching out she touched his cheek, his hands, in what he recognized as the habitual gesture by which she ascertained whether the children were dressed warm enough. "You're cold through and through. You'll catch your death."

He laughed. "I'm sure Planchett will agree."

~ ~ ~

Planchett insisted on rubbing his hair dry, too, and through his cautious towelling, Justin heard the clap of the door without at first seeing who had entered. It was Claire.

"Thank you, Planchett, that will do," he said. A sidelong glance showed her pale and tense. "Has the doctor arrived?"

Shaking her head, she put her hand to her eyes.

"He will be here quite soon. And she's a healthy child. Surely if the metal has not touched the flesh, there will be no infection."

"I hope so. Oh, I do hope so." She looked at him. "And you? Are you warm? Dry? I'm sorry; I ought to have sent you straight upstairs. Did Planchett remember to apply the tincture?"

He grinned. "I'm not one of your charges, *amor*. I can look after myself."

"Yes, I suppose you can." With a little smile she added, "And not just yourself, either." There was a moment of perfect accord.

Then she cast down her eyes and at the same time drew herself up. When she spoke again, the mood had changed entirely. "I am told you have Persephone waiting for you in the library," she said in a level voice. "I believe the duty to punish my sisters is mine. We agreed that you would not interfere."

"Is she indeed waiting there? Good girl. But this is between Percy and me. I told her never to venture on Manvers's land. She knew very well that she was doing mischief, choosing Miss Quinnault's afternoon off for it, and a day I was away." Some fool had brought his riding crop upstairs. With a vague notion of restoring it to its proper place, Justin picked it up and abstractedly tapped his boots with its tip. "This is between Percy and me."

"Captain." Claire laid a hand on his arm. "Please let me deal with Percy."

He covered her hand with his. It was cold. "This is not like you, *cariño*." He let his fingers close around hers and planted a kiss on her wrist.

He meant to leave her then, but she clung to his hand and took a sobbing breath. "Please." Her behaviour puzzled him extremely. There was no cause for such drama. "Please." With an apologetic smile, he shook his head. "Please, Justin. I will do anything, if only you will let me deal with Percy."

"Now that's promising." A bit of teasing might dispel the tension. "I'll be lenient, then." It did not; Claire dropped his hand as if it had stung her.

He was not sorry, however, that Percy had had to wait for him, although she might have found herself a seat instead of remaining motionless in front of the desk. "I hope you have used the time to consider what you have done," he growled, laying down the riding whip. "Come here." He took her by the shoulder, intending to stand her at his knee and give her a severe scold, but she threw up her arms, hiding her head, and flinched away so violently that he must have hurt her had he not already released his grip. "Stop that nonsense, and come here."

Slowly she lowered her arms. Her eyes were huge and staring in her pale face. "Please, sir, I know I did wrong," she said breathlessly. "So please beat me straightaway and scold me later. It was all my idea, so please don't punish Lucilla."

"Don't be silly." All this drama was beginning to sap his patience. First Miss Alba, then Claire, now this. "I'm not going to beat you."

"But I did it on purpose!" she cried. "I knew you were away, and I did it on purpose, because you had told us not to!"

Had it not been for her desperate manner, he would have laughed. "Now that's what I call a full confession." He sat down and regarded her, his hands loose on his knees.

"And I persuaded Lucy to come with me! I told her it was alright! I said I had permission!"

With some effort he suppressed a smile. "And she believed that?"

"Yes!" After a moment she added, as the ultimate sin, "I lied!"

"Now that is all very dreadful." Although she flinched again when he reached for her, she yielded to the pressure of his hand. Her whole being was taut with fear. This must be hysteria. She could not possibly believe that he would beat a child, a girl, but when he spoke to her, there was no response, although her breath coming in rapid gasps and her fixed unseeing eyes told their own tale. "Well, I won't beat you," he said crisply.

She glanced at him briefly, looked away, glanced up again. Her gaze focused. "No?"

"No."

"Later?"

"Never." He patted her shoulder. "Never ever."

A tremor went through her. There was a small moment of absolute stillness, then she burst into a passion of tears. He lifted her to his knee, cradled her head, and let her weep.

When sobs turned to hiccoughs, he said, "Now it's time to stop." He made her sit up and blow her nose. "Percy." He cleared his throat. "You know you did wrong, don't you?"

"I wanted to do wrong." Quickly turning her face into his shoulder, she added in a hoarse whisper, "I wanted to get at you, and instead I've hurt Lucy."

He considered this. "That's not really the point, however. Do you know why you weren't to cross onto Manvers's land?"

"Because you said so," she mumbled into his coat. "Well, no."

She sat up. "No?"

He shook his head. "Clearly I didn't explain very well at the time. Come to think of it, I didn't explain at all, did I, since you were there when Manvers took his noisy exit . . . No. The reason you weren't to go on his land is that there's a bit of an argument between him and me, and I wanted to keep you children out of it. I thought he'd probably make a fuss if he saw you. He doesn't like trespassers. But I never thought he'd place man-traps." Seeing her frown, he added, "That trap wasn't set for badgers, you know, but for trespassers."

The girl swallowed. "That's horrible."

"Yes, it is. Poor Lucy. I'm sorry. I suppose it's partly my fault."

Her eyes narrowed, and there was patent disbelief in her voice when she spoke. "Your fault?"

"You don't think so?"

"No." She shook her head. "I think we should do as you say. But even if you had explained, I would have done it, because I didn't like you. But not if I'd known about the trap." She cast him an agonized look and sought refuge at his shoulder again.

He patted her back. "*Anda, bobita.*" Setting her on her feet, he rose. "Now we will go and tell Lucy and Claire how sorry you are, and it will be alright."

~ ~ ~

"Don't be silly." His angry voice penetrated the door. Claire pressed her forehead against the jamb, ready to rush in at the first sounds of violence. Her heart slammed against her ribs in painful strokes. The voice went on, "I won't beat you."

Percy's desperate defiance provoked only the mildest of responses. It was hardly credible. Claire leaned against the panelling, weak with relief. He was not going to beat the child. If he had so much as lifted a finger against her, she would have gone in like a lioness. But he had not. He had not.

The remainder of their talk washed gently by. Too shaken to leave her post, she just stood there, her back against the wall, until the door opened.

Percy ran straight at her, hugging her around the waist. "I'm sorry, Claire!" Then she tilted back her head to give her a gleaming smile. "He didn't beat me. I think I like him, after all."

The remark brought no smile to Justin's lips. He looked stunned, as if the blows that had given him his bruises had only just fallen. Except that when they fell, he had not been stunned but had fought off his assailants with alarming presence of mind.

Without a word, he took Percy's hand when she said that he would come with her, wouldn't he, to see Lucy. Nor did he comment on the sense of intimacy arising from being linked together thus, with Percy in the middle. Perhaps he did not feel it. Claire cast him a quick glance. His eyes when he turned his head were haunted.

Chapter 13

There is no fear in love;
but perfect love casteth out fear:
because fear hath torment.
I John 4:18

LUCILLA'S forgiveness was instant and complete, and it threw the older girl into an agony of remorse that was beyond the reach of human communication. She did not respond when Alba tried to console her, nor when Claire called her to order, nor did she show the slightest reaction when Dr Hurd arrived.

Trying to ignore the child's sobs, Claire went to greet the doctor. Justin had been speaking to him in a rapid undertone, but now he said, "You remember Dr Hurd, Claire? You met him at our wedding."

"Yes, indeed. How do you do, doctor?" She inclined her head. "Have you met my sisters? We are not usually such a tearful lot," she added, "although you see nearly all of us assembled. Stella is the only one missing. Could you perhaps find her, Captain? She may be able to deal with Percy."

"Brave girl," Justin said. Instead of complying with her request, however, he stepped past her towards the bed. He touched Alba on the arm and made a speaking gesture with his head that hurried her from the room. His voice when he said Percy's name was calm and compelling. The girl raised a stormy face. "Pull yourself together, Percy."

"I'm sorry, Lucy." Percy gave a great sniff and a gulp. "Can I hold your hand?"

"You're already holding it, you gowk." Lucilla managed a ghostly smile.

"This is Dr Hurd, Lucy," Justin added. "He'll examine your leg and it will be painful, but he'll make you better."

It made sense for Justin to stay throughout the examination, since there were questions to which only he could reply, and he did this briefly and to the point. He even produced the mangled boot he had cut from Lucy's foot. All the same, he was taking rather much upon himself, to ignore Claire's request for Stella, order Percy about, send Alba away before the bandages were removed, and prepare Lucy for the doctor's probing hands

Good, firm hands and a tiny dose of laudanum. Whenever possible, the doctor requested Claire's assistance, clearly aware that her familiar touch would soothe where his might scare and hurt. But it was Justin who called for more hot water and had tincture, lint, and bandages ready when required. "You go and wash your face, Percy," she heard him say at last. "Alba is waiting for you."

Lucy was very pale, her lip bruised where she had bit it, but her forehead was cool and her eyes drowsy. The laudanum seemed to be taking effect. "We can move her now," the doctor said, bending over the child, but Claire stopped him.

"Captain Sumners will carry her."

When he knelt, Lucy immediately put her arms around his neck, making it easy for him to lift her. As he rose with the child in his arms, he looked at Claire. "Your bed?"

"If you please." Miss Quinnault would have returned by now, making everything ready, down to a hot brick and Lucy's own pillow. "You will stay for dinner, Dr Hurd?"

Everything was ready, Miss Quinnault as quietly efficient as ever. "What an ending to your free day," Claire murmured as they tucked up the child. Over her shoulder she added, "Do persuade the doctor,

Captain. I will join you shortly." And to Lucy, "Try and sleep, love. I'll be back soon." The governess was adjusting the bed-curtains, positioned a lamp. Everything could be left to her. "What would I do without you, Miss Quinnault?"

"What you cannot do without much longer, Mrs Sumners, is your dinner. Now, you must shed your apron, wash your hands, and go down to join the captain."

As Miss Quinnault tidied her hair, Claire wished that she might tidy her thoughts as well. The captain had had no business interfering; but he had done extremely well. The sense of combined gratitude and resentment was oddly familiar, although shame came into it, too, for some as yet unidentified reason, and pride. He had dealt swiftly and intelligently with the crisis.

Even now he was dealing with it, explaining the doctor's presence to Lord Hawksfield at precisely the right moment, when the arrival of the soup could be counted upon to distract him.

"I must give you fair warning, doctor, that we like our soup served hot and hot," his lordship said. "Many a guest unused to our modern conveniences has burnt his tongue. A warming room behind that door," he pointed with his chin, "that is the trick."

The doctor blew on his spoon, took a cautious mouthful, and made appreciative noises. Claire slanted a quick look at Justin, next to her, but no tell-tale lines fanning out from the corners of his eyes hinted at amusement. From this side, his bruise was invisible. It would hurt if he smiled, but this was unlikely to affect his mood.

"You have my sister Stella to thank for your dinner," she said to the doctor. "She looked in on the kitchen. People do lose their heads."

"It may be a superstition," Stella added, "but we believe chicken soup is good when you have had a chill."

"A chill of the soul, too?" Justin's words were inaudible to anyone but Claire. She recalled his stunned look when he saw her waiting outside the library and knew that it was she who had dealt him that stunning blow. Her promise, her protective presence had made amply clear of what she believed him capable. And she had believed it. "That sounds promising," he had said, laughing, and she had taken it as confirmation of her belief. Now it seemed inconceivable to have believed that of him.

But it was a promise, and she would keep it. If she had meant it as a bribe, perhaps it could be offered by way of apology, too.

Lucilla was sleeping soundly when Dr Hurd paid her a final visit before departing. Miss Quinnault said goodnight, Claire got ready for bed. She was tired without being sleepy and sat for a long time watching the child, waiting for Justin's footsteps in the hall. How trustfully the little one had clung to him; the only one among them who really could trust. A posthumous child, she alone was untouched by the fear that casts out love.

The shouting; the blows. Nothing but complete intoxication and incapacity could prevent either. The question had been, rather, when it started and who got them. To an extent, it was possible to influence both, to bring things to a head quickly so at least to be spared the agony of waiting for the first blow to fall, and to put oneself in the way of it when it did fall. Claire felt that it was better if it was she, because Mama intervened sooner then. But Robert argued that he could stand it better, and he wanted to protect Mama, too, even though she was only his stepmother. Claire despised her for her submissiveness, and for letting Papa comfort her when he had finished his beating. Robert saw these things differently. He said Mama had no choice.

She herself had had a choice, and for Robert's sake she had chosen to marry, despite all she knew about the conjugal tie. She had not credited Justin's claim to expect nothing of her, but she was coming to credit it. He had accepted her refusal. He had also made plain that an affirmative would be welcome.

Perhaps it would not be so bad. But that was the rub. It was not the violence that scared her – she had had enough of that to know she could bear it – it was the power over mind and soul that love conveyed to the beloved, the dependence of the loving one. What if her brother was right about her, and she was more her mother's daughter than she knew? She had kissed Justin, after all, and the sensation of his warm, pulsating body against hers was akin to nothing she had ever felt before, except perhaps the sensation of holding the newborn Lucy in her arms. If the mere touch of his skin made her feel like that, what might his embraces not do? No wonder Percy had chosen to defy him now; she must have sensed a change in her sister. And she, too, must defy him, for if he did not prove brutish and violent now, what was to prevent her from succumbing completely, losing any independence she might have?

Voices in the hall, the creak of oak, a soft clap of doors. It was time to keep her promise. He had been so shocked. Hurt and shock often turned into anger. Perhaps his anger would help her. With a glance at the mirror, she banished the unhappy frown, flung back the dark mass of her hair, and dabbed lavender behind her ears.

Nicola's wedding gift had not been as inappropriate as Claire had thought at the time. The white nightgown fell to her ankles in soft folds, cool and smooth against her skin, which the fretwork of narrow straps left scandalously bare on arms, shoulders, and most of her bosom. Although the exquisite gauzy robe that came with it covered her arms and shoulders, it did not lend the ensemble even a modicum of decency.

A last look at the sleeping child and she slipped into the hall. His reply to her knock came on a questioning note. "Enter?"

A branch of candles burned on the bedside cabinet. He lay propped up on one elbow, his bare arms and chest tawny against the bedclothes, a book open before him.

Yet this was only the briefest impression. In a flash, he was out of bed and holding her by the shoulders. Instinctively she braced herself, but his grip was light. When he spoke, his words were entirely unexpected.

"Is Lucy worse? Do you need me to get the doctor?"

Unable to utter a sound, she shook her head. The clean scent of his skin mingled with the sleepy warmth he radiated to form the image of an over-powering force that made her flesh tremble. His dark eyes held her gaze.

"You're trembling, Claire. What is it?"

Only his hands and his eyes were holding her up. If their hold relaxed, she would fall. "Nothing. All is well." The grip on her shoulders diminished, but his gaze was no less keen. "I came to thank you for . . . for all that you did today."

He moved his hands in a caress so gentle that it was imperceptible except for the friction of fine lawn against her skin. "Thank me?"

"Yes." Breaking his hold with a slight shrug, she stepped into his embrace and, for the second time, slipped her arms around his bare torso. This time she remembered his bruises and kept her hands clear of his shoulders.

Too tense to see beyond her own fears, she had not perceived him very clearly, and it was only when she felt his warmth through her thin gown that she knew him to be quite naked. She lifted her cheek from where it had lain against his collarbone, sought his mouth with her lips and, imitating his response the first time she had kissed him, idiotically, in the stillroom, took a cautious taste.

Again his reaction was unexpected, for although he did take her in his arms, he broke the kiss. "This is how you thank me?" His voice was low and intimate in her ear, his jaw rough against her temple

"Yes," she said again. "And do you remember what you said when first I kissed you?" A tremor went through him. When he spoke again, she knew it had been a tremor of amusement.

"I didn't have a chance to say anything. You ran away before I could so much as open my mouth."

"The next day, then. You said you wished it had not ended there." She drew a deep breath. "This need not end here, if you wish."

But he did not throw her on the bed and himself on her. Instead, he untangled her embrace and held her away from him.

"I don't believe it." His grip tightened. "And I don't want it." Although the words startled her, the suppressed anger in his voice did not. "It's not what I have done but what I haven't done that you're thanking me for, isn't it?" In a moment he would start shaking her. "Isn't it?"

She kept her eyes on his face, trying to gauge his reactions, wondering which reply might best hurry events to their inevitable end.

"You really thought I would beat her?"

"I am sorry. It was the whip."

"The whip?"

"The riding whip you carried downstairs with you."

His brow furrowed. Perhaps now the storm would break. "You have every right to be angry," she added contritely.

"Of course I'm angry! What on earth have I done to you to make you think I'd beat a little girl, my sister-in-law, for God's sake!"

Now it would come; she could feel it coming. But all that followed this outburst was a long silence, and then he said, in quite a different voice, "You're doing it, too."

She had no idea what he meant, but it seemed better to agree. "Yes. I'm sorry."

He ignored her apology. "When I tried to talk to Percy, she asked me to beat her first and scold her later. That's what you're doing, isn't it, trying to hurry a beating to get it over with? Only in your case it wouldn't precisely be a beating . . ." Her thin robe seemed to evaporate under his burning gaze. "This is what you were doing on our wedding night, too. You're even wearing what Lucy calls your special nightgown." Unhanding her, he stepped back a pace. "Look at me, Claire. Do I really look like the kind of man who would force his wife and beat his sister?"

She hardly knew where to look. It was only upon her inarticulate noise of protest that he seemed to become aware of himself. His astonishment was almost comical. With an oath, he flung away from her, and when she hazarded another glance, he had wrapped his dressing gown around himself.

"Forgive me, Claire, I —"

An absurd urge to giggle assailed her. His look of chagrin was too much; a choked laugh escaped her. When he cast her a quick, surprised glance, her mirth overcame her, and then they were both laughing.

"Time for bed, I think," he said at last.

"Of course." Quite sober now, she stepped past him. His book – the book she had given him – still lay next to his pillow. Careful not to lose his page, she lifted it to the bedside cabinet. Then she sat on the edge of the large four-poster, her hands outspread at her sides.

He had turned to follow her with his gaze but made no move to join her. "Have you been listening to a single word I've said, Claire?"

She looked up in surprise. "You said it was time for bed."

The clock ticked, a log snapped in the fire. He went to the hearth and laid his arm along the mantelpiece, staring into the flames. "Love isn't a reward, Claire," he said. "You're not the first woman to offer herself to me in payment for some imagined debt. I thought it was a form of currency used only in war; but apparently I was wrong. Love isn't a reward, nor an apology, nor a punishment. Never that. Never."

"I'm sorry." There was a lump in her throat. She tried to gulp it down. Somehow his meaning eluded her. "What is it, then?"

"It simply – is."

That was clearly nonsense. There was nothing simple about love. Love was power and dependence; violence and submission; twisted pride and humiliation. His stern expression dissolved in the sparkle of tears filling her eyes. She blinked them away, but the breath she drew to control herself turned into a great, gasping sob.

~ ~ ~

She stared at him, her eyes swimming, then she was staring through him into some dark abyss. As her body wound itself into a tight ball, she slid off the bed, covering her mouth with her hands – biting her hands. Her head struck against the cabinet, but the pain did not appear to register. The source of her anguish was elsewhere.

He leapt to her side, knelt, and put his arms around her, holding her close to prevent her hurting herself any more. Then he found purchase on her cramped limbs and lifted her back onto the bed. Cradling her against his chest, he hushed and soothed her as only some hours before he had soothed her little sister. But there was no response, and he understood what was happening. At least she stopped biting her hands, and instead twisted them into the front of his dressing gown.

His sergeant had told him that the most effective remedies were a few slaps in the face or a bucket of cold water. The soldiers called it madness, raving, fits; the officers, nerves or hysteria, but mostly no one called it anything at all, preferring to keep silent about the shattering effect that war could have on a man's spirit. There was no logic to it; anything might set it off, and he had seen a strong, brave man cowering before the shadows of his past while a coward might remain unaffected.

I have nightmares. Percy's half-proud, half-defiant assertion, and the girls preferred sharing their bed-chambers even though there were rooms enough in the house. He knew the sisters had been adopted into the secure comfort of their grandmother's home some six years ago, taking her name. About what had come before, they kept silent. All he had learned was that they had lived in Edinburgh, their father and mother had died, Claire had not learned to ride. *Family dissension, domestic unhappiness.* Percy would have been five years old at the time. "*Dios me libre,*" he muttered.

In the same language, he murmured softly in Claire's ear until the tormented gasps subsided and

161

she was weeping childishly into his shoulder. After a little of this, he said, "Pray use a handkerchief, *mi amor*. Planchett will break his heart if he finds my dressing gown all snotty."

She sat up abruptly, her face averted. "I'm sorry."

"And so you should be." Leaning away from her, he rummaged under his pillow and drew out the clean handkerchief Planchett placed there every night. But her face looked pale and bruised, her eyes were red and swollen, so he soaked the stiff linen in his washbasin and only then handed it to her. With an inarticulate sound, she pressed it to her skin.

Several long breaths later, she lowered her hands, slowly, wiping her nose in a final way. "Thank you." Her eyes were downcast, and he recognized the same profound shame that Private Muller had suffered after his fit. "*Bobita*," he said softly, "don't be ashamed."

"How could I not be?" Her voice was rough. "A hysterical female." He saw her throat move as she swallowed. "Rest assured that it doesn't happen very often. Grandmama gave me two sharp slaps when it did, and that helped."

Apparently she thought he should have applied the same remedy. "I considered pouring the washbasin over you, but didn't want to ruin the carpet."

She raised her eyes to his and looked at him for a long time. "You're laughing," she said at last.

"At fate." He smiled. "Not at you."

"At fate?" She tilted her head, considering, then returned his smile. "I like that." Leaning towards him, she kissed him, once, on the corner of his mouth. "I'd better get back to Lucy. I never meant to stay this long."

Justin rose with her, letting her into the hall, where he stood and watched her receding form. At the door to her bedchamber, she turned and lifted her hand in a silent farewell. Not more than thirty minutes had elapsed since she had entered his room. What the devil had she been expecting? *She was asking for it, she wanted it* – quite literally she had asked for it, but it had been the mere physical act that she offered him.

And he had talked about love. That, on top of everything else – no wonder she had collapsed. But he was flattering himself; if he had given himself away, she had not noticed it. Her gaze had been drawn deep into some dark abyss; it had nothing to do with him. She would have clung to anyone who pulled her back from its depth.

He wanted a cigarillo. Lifting aside the curtain of the hall window, he scanned the night sky, listened to the wind; he would have to put some clothes on. A flicker of light on the other side of the courtyard drew his attention. It came from the Long Gallery, which at this hour ought to lie in darkness. He had better see if all was well. In three strides, he was back in his room, fetched up the counterpane, and ran across the hall.

But the house was not on fire. The fire was in the fireplace, where it should be, the bright light emanating from a branch of candles on the mantel-piece that illumined the outlines of two wing chairs and, above it, the portrait of his mother, a family group by Lawrence with Stephen and himself as rosy infants. The rest of the gallery lay in shadow.

A head peered around the wing of one chair, white hair shimmering in the candlelight. "It's you, is it?" Lord Hawksfield said. "I should have known. Pray, is there any reason for you to burst in like this, or is that your usual way of entering a room?"

Justin had to grin. "There is, and it isn't," he said. "I thought the house was on fire. Don't be alarmed in your turn, sir," he continued, "if you hear the side door opening. I want a cigarillo."

"It's a vile habit," Lord Hawksfield commented. Justin was about to turn and go when the older man added, "At least you don't indulge in it inside the house, or obtrude it upon Mrs Sumners. Would a glass of brandy do instead?" He gestured vaguely. "I've been too idle to get up. Pour me a drink and join me, won't you?"

Despite his surprise, Justin did not hesitate. "With pleasure." He advanced into the room and let the counterpane drop on the other chair. When he returned from the cabinet at the gallery's farther end, Lord Hawksfield was contemplating the portrait with a wistful smile. Justin bent to make up the fire. "That's better," his lordship said as it leapt to flame and warmth. "Your mother has been much on my mind since your wedding. I couldn't think why, until tonight. You have a look of her when you are with Mrs Sumners."

"Did you think I married her only because you wished it? You, who have always lamented how disobliging I am?"

The dark eyes – so like his own – slid to his face. "Disobliging, contrary, obstinate. I have little hope that your recent, painful encounter will cure you of your sad predilection for low company."

Justin had placed the glasses and decanter on a side table. Now he poured two stiff tots and pushed one glass within the older man's reach.

"Thank you." Lord Hawksfield took some slow sips. "You have changed," he said at length, adding with a rare gleam of amusement, "and I don't mean since that portrait was taken. Why did you exchange to the Riflemen?"

It was a question, not an accusation. Even had he followed the Peninsular campaign more closely than Justin thought likely, his father could not have known what it was like – that it was not all marching and fighting, but quite a lot of talking and listening, too. If he had heard of the guerrilla at all, he probably classed them as bandits and cutthroats, and not without reason. Justin wrapped the counterpane around his body and ensconced himself in the other wing chair, tucking his bare feet under him.

"Are you a savage, young man? Is that a way for a gentleman to sit?" This was an accusation. Justin murmured that his feet were cold; his lordship submitted him to disgusted scrutiny. "Why, you're practically naked! What can you be thinking of, to be prowling around the house in a state of nature!" He broke off, drank some brandy, coughed. "Well." He cleared his throat. "Where were we?"

"You asked me why I exchanged to the Riflemen," Justin said mildly. He picked up his glass and cradled it in his hand. "Do you remember when I lost my regiment, back in the year eight?"

"Do I remember?" Lord Hawksfield burst out. "Yes, Justin, I remember quite well what it was like, thinking I had lost you, and likely to take Stephen with you as well, the way he went on after we had the news. I may not be a very demonstrative parent, but I had only the two sons, and I loved you, confounded nuisances though you were, both of you!"

"I'm sorry," Justin said. "I had no idea." He had been certain that his father never spared a thought for him once he was gone, apart from condemning his exchange. The older man finished his drink in a gulp; Justin replenished his glass.

"Anyhow, during that time I made the acquaintance of some local combatants opposed to the French, and learned the language, so once I'd found Wellington's army, I was able to act as a liaison – and the Riflemen are simply more suited to that kind of service. Not least," he added with a grin, "because their uniform is much less conspicuous than a Hussar's."

His father grunted. "So it was to make better use of your skills, and better serve your King, that you exchanged to a less prestigious regiment." That was not quite the way Justin would have put it, but he let it rest.

"Is that why you're not interested in taking up our seat? You're aiming for the Foreign Office?"

"My aim," Justin said as explosively as his father had spoken only a moment before, "my aim was to save you from ridicule. What do you think would have happened, had I chosen to destroy the splendid web you had woven – Boughton and Lyster and you – around Claire and myself? How do you think she felt when she learned she was to marry me?"

His father shrugged. "I should say she's done pretty well. Certainly, her grandmother was a Scott of Harden, her grandfather an eminent judge, and she's a woman of property, but she could hardly expect to marry a Sumners."

"That's precisely the point," Justin said acidly. "She didn't." But she, too, might have expected him to be employed abroad. He found himself assailed by a strange doubt whether that had influenced her decision to accept his hand.

"Well, you needn't frown so fiercely, Justin. I'm proud of you, and I'm sure your mother would have been, too." Once again he glanced up at the picture. "I was a better man when she lived, and loved me." He sighed.

And then they talked, for the first time, without any of the old rancour intervening. Not about Manvers or Lyster or Claire, but about the estate, the people, the war, the national economy. Only when they parted did his father say, with emphasis, "*I* will speak to Manvers tomorrow. No," he forestalled a contradiction, "it will be much better coming from me. Man-traps, forsooth," he muttered.

Chapter 14

What seest thou else
in the dark backward and abysm of time?
Shakespeare, *The Tempest*

SHE ought to have lain awake for hours, but Claire fell asleep as soon as her head touched the pillow, and slept deeply and dreamlessly until Alba woke her at four o'clock in the morning. Even then she felt refreshed and more at peace with herself than she could remember having felt for a long time. "What is it, Alba?"

Her sister stood in the door, dramatically lit by the flame of the candle she carried.

"Do come in, love."

"I can't." One hand holding the candle aloft, the other laid upon her bosom as if to still her quickened breathing, Alba stood rooted to the spot. "Oh, Claire!"

"Won't you tell me what is wrong?" Beside her, Lucy stirred. Claire pushed aside the covers and swung her feet to the floor. They had better talk in the hall.

Alba gave a faint shriek. "Don't come near me!"

Lucy mewed sleepily and knuckled her eyes. It was too late to worry about waking her; she was sitting up, blinking into the light. Then she saw Alba and cried, "No! It's not fair!" In a half-lurch, she grabbed Claire's arm. The tent they had constructed over her leg to minimize contact with the bedclothes swayed dangerously. She was hurting herself, but it was not that which caused her to cry out again. "It's not fair, Percy always gets everything. I want Claire to stay with me!"

"You mustn't be selfish, Lucy," Alba cried.

"For Heaven's sake, Alba!"

Again it was too late. "I am not selfish!" After this enraged protest, Lucy not unnaturally burst into tears.

"Oh, Alba. At least close the door, she'll wake the whole house."

"I cannot come in," Alba declared.

"Would you mind if I do? Good morning, Miss Alba. Morning, Claire." Justin briefly raised his eyebrows. "We needn't have worried, *amor*. Lucy's voice penetrates loud and clear to my bedchamber." He propelled Alba into the room and shut the door.

With a sense of relief, Claire turned to the little one. In the few moments that had passed, Lucy had worked herself into a fine tantrum, and at first Claire merely applied herself to preventing damage or hurt to the strapped-up leg, letting the girl have her cry out. When screams turned to gulps, however, it was time to soothe and comfort. "Certainly I'll remain with you, love. Of course I will. What's that you're saying?" She bent her head to catch the words Lucy was mumbling into her bosom.

"I thought you were going to leave me."

"No, nay, never." With a damp sigh, the little girl snuggled closer, small fists curled tightly into the fine stuff of her gown. Cradling her gently, Claire looked up. "Well, Alba, it seems Lucy has much quicker wits than I do. Did you indeed want me for Percy?"

Alba had not altered her stance, except that her gaze was now fixed on Justin, as though he were a bear that had unaccountably got into the room.

"Alba!"

She gave a start. "Yes – no," she said. "I woke up – oh, a little while ago, and heard strange sounds, so I got up and found that it was Persephone. She had difficulty in breathing, and when I felt her forehead, it was glowing with heat, although her hands were icy."

"So she's caught cold," Justin said matter-of-factly. "Not entirely unexpected, is it?"

Alba threw him a sidelong glance, but did not reply. "I called Miss Quinnault," she told Claire. "She is with her now."

This could be serious. "Is it Miss Quinnault who wanted me, then?"

"Oh, no. Miss Quinnault said you mustn't be disturbed. I must go back to bed, she said, and she would look after Percy. There is the risk of infection, after all. But I felt you had to know!"

Drat the girl! Why could she not have heeded Miss Quinnault? What use was it waking half the household at this hour, when there was nothing anyone could reasonably do? "She did not ask for the doctor to be sent for?"

Alba shook her head. "But Persephone is so delicate, Claire. What for any other child is a cold, turns into an influenza with her. You know her constitution."

"Yes." Miss Quinnault was perfectly acquainted with Percy's constitution, too; if she wanted neither Claire nor the doctor, then neither was wanted.

"Alright, Alba. Thank you. Go back to bed now, love, and trust Miss Quinnault to know best. It was sensible of you to think of the risk of infection. You will take care, won't you?"

"I'll keep myself apart as much as possible." Alba threw out her hand in a valedictory gesture. "Goodnight, sister. Goodnight, brother." And she swept from the room.

"Goodnight," Claire said absent-mindedly, her attention claimed by the child asleep at her breast. "Goodnight, Lucy-love," she murmured as she lowered her onto the pillow. A small snort was her only reply.

"Asleep and dreaming." With a smile she looked at Justin. Alba had been so shocked, but at least he was not naked. He was even wearing slippers.

He exclaimed in Spanish, as was his wont, and rolled his eyes. "I admire your patience, Claire," he added. "I could have told her to go the devil with her histrionics."

"That might not have been all that useful, unless you wanted her to weep all over you, too, braving the risk of infection. I'm sorry, Justin, this has been a weepy day, and you've borne the brunt of it."

"You had full cause of weeping." He frowned. "But Claire, is the risk really that great? Surely this is only a cold?"

"I daresay it may seem excessive, but I do try to keep contact among the children to a minimum when one of them is ill. It hasn't always been possible . . ." Only too well did she remember the three cramped rooms in Edinburgh and how they had seemed filled, absolutely filled, with coughing, retching invalids.

~ ~ ~

For the second time that night, there was that faraway look in her eyes, but when he said her name, she turned her head on her pillow to face him as he knelt by the bed.

"We only had three rooms, you know, and there were six of us – Mama and Papa, me and the boys and Alba – when the epidemic broke out. We all had the fever, but James and Frederick died. Papa blamed us, I suppose; it was then that it started. And there were no more boys, only girls, and he blamed Mama for that. After Percy was born, he brought Robert to live with us. I don't know what I would have done without Robert." Her eyelids were drooping, her voice drowsy, making her terrible

170

little narrative sound like any bedtime talk. At last she yawned and added, as though coming back to the point after a perfectly normal explanation, "So perhaps I am a little overcautious when it comes to infection."

The lips that formed those chilling words were the same he had felt so warm and soft against his own some hours before; the same young woman, the same remote beauty. He stared at her, but he still saw what he always saw when he looked at her. Yet something had changed, although it might be no more than the aftermath of the crisis, or sleep. For she was rosy with sleep – not cool and remote or controlled at all, but sleepily there, so close that he could see the shadows that her eyelashes cast on her cheeks.

Beyond all doubt, something had changed within him. Her self-contained poise was not, after all, as natural to her as her beauty was, or her cool intelligence, the qualities that had first attracted him; before he knew her loyalty where she thought she owed it; her sense of honour, her courage – the immense courage it took to face and overcome the life of which he had had a glimpse that night. Inside the cool, controlled woman, there was a terrified girl fighting tooth and claw to sustain that coolness and control, fighting demons unknown to him, and here he was shaking, literally shaking, with protective passion.

"You cannot be comfortable kneeling there," she murmured, moving aside to make room for him to sit on the edge of the bed. Unconfined under her nightdress, her breasts nestled against her arms. Her neck and cheeks were a little flushed.

Clearly it had never entered her head that he might love her, although she seemed certain that he desired her. Not that she was wrong, but – his heart began to slam in short, quick beats. He had talked to her about love as though he knew what he were talking about. But he hadn't. "I've been in love, and it was nothing like this," he had told Matthew. He had never felt anything like this. Love was simple, giving and receiving in equal measure, and if that equality was not there, he had declined whatever was offered as love, accepting neither sacrifice nor reward. If he loved a woman, he did not care if she merely sought the pleasure or distraction of an affair. It was agreeable to be loved, certainly, but it had never mattered much to him. And now it did. It was an uncomfortable thought. With a last look at Claire's restful form, he rose.

"Justin?" Her eyes fluttered open.

"I didn't mean to wake you. Try and get some sleep."

"Yes." Her head moved against the pillow. "Have you loved many women?"

"What? No – maybe three or four." Why did she ask? And was it a good sign, or a twisted kind of jealousy?

His startled reply seemed to have been the right one, however, although her response was again startling. "How splendid," she murmured. Correctly interpreting his silence, she added, "To be able to love like that." She smiled dreamily. "You see, I was wondering if that really is your experience, that love is simple."

"It is," he said, determined that it should be so.

Chapter 15

Land of my sires! what mortal hand
Can e'er untie the filial band?
Scott, *The Lay of the Last Minstrel*

Up until then, it had all been a game. An absurd twist of fortune had thrown this girl into his life, and he had laughed and assured her that things would look after themselves. And she had expected violence and seduction.

Not that she was entirely wrong. If he had thought about it at all, which he hadn't, he would have had to admit that what he meant by things looking after themselves was that she would come to accept her situation, their marriage – him.

But he had changed. Even Lord Hawksfield had seen it, and he was not the most observant parent. He was no longer the irresponsible younger son setting out to make his own way in the world. Not that Stephen had ever possessed any great sense of responsibility: if he had, he would not have got himself killed in that foolish manner. Matthew felt responsible there, and with a sudden sense of a weight lifting, Justin realized that he, too, had felt guilty about his brother's death. Yet even if his leaving England had caused the mood of splenetic ennui that Matthew had described, if any blame were to be apportioned, it belonged equally to both brothers. Now Stephen's place was empty, and it was his part to take it.

The candles were nearly burnt out, but a grey light was seeping through the gap between the curtains. Pushing them aside, Justin saw that dawn was extending cold fingers over the park, the trees dark and dripping, a white brume hovering over the ground.

Not many minutes later, it swirled around his boots as he made his way across the pasture down to the old willow growing aslant the stream, where Stephen and he had been used to meet up with Dick Gurney when they sneaked out for some early fishing. Justin settled on the gnarled trunk, felt in his pockets for his tinderbox and lit a cigarillo. On an empty stomach and after the broken night, the smoke was as heady as the brandy he had shared with his father, burning sharply on his tongue.

He looked back at the dark trail he had left in the silver grass, the wide sweep of land rising from the stream, the solid limestone walls of Hawksfield Manor floating in the twilight. He saw Claire, fast asleep with the little one beside her; his father in the fitful morning hours of the aged. In his room above the stables, Pepe would be yawning widely as he climbed into his clothes, the horses snorting sleepily in their boxes.

A curious sense of connectedness seemed to tie him to everything that lived among these rolling pastures, human and animal creation alike. A sheep bleated plaintively. A blackbird tried its voice. Somewhere in the undergrowth a badger sneezed.

Sheep and badgers, for all love! A spurt of laughter shook him out of his trance. The image of stability was deceptive. He had seen houses like this gutted and burnt, the inhabitants fled or killed, the livestock slaughtered. Not that this could ever happen in England, he told himself with a wry grin.

It had begun to mizzle, but a change in the pervading grey told him that the sun had shouldered its way over the horizon. In the growing light, the furry catkins clustered along the willow's as yet leafless branches shone like silver. The pale flowers of a clump of fumewort growing at its foot glowed softly purple.

The blackbird broke into song, was joined by its brethren, wrens, blackcaps, a chiffchaff. On a wave of birdsong, jubilant, he returned to the house. A faint light showed in the kitchen windows. He rubbed his jaw. There should be a chance of hot water. He wanted a shave.

A wash, a shave; now for some coffee. The open door of the stillroom turned him aside, however, and he entered with his heart in his mouth.

The words died on his lips. It was Stella who stood by the table in her apron, mixing herbs, not Claire. "Good morning, Miss Stella. You're an early bird."

With a slight smile, she returned the greeting and the compliment. "Claire is still upstairs," she continued. "Asleep, I hope. Alba roused her at about four o' clock in the morning because Percy has come down with a fever."

"I know. Is there anything I can do?"

"I don't think so." She put a handful of dried blossoms on the scales and carefully added more.

"How bad is she?"

"I haven't seen her, or Alba, or Miss Quinnault. Claire is very careful about the risk of infection." Misinterpreting his silence, she added, "I daresay it may seem excessive to you, but Claire does not see why she should lose Percy or any of us to a mere fever when she and Alba pulled through typhus."

Before his mind's eye flashed a recollection of the Belén hospital in Lisbon in the winter of the year nine. "Hospital fever? *Dios me libre.*"

Stella tilted her head. "Claire never told you?"

"An epidemic was all she said."

The girl's face opened up in unexpected laughter. "That's Claire all over. I'm surprised she said as much as that. She never tells anyone anything. She never told us she was going to marry you, either, although her letters were rather full of you."

"Don't deceive yourself," he said dryly. "She did it to oblige her brother."

Even in jest, it was an inappropriate thing to say to a girl of her age, much less his wife's sister. But she was clearly and intelligently amused. "And you married her to oblige your father. Tell that to the tinkers, brother. It was clever of you to pretend that was the reason, though. She'd never have married you if she'd known that you love her."

His knees felt suddenly weak. He leaned against the door jamb. "No?"

"No."

"And do you think she . . . No, I'm sorry, you cannot possibly tell me that."

"I can tell you this much, however, for it is obvious and I only point it out to you because the significance may have escaped you: Claire trusts you. That may not seem a very great thing to you, but for us, for any of us except perhaps Lucilla, it is a great thing. And to trust anyone so far as to marry him . . . well, I never thought it possible." She was occupied with her herbs and did not look at him when she added, "Mama loved Papa very much and yet theirs was a cruel union; and when he died, it destroyed her." There was a tremor in her voice, and her hands were no longer quite steady.

"What an extraordinary girl you are. Is that why you are usually so quiet, so as not to be perpetually exclaimed at?"

Again she laughed. "As a matter of fact, it is." She put the lid on the jar containing her herb mixture. "I need to take this to the kitchen; you go on to the breakfast parlour, I'll ask them to send up a pot of coffee."

He let her pass, closed the door for her. "You're very like your sister, aren't you?"

"I wouldn't mind."

"There seem to be a lot of early birds abroad this morning," she commented later, when a footman came into the breakfast parlour to announce that Mr Lyster wished to see Mrs Sumners.

"At this unchristian hour?" Lord Hawksfield muttered. "Thank you, my dear," he said more distinctly as Stella poured him his first cup of tea. "Certainly not. Would you speak to him, Justin?"

With a quick nod, Justin rose. Catching Stella's dispassionate glance, he said, "Let Claire know, would you?"

~ ~ ~

"How is she?" There were dark smudges beneath Lyster's eyes. He must have spent an uncomfortable night, if not nearly as uncomfortable as most of his sisters.

"Going on as well as may be expected. She's in a good deal of pain, of course, since the doctor is reluctant about laudanum for such a small child."

Before he had quite finished, Lyster interrupted him. "Not Lucy! I mean Claire – how is Claire?"

What right had he to feel concern for Claire? "She was in perfect health when I left her at about half-past four this morning," Justin said coldly. "Do take a seat." He perched on the edge of his desk, one booted foot dangling, and watched the other man as he fidgeted about the room.

"Half-past four?" Lyster stopped by the window, twisting his fingers into the curtain. Against the light, it was impossible to read his features, but his hoarse voice was revealing enough. "Surely you do not claim her duty at a time like this?"

Remorse, it seemed, had caught up with Lyster. One might almost feel sorry for the pitiful figure he cut. But not quite. Justin raised his eyebrows. "Are you casting aspersions on my virility?"

The other man drew a sharp breath. "There wasn't any blood," he muttered defensively.

Silence hung in the room. When comprehension dawned on him, Justin found that he was shaking with rage, his hand gripping the pen-knife that lay on the desk behind him. But he had known all along that Claire's maid was niece to Mrs Lyster's, and had devised his own stratagems to benefit by the channel thus established. He unclenched his hand. "You're very well informed. No, unlike the Spanish gypsies, the Sumnerses do not celebrate their consummations by displaying blood-stained sheets. Nor were there any."

Inwardly begging Claire's forgiveness, he added, "Don't be so conventional, Lyster. Flat on her back in a bed is not the only – nor the most satisfying – way to have a girl."

Lyster dropped into a chair and covered his face with his hands. "What have I done!"

"You have profited by her sense of duty, Lyster. As do I." He let the words hang, and when the other man cast him a haggard look, he added, "How have you been deluding yourself?"

In a queer voice, Lyster said, "It's just that she seems so . . . untouched."

And yet he knew what had touched Claire, he had been there, had seen it, had even tried to stop it. His betrayal was all the greater. It seemed that he had sought to console himself with two irreconcilable illusions: one, that she was but a woman, and the other, that it had never happened.

"If she seems untouched," Justin said harshly, "it's because she's constructed a beautiful white shell around herself so that nothing can touch her."

"She told you about – that?"

"I know enough." The rest was not for Lyster. Again the man groaned, his head in his hands.

"It's a fortnight since you gave her to me, and it's taken you this long to understand what you've done? You know what it is that touched her, when you were both children. You sought to prevent it and were touched by the same horror. Yet you betrayed her." Lyster writhed in his seat. "Now you may suffer the consequences of your actions: ignominy, obscurity, forsaken by the one who loved you most in the world."

A little surprised by his own eloquence, Justin paused, letting his words sink in, and apparently they were sinking in. An occasional strangled sob was the only sound in the small study, but after a while, Justin became aware of a quickening in his breast, a quick footstep in the hall. And suddenly she was there, standing in the middle of the room, quietly bidding them a good morning.

At once Lyster was at her feet, hugging her knees as he mumbled into her skirts. Justin countered her look of mild surprise with a shrug.

"Is it your ambition to be wept at by every member of my family, Captain?" She touched Lyster's head. "Contain yourself, Robert. I have neither time nor inclination for these demonstrations." Somehow she made him sit down again, but that done had no more attention to spare for her brother. Instead she turned to Justin. "I only came down to inform you, Captain Sumners, that I do not ask you to withdraw your support for my brother's candidacy."

He nodded slowly, his gaze never wavering from her face. Now that he knew what her remote poise concealed, he loved her all the more. Her colour rose. "In all other respects, I believe you know my mind."

"I believe I do," he said. "Thank you, Claire. There is one thing that I've been meaning to tell you, however, which may change it." Lyster made a sudden movement. Justin ignored him. "I'm sorry if this hurts you, *cariño*, but you must know that the attack on Pepe and me was staged by your brother."

Her smile was entirely unexpected; not only that she smiled, but the quality of her smile, the tenderness. "I've known that all along, Justin, and my brother knew that I did." For a small eternity, she let him hold her gaze, then she gave him a nod. "I must go back to Lucy. Gentlemen." With a gesture of her head, she turned to leave.

He held the door for her and did not close it until the sound of her retreating footsteps ceased to be audible. Over their swift continuo, he kept hearing Stella's voice as she said, *Claire trusts you.* He had just had proof.

Like a swimmer surfacing after a long dive, he took a deep breath before turning back into the room. Lyster was palely staring at him.

"You're very fortunate in your sister."

Lyster gulped. "Do you indeed mean to continue your support, merely on Claire's word?"

Merely? "I scarcely believe the man-traps were your idea." Not that Lyster's remorse was about man-traps, but what it was about Justin had no intention of discussing. It was enough to make Lyster understand what he had done to Claire, and either he was a good actor, or it had indeed come home to him. And Claire knew Lyster through and through. If she did not ask him to withdraw his support, then he would not. "Nor do I suppose that you make a habit of hiring thugs? I don't much mind my own temporary disfigurement, but to be playing with the lives of men who, if not too innocent, are at least too stupid to know what they're about, strikes me as iniquitous. Once again you have your sister to thank: being a bride, she was able to beg them off, so you have only to blame yourself for two men's transportation rather than four men's deaths, and they were as pretty a pair of rogues as one could wish."

Not that Bouverie's pardon made any difference to the real offence; Lyster could not have known that the men would come off so lightly. A similar thought seemed to cross his mind, for he said, "I didn't expect them to be taken, you know. In fact, I was certain they'd get away. I mean, four armed men to two very surprised unarmed ones . . ."

Justin suppressed a grin. "That reasoning is unlikely to reconcile me, Lyster." He pushed himself away from the desk, against which he had been leaning. "You haven't had breakfast, have you? Come along, then. My father was just having his first cup of tea when you called, so when you've both finished, we can talk politics."

Lyster gave a snort. "Given the position in which you've put me, I'm unlikely to object to anything you propose."

Claire was right; a man whose armour was so swiftly back in place must be made for politics. "Are you accusing me of blackmail? You've put yourself in that position, and yes, it is not one from which to cavil at my methods of persuasion."

~ ~ ~

Although the methods of persuasion he brought to bear on the electors were rather different, they proved equally effective when the time came for them to cast their votes.

"You have put me in this position." Lyster shook Lord Hawksfield by the hand, then Matthew. "I am deeply grateful to you, and to Lord Boughton." Turning to Justin, he added, "And I thank you, from my heart, for employing your gifts on my behalf. I know full well that I would have had no chance had you decided to stand for the seat yourself. Goodnight, my lord. My lord, goodnight. Captain." He alighted from the chaise and stood with his hat in his hand until they had rounded the corner.

"That's handsome enough," Lord Hawksfield said. "Let's hope he doesn't get above himself once the grateful flush of victory has passed. Not that there was any great doubt about his success. But he is right about you, Justin. If I had known how good you are with people, I might have spared myself the effort of grooming Lyster, and all the trouble I've had with Manvers."

For the remainder of the short drive, he passed the events of the day in review. Lord Hawksfield was in an unusually mellow mood, expressing himself satisfied with Reverend Meynell's sermon, the weather, the refreshments provided at the Crown, the behaviour of the electors. Matthew was mute in his corner, although he did give a low affirmative when his lordship asked if he was likely to bring his pack out any time soon. "With all this political business to look after, I haven't been out at all this winter," Lord Hawksfield said. "In fact, I haven't been out since . . ."

Justin knew why he did not finish the sentence. His father had not hunted since Stephen had died. "Why don't you go up to Dallington Hall for a few days?" he suggested with a glance at Matthew, who made another affirmative sound. "Hawksfield Manor cannot be very comfortable for you at the moment, with our two invalids."

Lanterns had been placed at the gate to the forecourt, and a footman threw open the doors before the chaise had even halted. "I was going to suggest a nightcap," Lord Hawksfield said as he climbed down, "but you have better company awaiting you, Justin, and I've had too much to drink in any case. I'll say good night." Once inside, he extended his hand and, when Justin took it, looked him straight in the eyes. "Yes, if I had known you better, I might have saved myself a lot of trouble."

"I don't know." Justin rubbed his chin. "I can't have been very promising. As you have said, I've changed a great deal. Besides, if you hadn't taken the trouble to foster the acquaintance of Manvers and family, why, I wouldn't be married now, and that would be a great shame."

"So it's all for the best? Handsome of you to say so, Justin. I must admit, however, that I had no idea initially what an uncommonly . . ." He cast about for a suitable attribute. "What an uncommon young woman Mrs Sumners is. Yes, very uncommon." He trod up the stairs.

Matthew was silent. In the lamp-lit chiaroscuro of the entrance hall, it was impossible to tell if he was drunk, tired, or merely morose. With a notion of conducting him to his room, Justin slid his hand under his cousin's elbow, but Matthew pulled away. "Leave me alone," he hissed.

"Turtle." Justin felt a stab of guilt. The alarums and excursions of the past three weeks had let him forget the hurt that had left Matthew sick and incompetent after the wedding. "I'm sorry, Turtle."

"Papa thought it would make a good impression if your candidate were seen to have the support of the Earl of Boughton." Matthew had half averted his face. "And I thought I could stick it out. Being with you is bad enough, but hearing you talk about her is the limit. The absolute limit." His words came in a hoarse whisper and were only a little slurred, but this and the fact that he said them at all told Justin that he must be very drunk indeed.

"Come along." He propelled his cousin into the large courtyard. The old staircase leading straight up to the guest quarters was unencumbered by occasional tables and flower arrangements; he would have an easier time there. As expected, Matthew's legs buckled under him after the first landing. Fortunately by this time he was too far gone to object to Justin's arm around his middle or his own around Justin's shoulders.

"I don't even know if it's young men or just you; whenever I look twice at a young man, he looks like you," Matthew breathed in his ear. "It's always been you. Always you."

It was better not to hear; it would be unfair to hear. By morning, Turtle would have forgotten how far he had stuck his head out. Remembering how he had described Claire to her brother, Justin thought, "I am surrounded by shells," and fought down a crazy urge to laugh.

~ ~ ~

Awaking with a start, Claire rose swiftly from the easy chair in which she had meant to await the gentlemen's return. She lifted aside the bed-curtain, but it was no sound from Lucy that had woken her. The little one was fast asleep. The noise came from the hall: someone was mounting the stairs, trying to be very quiet and not quite succeeding.

Not succeeding at all – a sudden burst of loud, indistinct speech and murmured hushing revealed Dallington and Justin, then the voices receded in the direction of the guest bedrooms. She yawned and stretched, made up the fire, lifted the kettle to ascertain by its weight that its contents had not evaporated, and set it back on the hob.

It seemed a long time before footsteps returned down the hall; not the trod of boots but a hesitant shuffle, and muffled sounds she could not identify. Just as she was about to investigate, she heard a heavier footfall and Justin's voice, low and yet clear. "Miss Alba!" he said. "What's the matter?"

Now she knew what the unidentifiable sounds had been. Still she hesitated, chiding herself a moral coward. But indeed it seemed that she would not be called upon to comfort Alba, who was alternately sobbing and exclaiming. Far from telling the girl to go to the devil, Justin spoke to her calmly, mildly, precisely. Finally she heard him say: "Go to bed, Miss Alba."

The light tread receded. There was a muttered string of foreign words, probably foul, presumably Spanish, then footsteps, the clap of a door, silence. A long silence; no sound at all.

But he had not collapsed in drunken stupor. His reply to her knock was distinct enough, although he took a long time to lift his face from his hands and stared at her for another long moment. The fire had burned down. Apart from her candle, there was no light in the room.

"Please don't rise," she said quickly, but he was already on his feet. She set down her candle and made to lay her hands on his shoulders. He prevented this by the simple expedient of taking two steps backward. "What's the matter, Justin? What's happened?"

"Nothing." He shook his head. "It's alright. Your brother won."

Not that there had been much doubt. But it was over. There was no satisfaction in his expression, however; he looked sad and strained. Although his speech was a little heavy, his gaze was focused, and he had been quite rational with Alba. "Are you drunk, after all, Justin?" It was better to be sure.

"A little." He wrinkled his nose. "I'm afraid I smell like a pothouse. I expect I was spilled upon by the celebrating crowd."

So that was why he would not let her near him. "I believe," she said, "you could do with a cup of coffee."

His eyes crinkled. "I certainly could. And a wash, too." His gaze drifted to the ashes in the grate. "Ah well, cold water is good for the fibres." He began to shed his coat.

She picked up her candle. "I've a kettle on the hob. Bring your dressing gown, will you?"

An invigorating scent rose as she poured boiling water into Rumford's patented coffeemaker. Closing the lid, she carried the kettle to her dressing table and half filled the washbasin, adding cold from the pitcher. Justin had already pulled off his boots and unwound his neckcloth. Now he drew his shirt over his head with no apparent sense of gêne, so she retreated behind the half-curtained bed until the splashing ceased and he inquired, softly, "How is the little one?"

"Going on quite well." The inn at which Robert had chosen to celebrate must have been crowded and extremely stuffy: Justin had even washed his hair. His damp, untidy head made him look boyish and innocent. "Sit by the fire, you'll catch cold." He had left his clothes in a neat pile, the towel draped over the back of a chair, the soap stowed in its box. There was nothing left for her to do.

"Claire?" The coffee must be ready. He was waiting for her to pour. But when she came to the table, he was already filling a cup. "Are you having some, cariño? No?" He swallowed a mouthful. "Heaven. Thank you." With a sidelong glance, he added, "We seem to spend a lot of time half-dressed in each other's bedchambers, considering we're not lovers."

Not as innocent as he looked, and while he had appeared to be unaware of himself, he had clearly taken notice of her attire, although made of decent and sensible flannel. Never before had he alluded to any of this when they were alone. But they were not alone, and he was balancing a cup of hot coffee. Her certainty that this would prevent him from doing anything untoward surprised her. Neither a child's presence nor hot liquids had ever prevented her father from doing precisely what he wanted. Her shawl still lay in the easy chair. She wrapped it around herself and sat down. "It's not my fault if we aren't."

He laughed. "No, I don't suppose it is. Whose do you think it is?"

"Yours, of course. Do take a seat." Claire let her gaze roam from the blue damask of the armchair opposite her to the bright hearth and the gleaming mirror above it, the lesser gleam above the dressing table, the tall bed with its midnight hangings, half-drawn to shield the sleeping child from the light. Her bedchamber was a warm, comfortable, even opulent place, and entirely devoid of violent or fearful memories. "If you weren't so honourable and selfless, we'd have been lovers long ago. Well, not long ago, since we've not been married all that long, but certainly from that day."

"You wouldn't have resisted?"

"No. But I would have hated you." She laid her arm along the back of her chair and rested her head in the crook of her elbow. "It would have been simpler. You're letting your coffee grow cold."

"A timely reminder that I'm here to talk about your brother, not you or me." He drank and poured some more.

It was over, she thought again as he told her about the election. She was free of her obligation to her brother. She had loved Robert, and would have done almost anything he asked, but that had not been enough for him. So he had tricked her, and love had turned into duty. But that was over, and with the tie between them dissolved, perhaps their shared past would also recede. He had celebrated that evening, and she, too, felt a drowsy sense of celebration.

"So there we are," Justin was saying. "Tomorrow, Matthew returns to Dallington Hall, and my father may accompany him."

She sat up. "Your cousin is not happy, is he?"

"No." His shoulders moved as he heaved a sigh. "There's nothing anyone can do about it, however, and it's better not to say anything about it, either, neither to him nor anyone."

His expression had been rather grim, but it was replaced by a look of amusement and then surprise when she commented, "At least it's not the election results worrying him. Nor Alba, either, I expect?"

"You heard us?"

"Not very clearly. But I did notice that you did not tell her to go to the devil."

"That girl!" He made a grimace. "It's hard to tell. Either she's a shirker with a turn for tragedy, or she's genuinely exhausted."

If he thought that was tragedy, it was because he had never seen Alba at her best. Their contretemps had been far too short. "Poor Alba," she said. "I've overtaxed her. She's only seventeen, and Percy is not an easy patient. But what do we do now? I can't change places with Alba, who may be contagious, and Miss Quinnault can't look after Percy day and night."

He rubbed his chin. "Perhaps I could help?"

It was the ideal solution. Percy no longer disliked him, and how good he was at telling stories she herself knew only too well. "Perhaps you could show her some drawings?"

"Certainly." Raising his elbow to stifle a great yawn, he made to rise. "I'd better get some sleep if I'm to relieve Miss Quinnault in the morning."

His dressing gown, not tied as tightly as usual, fell open at the neck. As her gaze slid down his silk-wrapped figure, Claire noticed that he was not wearing slippers. His feet and ankles, slim and bony, were quite bare. "And a fine example you'll be to the bairns!" Her burst of anger brought her to her feet as well, but she was standing too close to him and had to tilt back her head to berate him further, besides keeping her voice down so as not to wake Lucy. "Why did you not ask for a pair of woolly socks, or a rug?"

But he only said her name, on a note of surprise, and again, in a conciliatory tone, and again, in a low murmur. His arms came gently around her; she laid her head against his neck.

Then he tensed. From the bed a small voice made itself heard. Lucy had woken. "Justin? Are you there, brother?"

"I am." He pushed back the hangings and sat on the edge of the four-poster. "How are you, child?"

"It hurts," she informed him, and when he agreed, she asked whether he had ever broken a leg. He shook his head.

Standing behind him, Claire put a hand on his shoulder, her anger gone. "Justin was wounded in the war, however. That must have hurt vilely."

He slid his hand over hers. "It did, too, and I didn't have Claire or Dr Hurd to look after me."

"Or you," Lucy said. "Will you teach me another clapping song?" A few days earlier, he had shown her how the Spaniards made music by clapping their hands.

"Can you remember the first one?"

She raised her thin arms and clapped, keeping up a steady rhythm even when he joined in with a layer of syncopation. After a while, he told her that he wouldn't be able to teach her more, for the time being. "I need to help Miss Quinnault look after Percy, and you know how cautious Claire is about infection." Her brows sprang together, her mouth puckered, but then her face relaxed, and she sighed and said, "I suppose it is fair that Percy should have you, since I have Claire."

"I'll miss you." He gave her a kiss, made a cross on her forehead. "Goodnight."

He was leaving. Claire looked up at him. "I had not considered what it would mean if you help look after Percy."

"Apart from the risk of infection?" A corner of his mouth lifted. "I will miss you, too, Claire."

"I didn't say —"

"I didn't say that you did. I told Lucy that I'll miss her, and now I'm telling you."

Half in laughter, half in indignation, she gripped his collar and gave him a rather unsuccessful shake. And since his face was very close to hers, his eyes mischievous and his mouth tender, and because he made no attempt to embrace her, she kissed him.

Warmth, the taste of coffee, the drumbeat of his heart beneath her hand, the lift of his chest as he took a deep breath. "I think I'm going to faint," he said softly.

"So do I." She leaned her forehead against his chin. "I feel as though some dark cloud were about to engulf me."

"Don't worry, *cariño*. Once the rain is spent, there will be only sunshine."

She pulled back and narrowed her eyes at him. "There will?"

"It's a song I learned in Spain." He drew her into his arms and enveloped her in a humming rhythm of sharp sibilants, rolling trills, and sounds made in the back of the throat that reminded her of Lowland Scots.

Chapter 16

Will the unicorn be willing to serve thee,
or abide by thy crib?
Job 39:9

HIS voice had been husky in her ear, low and yet true. Claire picked out a few notes, was led astray by habits of harmony, went back to the beginning and concentrated on the song's curious scale, won confidence and played through the whole.

The sunshine promised in Justin's song failed to appear, however. The day was so gloomy that she had lit the candles in the piano sconces. Low clouds hurrying across the sky threatened rain, and the invalids were far from recovered, although a hasty scrawl early that morning had informed her that Percy's fever had broken at last. Lucy had been mending slowly, steadily, fretfully from the first day; the doctor saw no complications, nor did he expect any. It was Stella's turn to sit with her this morning.

Claire played the Spanish song once again, added some chords, lost herself in the music, her fingers wandering at will. Corelli, familiar and comfortable as an old glove, a German dance, and then a melody so light-hearted that it ought to have banished all clouds and troubles. 'Cello and violin, a cheeky pizzicato – it was the Boccherini they had heard at the Academy of Ancient Music. Although the pianoforte could not do justice to the piece, Claire continued to play, her mind supplying the missing orchestra, even to the triumphant finish. The nocturnal music of the streets of Madrid: hopefully Percy would soon be well enough to be entertained by foreign tales. Justin could be trusted to adapt them to her age.

A slight cough made her start. "Excuse me, ma'am." The butler was standing next to one of the fluted columns that set off this part of the drawing room. "May I inquire whether you are at home to visitors?"

An hour's solitude had been too much to ask. Claire sighed. "I suppose I must be, with the noise I've been making." She touched her hair. "Am I presentable?"

"Certainly, ma'am, certainly. I might still deny you, ma'am; I would have denied you, only it is Mrs Lyster, ma'am, with your brother."

"You're quite right." She played some valedictory chords in D minor. "Do, please, show them in."

Robert hung back, his greeting barely audible, but his sheepish reserve was covered by Nicola's flow of sympathy. "How dreadful for you, Claire, and after you said you were prepared for the worst, too! It is most unfair for things to turn out this way, when you were only jesting! Who could have imagined such a string of calamities? But at least you are well, although I wonder at it, with all the strain of looking after three invalids!"

"Three?" For all Nicola's lack of arithmetic this was a puzzling figure. "Why three? Please." She gestured for them to be seated. Bootle was lighting the fire, the candelabra on a side table; he threw her an inquiring look and upon her nod procured wine and set out a dish of biscuits.

Nicola drew her to the sofa. "You're very brave. But Percy's influenza, on top of Lucy's broken leg and the captain's wounds ... So gallant of him to face the crowds after what happened." Somewhat inconsequentially, she cast Robert a melting look. He sipped his wine.

"Oh!" Finally it dawned on Claire. "I'd forgotten Justin's bruises. But he doesn't need tending. In fact, he's helping to look after Percy."

"Is he? How domestic." From Robert's mouth it was a taunt. "You've been quick to tame him."

"You confuse me, Robert." How dare he sneer at Justin? "I thought you meant for him to tame me?"

"So I did." His lips curled. "I did not expect such instant success, however, although I should have known. He must have a great deal of experience."

Claire struggled to suppress a laugh, but the expression on Nicola's face was too much for her. "Do not look so shocked, dearest." She patted her hand. "Of course I'm not his first love." His fourth or fifth, she thought hilariously. "It would be very odd, to be sure, if a man as tender and passionate as he had never loved before."

"Robert says he never loved anyone until he met me." Nicola frowned. "Does that mean –"

It meant that Robert had a calculating nature and did not waste affection on anyone who might not be of benefit to him. Briefly Claire met his eyes, saw a panicked plea in them, and kept her counsel.

"It means that no one but you, ma'am, would have been able to inspire Lyster with love."

Claire felt the jerk in Nicola's hands, and Robert, too, gave a start. "Good heavens, Sumners, where did you spring from?" he remarked. "But I need hardly ask."

It was true enough. Although it was clear that someone had taken cloth and brush to Justin, it was equally clear that he had been riding, and riding hard. He still carried his whip in his hand. Had she misread his message about Percy? Had he gone for the doctor? But he caught her gaze and shook his head, so all must be well, despite the tired dark smudges around his lids. His bruise had turned an interesting shade of green. Yet he brought a breath of fresh air into the room, a sense of vigour and also laughter, laying aside his whip with a conscious, complicit grin.

"Should you really be here, Captain?" It was impossible to be stern with him. "Are you not spreading influenza?"

"You're safe if you don't kiss me." Leaving her speechless, he gave Robert a nod, bowed to Nicola. "Forgive me for presenting myself in all my dirt, Mrs Lyster. I did not want to miss you, having just missed you at your papa's house." So he had called on Mr Manvers. "You've come to take your leave, Lyster?"

"Indeed I have. We're going back to town, in preparation to my taking my seat – or perhaps I should say your seat, Captain, considering the debt I owe you."

How galling it was that Justin should be able to steer the conversation with no apparent effort, when she had been struggling to keep afloat! Now Robert was all politeness and gratitude, with more thanks to Justin, wishing the invalids a speedy recovery. He hoped to see them all in London soon, so did Nicola, and they parted in perfect amity.

At last she could ask about Percy. The wider world was dismissed. Questions tumbled from her lips, hardly waiting for his answers. A nod or shake of his head, a smile or frown must suffice.

"And when did you go to bed, Justin?" she asked finally. "You look . . . tired." *Trachled* would have been a better word for the exhausted heaviness that had descended on his shoulders, but she was not sure he knew it. "Tell me."

"It was a long night." He walked over to the fireplace and leaned his arm on the mantelpiece. For a moment he looked up at one of his ancestresses, a lady in a flimsy dress whose stance was a mirror-image of his own. Then he turned his head. "But believe me, Percy is better." The description he gave her of the little girl's ordeal amply explained why he thought such a rider necessary, and he repeated it at the end. "She's been sleeping since daybreak. Miss Quinnault is with her now."

"Thanks be to God." Her voice refused to remain steady.

"Don't, Claire," he said. "Don't weep when I can't put an arm around you. Good girl," he added when she squared her shoulders. But there was no real warmth in his eyes when he looked at her; he was almost frowning. "Claire," he began. He took a few turns about the room and finally alighted on the edge of an easy chair several yards away from her, keeping a medicinal distance. "It's hellfire difficult to say this without holding your hands."

Without conscious volition, she had picked up some linen and begun to set stitches. Now she let it sink to her lap. "To say what? You're frightening me, Justin."

"I'm the one who should be afraid." His face was dark and troubled. "Listen, Claire. Do you have any money?"

Her eyes dropped to the pillowcase on her knees. Her fingers had twisted themselves into its folds. She extracted the needle, which had slipped the thread, and pushed it into a pincushion. Her mind was racing, but she managed to say matter-of-factly, "I thought you knew quite well how much money I have, safely tied up with your help and Mr Scott's."

He took so long to reply that she almost risked a glance. "I'm not putting this very well," he said at length. "I don't mean your fortune. I mean whether you have any money on you for an emergency, should you need to make any unexpected purchases, or . . . or travel any great distance."

This was puzzling. "Where would I want to travel? And why? You don't want money, then?"

"I'm sorry, Claire." When he said her name, she looked up, but only briefly, disturbed by his grave countenance. "I'm finding this very hard. You see, Percy was not herself last night, and I learned things – things that I should have known, that I did know, from her and from you, but seeing her like that . . ." He drew a deep breath. "I want to know that you have the means to leave me, Claire. You have somewhere to go, you and your sisters, you have Sunderland Hall, and I want to know that you can get there if need be. If all this becomes too much for you, if you feel you can't bear it, you must go home. Don't stay for some mistaken loyalty or honour. You've paid your debt to Robert ten times over. Nothing can justify such misery as you girls lived through when your father was alive."

Her eyes stung, and her hands felt limp. More than anything, she wished that he might indeed be holding them.

But he did not seem to lend his extraordinary statement any great weight. "Why didn't you go, back then?" he asked instead, intent on her story. "You did go to your grandmother's in the end. Was it the money?"

There was a lump in her throat; she swallowed. "Not wholly the money. Grandpapa wouldn't allow it. He never forgave Mama for eloping with Papa. I still don't know if it was right not to leave her, although I had to face the decision almost every day, while Papa lived."

"I see," he said, and by the fierce Spanish phrases he growled under his breath, she thought that he probably did. After all, he had lived through much worse in Spain. But when she said so, he shook his head. "I may have some impressive scars, and at the time I was pretty miserable, to be sure, but I am a soldier. Not that I knew what I was letting myself in for when I joined – no one can imagine what war is like, nor believe that one will be wounded, or even killed – but war is itself such a grand scheme that it is, somehow, easier to believe in a grand scheme. The end is clear, and you have daily proof that the ways by which it may be achieved are very mysterious indeed."

The rigid set of his shoulders had relaxed. He seemed perfectly at ease saying these things.

She stared at him. "You're so philosophical, you make me feel ashamed." How often had she not rebelled in her heart, and in deed, too, her anger and despair growing with every defeat. It was Mr Scott who had saved her in the end. When he accosted her in the street one day, she had thought he was another one of those – and she had been so worn down that she might have gone with him if he were. She never knew exactly how he did it, but he knew her grandparents, and things became easier from that day forwards. There was more money, and Mama had been able to employ a maid of all work.

"'The Lord gave,'" Justin was saying, "'and the Lord has taken away, blessed be the Name of the Lord'? Not really. I've charged God often enough. He can be cruel."

That was certainly true. A silence followed. Was this the time to ask about Corunna, his escape from prison, loves he had lost?

Suddenly he grinned. "Although I do adore the Book of Job, don't you? When the voice from the whirlwind asks him if the rain has a father?"

Her tension ebbed. How cleverly he had changed the subject, the whole mood of their conversation. "Who hath begotten the drops of dew? Wilt thou hunt the prey for the lion?" she replied.

"Or fill the appetite of the young lions? Who has sent out the wild ass free?"

"Will the unicorn be willing to serve thee, or abide by thy crib?"

"I hope it will." A smile hovered about his lips. "But do you have that money?"

The way he sprang the question upon her, again changing the subject, made her laugh. "I do." A disturbing thought occurred to her. "Would you prefer us to go?"

"No!" His reply came without hesitation. "That's why I was so worried about bringing it up." He did not look worried now. There was an unsettling glow in his eyes. "Let the unicorn – the whole pride of unicorns – abide."

"Don't unicorns come in herds?" The quibble helped her cover her confusion. "What wonderful rhetoric you have, Justin. I am filled with envy about the way you handled Robert, too, when I was floundering in the sea of his innuendo. I nearly told him exactly how many loves you have had. '*Ma in Spagna, mille e tre.*' It might have been worth it, just to see his face!"

"Come now, it's not as bad as that. And he was looking pretty blank as it was." His dark eyes were full of warmth. "Your repartee was perfectly beautiful. But do you mind, after all?"

She shook her head. "Although I do wonder –"

He frowned. "Yes?"

"Why three or four? Why not three, or four? Surely you must know how many times you've been in love."

His troubled expression faded into a look of pure delight. "You do like to have things clear, don't you? And it's quite simple. Rosie, Elena, and Teresa I loved with all my heart. But there was one lady who took notice of me when I was a callow youth, and that may have been a case of gratified vanity merely. Especially after Rosie had never had a glance to spare for me." His voice changed. "Elena was like you. She meant to sacrifice herself for the safety of her family, so nothing ever came of it. Teresa was a guerrilla. Like you, she was a brave young woman."

198

Perhaps she was jealous, after all; her heart gave an odd twinge. "I'm sure I do not have that kind of bravery."

He regarded her in silence. "Claire," he said at last. "You sit there mending linen, in your mind the mechanics of several households, regulating the lives of I know not how many people, with thoughts to spare for enclosure, local elections, the national economy, the war, and yet you know . . . you know as well as I do that our world is as fragile as the ice of the Thames, with cold dark chaos underneath. A few blows of the axe may fell an ancient oak, a blow of fate may unhinge a man. And still you mend linen and play the piano and comfort your family. I call that brave."

She had to smile, for in fact, the pillowcase was lying untouched in her lap. She ran her fingers along its stiff folds, searching for the frayed bit at the centre, and raised it for him to see. "It would be a shame for it to fall apart for lack of care. Perhaps that is why –" She caught herself up, changing what she had nearly said. "That is what I like about you. You know that our world may well collapse if we do not care for it. But it frightens me, and you're not afraid."

"No. But I'm a man; more than that, I'm a noble-man. I can defend myself, and I can make laws. All the same, it was a relief to learn that those thugs were hired by your brother, and not the spearhead of revolution."

He glanced over his shoulder. Behind the Grecian screen the open pianoforte was showing ivory teeth in the glimmer of its candles. "And he spoiled your solitude. I had meant to spare you his visit. Will you play for me, Claire, before we both return to our various duties?"

She walked over to the instrument. Outside, the rain was pouring down with a steady roar. Settling in a window-seat, he remarked that he had not noticed the weather change; nor had she. She played a few bars of his song, asked for his help, and so he sang, and she played. Despite their foreignness, the simple harmonies reminded her of the ballads and folksongs she knew so well; her fingers found their way into familiar tunes, his voice joined hers in familiar words.

"Well, this is a far cry from old Job and his comforters," he said finally. "Mama used to play those songs."

"So that is how you know them." Claire felt pleased. "Well, we had better go and practise our arts upon our invalids."

Chapter 17

You cannot love, my independent heart, and why?
Drayton, *Idea*

"JUSTIN knows wonderful stories, Lucy, and they're all true! And he illustrates them with drawings of his own! I'm well," Percy protested as Claire started up to prevent her saluting the little one. "Dr Hurd is here," she added as an afterthought, and indeed the doctor was knocking on the frame of the door that Percy had left gaping. Unimpeded now, Percy climbed onto Claire's bed and gave Lucy a cautious, horizontal hug. "How are you? How's your leg?"

"That we shall see," the doctor said. "Good morning, Mrs Sumners."

"Forgive the invasion." Justin followed him into the room. "There was no holding Percy when she heard there is no longer any risk of infection."

The two girls were chattering away breathlessly, like swallows in their nest. Their attention turned to the doctor when he lifted the covers to inspect the injured leg, but they never stopped talking and subjected Dr Hurd to a barrage of questions. They were used to him now; no recourse to more familiar hands, to hold or to assist, was necessary.

"Is Percy indeed well?" Claire twisted round to look up at Justin.

"You'll get a stiff neck." He folded himself onto a footstool. "It's only because she's been inside so long that Percy is so pale. So are you, by the way. Why don't you go and lie down on my bed for a spell? You look all done in." He rose briefly to give the bell-pull a tug. "Those two will keep each other entertained." With a soft smile, he regarded the two girls. "Would it be presumptuous in me to suggest employing a drawing master for Percy? I think she may soon outgrow Miss Quinnault's not inconsiderable skill. Her talent is remarkable. Drawing was one of our main pastimes when we weren't studying the expurgated and abbreviated history of the Peninsular War or the geography of Spain and France." He grinned. "I should have been a governess; I have all the right qualifications."

"Oh? But you don't play the piano." Clearly he was in a funning mood, although it was not really funny. Yet she could hardly point out that what he called his qualifications equipped him not for the post of governess, but would make him a charming father – not his knowledge or his skills, but his way with the little ones.

"Ah, there you have me. But I can sing, or at least I do." He reached for her hand and kissed it, then rose and pulled her to her feet. "Here's Hannah to put you to bed. Shall I sing you to sleep?"

"But I never sleep in the daytime," she said, and he, "Today, you will."

~ ~ ~

She never slept in the daytime; vaguely she recalled saying so, hours earlier. But here she was, just breaking the surface of consciousness, lapped in a sense of utter well-being. Behind her closed lids, the room was full of sunshine. Deliberately keeping her eyes shut, she breathed in the scent of the linen – comfort and safety, lavender and human warmth and tobacco – and blinked awake in surprise. For this was Justin's bed, his room, his scent that enveloped her like a cocoon.

His bed. When she turned over to locate the bell-pull, her eye was caught by a book lying on the bedside cabinet, the book he had been reading when she intruded herself upon him that night a fortnight

– was it indeed a fortnight? – before: the inscribed copy of *Marmion* she had given him for a bride-gift.

There are maidens in Scotland, more lovely by far, that would gladly be bride to the young Lochinvar. The imprint of his naked form was almost tangible beside her, so clear was her memory of the heat of his skin through her thin nightgown. Kneeling by her bed later that night, he had slipped his arm under her head, taking his leave with a swift kiss on her brow. How odd that she should be so aware of him now, when he was not there, while at other times his physical presence was hardly perceptible, hidden behind a screen of anecdote or abstract discussion. But she remembered other kisses, attempted and aborted, and all the memories came together to form the image of a possibility – to lie in his arms with limbs entwined, feeling his heat, yet feeling safe, too, in the gentleness of his touch.

When it came to imagining how it would go on from there, her invention failed. It seemed unlikely that he would strike her across the face, call her a slut, and mount her. He had not called her a slut when she came to his room so boldly, nor had he picked her up, thrown her on the bed and, sneering that all she wanted was a man between her legs, proceeded to supply one. Apparently it could take much longer than what Mama strangely called "comforting"; she had seen Justin's swift, surprised look at the clock when she remarked on the time. And thinking of time – had she not rung the bell some while ago?

"I beg your pardon, ma'am," Hannah laughed, and explained at some length how they had seen the bell in the captain's room go, and how Planchett had said that's funny, surely the captain was not there, and she had said, no, the bell was for her, as Mrs Sumners was resting in the captain's room, since hers had been full of little girls earlier. Yet still she had gone into Mrs Sumners's bedchamber, although she knew perfectly well ma'am was not there! But she had collected her dressing gown, which ma'am would please slip on; there was hot water in her own bedroom.

It was all very confusing. The hot water washed away some of her puzzlement, however, and by the time Hannah was dressing her hair she noticed how quiet the house was. "Where is everyone?"

"In the garden, ma'am."

~ ~ ~

The last time she had looked – really looked – the garden had been bare and bleak. As if she had leapt forward in time, the prospect that now met her eyes was bright with leaves, buds, even flowers. The spiky foliage of peonies and delphiniums clad the brown earth and made a dark background to light-green rounds of lady's mantle. Daffodils raised their slender necks; roses were unfolding leaves along the garden walls. Above the orchard, the flowering branches of plum trees hovered in a creamy white cloud.

The past fortnight fell away behind her like a long, dark staircase. Some few weeks after Mama's passing, the architect of Edinburgh's Nelson Monument had granted Grandmama and all the girls access to the unfinished tower. Its stairs had almost defeated Claire, but it had been meant as a treat, and it was that which had kept her climbing, climbing despite her exhaustion. The feeling she had now was much like emerging onto the viewing platform after climbing that endless spiral. The others had been ahead of her, and even now she heard their voices, childish and shrill in the bright sun.

But this was a different time, another place, and when she passed into the orchard, there was Justin among the girls. The little ones were snuggled up on a chaise-longue that must have been carried out with them on it. Alba was reclining in an armchair, Stella and Miss Quinnault sat on the stone bench, which was covered in sheepskins. The girls were all wrapped up in rugs, shawls, and pelisses; Alba's feet rested on an old muff. But this was the orchard's sunniest spot, catching the sun from the south and west: Alba had pushed back the collar of her pelisse, and Stella's shawl had slipped down to her elbows. Justin was hatless.

He must have heard her coming, for he was already on his feet. "Did you sleep, *cariño*? You must be hungry. Come."

A few moments later, she found herself tucked up warmly next to Stella, a plate of cold ham and salad in one hand, a glass of wine in the other. Only now did she notice the traces of a substantial luncheon having been consumed, a small table filled with broken meats, a lonely plate in the grass. She took a sip of wine, felt his shadow next to her.

"I'll hold the glass while you eat."

"Won't you sit?" She moved closer to Stella.

His legs stretched out before him, his shoulders against the sun-warmed wall, her glass in his hands, he looked deeply, lazily content. His dark hair would be warm in the sunshine, too, and she nearly reached out to touch it. Mistaking her gesture he gave her the wineglass, taking a sip himself when she handed it back. Their eyes met, but his gaze slid away from her to the girls, lingering on the little ones, the flowering branches of the plum trees, the glimmering surface of the lake, and in the distance the rolling pastures dotted with sheep and clumps of woodland. This was where he belonged.

This was what he had had in mind. Whatever Robert's plans had been, Justin had meant it. He had meant to marry her; he would have expected to have a family, too, quite apart from a wife who really was a wife.

"Tell us, Justin!" The request startled Claire, but of course Percy was not asking to hear his thoughts on his peculiar situation. She was merely taking up a thread interrupted by Claire's arrival. "You said you would tell us."

"I did not, you did. Who'd want to talk about December in Madrid when it's April in England? Or hear about it. Listen."

They all turned to him, but he did not continue. From the quality of his silence, Claire knew that he was not about to tell them anything; he was listening and meant them to listen, too. It did not take long for the girls to understand this. Ears cocked and eyes looking inwards, they listened.

The air was filled with skylarks. A breath of wind stirred the flowering branches, among which bees hummed busily. Sheep bleated in the distance.

"I see what you mean," Stella said after a while. "How strange it is: this life, and that."

"Isn't it?" Justin agreed, but his gaze remained intent on some faraway past. "At times that life is barely real to me. It's hard to believe that it was I who lived all that, and not someone in a poem – by your Mr Scott, perhaps."

"I think that it's the other way around." Percy scowled with concentration. "Like a dream, and I'll wake up with Mama . . . and Papa." The last word came out in a hoarse whisper.

Claire caught Alba's eyes, and her sister laid her hand on Percy's head as if to contain her thoughts. "You mustn't even think that."

But the girl pulled away. "I can think what I want!" She looked at Claire. "Can't I, Claire?"

"Certainly you can, and Alba did not mean to forbid you; she only meant that she wished you didn't have such thoughts, for your own sake."

Claire considered the little one, wondering if it was wise to ask the question that had sprung to her mind. "You don't think you might wake up and find yourself with Grandmama at Sunderland Hall?"

"No," Percy said unequivocally. "That was just a dream, too. Are we going to stay here for ever and ever, Claire?"

"I – I don't know," Claire floundered. They were all looking at her – Percy frowning, Lucy eager, Alba faintly apprehensive. Stella had turned away her face, but Claire knew that her expression would be deliberately non-committal. At her side, Justin inhaled softly, about to interpose, to say something that would spare her, as he always did.

Always. "Yes," she heard herself say, "I think we might. Would you like that?" Although speaking to the girls, she turned her head to look at him. His dark eyes met hers.

"Yes," Percy said.

Lucy grinned. "Well, obviously! Justin belongs here and you belong to Justin and we want to be with you."

"But couldn't we –" Alba began on an indrawn breath.

"Hold your tongue, Alba," Stella advised and kissed Claire on the cheek. "I am glad," she said simply.

"So am I." The corners of Justin's eyes crinkled as he smiled, but his gaze remained serious, deep, warm.

"Claire was not asking you, Captain!" There was a shrill note in Alba's laugh. "She meant us."

"I wouldn't be so sure." He turned his head, looking rather closely at Alba, but it was to Lucy that he spoke. "And Claire doesn't belong to me; with me, perhaps, if she happens to feel that way, but not to me. She can go wherever she pleases."

Again he lent no weight to his extraordinary statement, barely listening to what he had said, oblivious to Alba's astonished gasp. There seemed to be something tugging at his awareness. By the time Claire heard it, too, he was on his feet and running towards the fenced hedge that bordered the orchard on its western side. He vaulted it without slowing.

The sound of hooves, a horse at full gallop, and now it came within range of vision, flickering between the silvery trunks of the beeches along the avenue. Cupping his mouth, Justin called "Pepe!" – he would have recognized the lad by his handling of the horse, utterly familiar to him – then Pepe burst through the trees and held straight for Justin. For a moment Claire thought he would ride his master down, hallooing and waving his cap, and indeed he barely reined in his mount before he threw one leg over its neck, sitting sideways, and cast himself bodily into Justin's arms.

The horse cantered on for a few paces, then slowed to a trot and a standstill. Pepe was hugging Justin, thumping his back, jumping up and down. "Bonisbit!" he shouted. "Bonisbit!" Then Claire realized that he was speaking English, and what he was saying: "Boney's beat."

~ ~ ~

The wall at her back still retained the day's warmth, but the air was chilly. The flowering branches of the plum trees hung palely above her in the dusky sky. The lake seemed to emanate a light all its own. Apart from a blackbird thoughtfully singing to itself in the cedar, all was quiet, with only a faint soughing to indicate that the world around her was filled with meadows, hedges, and woods.

And people. Somewhere far away, there was noise, singing, and indeed it was astonishing that the night should be so quiet when people all over England and on the Continent, too, must be celebrating the capitulation of Paris. She thought of Justin and Pepe embracing, laughing for joy, their happiness spilling over in volleys of rapid Spanish.

She leaned her head back against the garden wall, turning her face sideways, but it had not really been necessary to come here to recapture the sense of affirmation that had suffused her when she heard Justin draw breath and knew that he would speak for her, even against his own interests, always. It had been with her ever since.

The sound of horses and another burst of song, closer this time, drew her from her reverie. The blackbird fell silent. This would be Justin and Pepe returning from their round among neighbours and villagers – yes, there was the clatter of hooves in the paved stableyard, a swift exchange, laughter, footsteps, the crunch of gravel.

The footsteps ceased. Had he gone into the house? Yet the sense of life and movement in the upper garden still remained. She stirred, debating whether to call out, and listened for the soft tread of boots on grass. The blackbird gave an interrogative chirp. A dark shape flickered in the entrance to the orchard.

"Justin?"

"Claire. Forgive me if I startled you." His voice came from an unexpected quarter. "I should have known it was you, *cariño*. What are you doing out here? Aren't you cold?"

"I have a rug." His concern for her well-being made her smile. "I wanted to be alone for a little while, after all the excitement."

"So did I, although I don't mind being alone with you. And you?"

"I don't either. Do sit down."

"I'm not sure it's wise to invite me." His dark shape loomed up before her. "I'm drunk, you know, on victory and all the different beverages with which I've had to toast it."

He did not sound drunk, nor did he smell drunk, or move like a drunken man. He did, however, have a cigar and tinderbox in one hand.

"Poor man. Perhaps you may find comfort in the thought that you did your duty. Your people must have been so pleased to get the news from you in person." She shifted her position to look at him. "And what news it is!"

It was too dark to make out his expression, only the gleam of his eyes. "For more than twenty years we were at war with France." He exhaled audibly. "Who knows what peace will bring?"

"It doesn't seem to worry you."

"Not right now, but I've told you, I've had too much cider – wine – triumphant talk. Right now I feel ready for whatever the future may fling at us. But that may also be because I have you next to me." His voice was low and intimate. "More intoxicating by far than cider and wine."

Perhaps he was drunk, after all. "You had better smoke that cigar," she said dryly, "to sober you up."

He threw back his head and laughed. "I need it." Then he added, "You mean it? You don't mind?"

"Not tonight."

He did not immediately open his tinderbox, but continued to regard her until she wondered what she might have said to give him pause. With a quick shake of his head, he slipped the steel over his fingers and struck the flint. A moment later, the tip of his cigar was aglow. He smothered the charcloth and stowed his materials, all with a practised ease that was a pleasure to watch. Leaning back against the garden wall, he smoked greedily. "That's good. Thank you, Claire."

"You've deserved it. It's not every day that we celebrate Bonaparte's downfall. Nor is that the only cause we have to celebrate." The glow of his cigar threw a fitful light upon his profile. "You've been successful on all fronts, at home and abroad."

~ ~ ~

She was laughing softly, but for some secret cause he could not fathom; something she did not seem sure whether to laugh at. "At home and abroad," he repeated. "I'm not at all certain about 'at home'."

"Are you not? You got Robert elected; you have a good understanding with your father; your people respect you; and your bruise has faded."

He was near to telling her that none of this mattered, but that was foolish: it did matter. Nor could he say that he had done it all for her, because that was not true, either. There was no omission in her list of his triumphs, for the one thing he wanted and had not achieved had nothing to do with triumph or defeat. Or had he? Not many hours since, in this very place, she had given him a "yes", although a qualified one. And she had chosen the same spot to wait for him – if she had indeed been waiting for him and not merely sought the garden's solitude.

Under the rough folds of the rug that enveloped her, the silk of her dress shimmered in the dimness, her skin as delicate as flower petals. The chain upon her neck was a little too long and its pendant had insinuated itself into the bosom of her dress. It would be warm between her breasts.

He dragged on his cigarillo; the awareness of its reek on his breath should curb his impulses. It was wonderful what civilization did for a man.

She was oblivious to all this. A slight frown around her eyes, her hands clasped tightly in her lap, she was in a fine study. After a while, she gave a small sigh and turned her head. "There is so much I wish to say to you, Justin, but I don't know where to begin, or how to end, nor even what to say in-between, or if it is wiser not to speak at all."

Slowly, deliberately, he pressed the cigarillo into the damp grass, where it expired with a hiss. "You may be right." Her name on his lips, he drew her close and hooked one leg around her to hold her in a three-limbed embrace. It had not needed the cigar to prevent him kissing her. The tension in the body he held sufficed.

"I'm frightened, Justin. You may call me a coward, but I'm frightened."

"You are one of the most courageous women I know. What are you frightened of, precisely?"

"You, of course."

She did not draw back, however, instead leaning her head against his.

"Not of what you might do deliberately, but of what you may make me do, simply by being the way that you are. I love you, Justin. But if I once admit that love, I will go up like the tinder in your box there. I would be completely in your power. For myself alone, I might risk it; but there are my sisters, who have been exposed to too much domestic unhappiness already. How can I take risks for them? And now you will go away and I am afraid that I will never see you again and may have missed the chance to love, and live a full life, and maybe be happy."

Somewhat dazed, he applied himself to allaying her most immediate fear. "What are you talking about, Claire? I'm not going anywhere."

She gripped the collar of his coat and gave him a shake. "Don't you see that if they have the slightest bit of sense at Whitehall, they will recall you as soon as may be and send you to Spain? You are just the sort of man our country needs at this juncture."

It was a possibility – a likely one, too, but for the moment the fate of the nation left him cold. "The devil fly away with Whitehall," he said. "Did you say you love me?"

"I did." She exhaled gustily. "But I don't know. It just slipped out. I don't think I know what love is."

"Well, whatever it is that made you say it – that made you kiss me, twice, and wait for me here – I'll settle for that." He let his lips touch the lobe of her ear. It was soft and warm; so was her cheek, a palpable blush. "Would whatever it is persuade you to come to bed with me now?"

"Justin!" She made a sudden movement, pulling back from him. "Is that all you ever think about?" But her voice was not quite steady, and when he said "Yes", she laughed shakily. "No, I know it isn't. But no, Justin. If I didn't care for you, it would be dangerous enough, but as things are . . . and no doubt you will be tender and passionate and I will end up totally infatuated and it frightens me! And don't say these things look after themselves!"

"They would, though, with me safely away in a few weeks or months. You'd be well rid of me and no regrets."

"Don't be daft. If you were sent to Spain, then obviously I would go with you."

He held her close, savouring her nearness and everything she had said. Then he replied, "I would not let you. Spain is no place for a woman, not at this time, not even Madrid." He felt her shudder; she whispered his name. "Don't worry, *cariño*, I can look after myself, or at least Pepe can. But all this is mere hypothesis. It may never happen, and meanwhile, things have looked after themselves." She made a noise suspiciously like a snort. Undeterred he continued, "Power, fear, that's all nonsense. It's simple: you say you love me, I know I love you –"

She laid her hand on his chest. "You do?"

"Of course I do." He might have left it at that, but her patent disbelief seemed to call for a more elaborate declaration. "I fell in love with you that day on the ice, Claire, and the feeling turned into an affection so strong and sure that for a while I thought I wasn't in love with you at all, it was so unlike anything I had ever felt in my life. You know I've been in love before." Softly he intoned, *"Ma in Spagna."*

She turned down her mouth in that way she had when suppressing a smile. Then her brows sprang together. "And you said love was simple, but if this is different, then how –"

"It's being married," he interrupted her. "I did not see it then – I was very young, after all – but I know now that I was not sufficiently part of my lovers' world to be quite real to them. It was simple because it had to end. But this," he drew a deep breath, "this is simple because it will never end."

~ ~ ~

Somehow his low, husky voice made his reasoning more persuasive than it should have been, smoothing over the flaws in his logic. Under her hand, his heart beat strong and fast. When her lips met his, there was a taste of tobacco, smoky and tart. No alcoholic fumes but the hot, bitter, exciting taste of coffee met her tongue. "Where did you get coffee?"

"At Farmer Martin's, strange to tell." There was a smile in his voice. She felt his mouth move against her cheek as he spoke, his breath warm, his upper lip and chin rough upon her skin – there had been no time for a shave that evening. Then his kiss found hers and all attempts at clinging to some form of rational thought were at an end. Something dark and powerful seemed to loom over her, but when she opened her eyes, it was to a shimmering brightness she did not immediately identify as plum blossoms illumined by a rising moon.

The moon lit their way back to the house, too, reflected in thin strips of cloud that brightened the night sky. White dots of narcissi lined the grassy path.

Before she went out, she had set a lamp on the table just inside the garden door. Now it made a golden circle as he lifted it. "Will you lock up, Claire?" The prosaic words were a caress. She shot the bolt and took his outstretched hand, joining him in the lamp's bright halo. In his bedchamber, he lit a candle on its wick, a whole branch of candles, and stirred the fire to an incandescent blaze. The leaping flames transformed the upturned bed into a nest of cream and honey.

Yet all this was as nothing to the glow in his eyes, the warmth of his tawny skin, or the ardency of his body.

Chapter 18

Methinks this time becometh lovers best;
Night was ordained, together friends to keep.
Drayton, *Idea*

"BONEY'S beat." The news of the capitulation of Paris was followed closely by that of Napoleon's abdication. Nearly all the guests treading up the stairs at Hawksfield House exclaimed at it. The Boughtons were among the last to arrive.

"And how fortunate this is for your sister!" Lady Boughton gave Alba a critical stare. "The girl looks charmingly," she told Claire. "An excellent notion to present her this Season. It will be extraordinary! What a chance for her!"

"Thank you, Lady Boughton." Claire linked her gloved hand with Alba's. "But my sister is not only charming to look at, she is also charming to talk to. Aren't you, Alba?"

Lady Boughton gave a deep guffaw. "Have I been talking across you? Forgive me, child. You look so young."

"I'm not sure I can talk." Alba's voice was low and diffident. "I feel quite breathless. One moment we were enjoying the sunshine in the orchard at Hawksfield Manor, the next we are receiving about five hundred guests to witness the entry of Louis XVIII into London."

"I believe there are only fifty, my dear, and the majority is here to meet you." In his rare attacks of gallantry, Lord Hawksfield was so like his son that Claire could not help looking at Justin. All the time they had stood bowing and curtsying – Lord Hawksfield, Mrs Sumners, Miss Lammond, Captain Sumners, lined up to greet his lordship's guests – she had not so much as glanced at him.

And with good reason, although Alba, between them, did not seem to feel anything. Perhaps the tension rising off his body was perceptible only to herself, nor could he know how it affected her.

"Mrs Sumners is in great looks," Lady Boughton was saying to Justin. "Much better than on your wedding day. Marriage is clearly good for her."

Justin did not reply, but when he turned his head, his dark eyes were scorching.

"Don't be vulgar, Mama." Briefly touching Claire's hand, Matthew gave her an approving nod. "Although you do look very fine, cousin. I'm glad to see Justin has at last given you the diamonds and sapphires I said you should have."

"The famous Sumners Sapphires, Dallington." Lord Hawksfield raised his eyebrows. "Surely you recognize the set? I got it out of the bank for Mrs Sumners." He looked down into the hall. "Looks like that's the lot and we can go in." To Alba he added, "You must be bored senseless standing here, when all anyone has to say is 'Boney's beat'. I know I'm parched."

"No, no." Alba's lids fluttered. "It is hard to believe, after all."

A moment later, Claire found herself alone on the landing with Justin, or as alone as one could be with guests milling about in the reception rooms beyond and footmen rigidly arranged in the hall below.

"I can't quite believe it, either," Justin said. "But that is only one of several things I cannot believe."

He was mad to talk like this; mad to stand so close to her. Her skin tingled with his proximity, yet when she raised her eyes, the distance between them was perfectly decent, although neither of them had moved.

She took a deep breath. "Such scepticism. You're hard to convince, Justin."

"Not really." He grinned. "I adore the process of being convinced, that's all."

~ ~ ~

He must be mad to talk like this. But the past hour had been maddening. Presenting her younger sister with simple pride, Claire had seemed oblivious to the appraising glances that slid around her own person, across her skin, heightening his own awareness. And then Aunt Boughton's frank remark – it was all he could do to maintain a safe distance, to recollect that they could be seen though not heard.

"You will have to take my word for it, this once," she replied with dizzying coolness.

"I will if you say it."

It was a challenge, and she rose to it with a lift of her chin. "Then I will say it yet again: Boney's beat." She looked past him into the drawing room. "They are handing around the champagne. We had better go in."

But when he gave her his arm, her clasp was firmer than the conventional gesture warranted. "Don't, Claire." He laid his hand over hers. "I know I started this, but if we don't stop now, I will do something mad, and Lord Hawksfield warned me not to interrupt his speech this time."

"This time . . . Did I ever thank you for acting so promptly, that other time, before I even understood what he was about?"

Her words chilled him more effectively than a bucket of cold water could have done. "You know I don't want your gratitude."

"You have it all the same."

A gentle pressure of her hand, then she withdrew it and preceded him into the drawing room. Her poise enveloped her like a mantle; the faint flush in her cheeks might be due to the warmth of the room, no more. With a graceful bow of her head, she accepted a glass of champagne from Lyster, chatted with her sister-in-law, turned attentively to listen to Lord Hawksfield's speech.

"Boney's beat." One day Justin might forget the date of his wedding, but he would never forget the day on which the news of the capitulation of Paris reached England: April 6, 1814, a day beginning with quiet contentment and ending in passionate fulfilment; the day Claire said she loved him. She had never said it since, and sometimes he wondered if it was not love, after all, but gratitude, the reward he had once rejected, a bowing to circumstance. Whatever it was, it was worth having. The complexities of her emotions did not cast into doubt the one simple truth, that he loved her and wanted her to be happy. If he could make her so, all the better; if she told him he did, he must believe her. There was no sense in searching questions.

And did not that very complexity argue the truth of her reactions? The extent of her knowledge had opened a grimy window onto her childhood – no gently bred girl ought to know what she knew – but it was limited to a factual, brutish physicality that had nothing to do with tenderness or love. "It's a bit like taking a beating," she had said early one morning. "You wake up sore and all anyhow, and wonder how you got so." Thoughtful, wondering, unaware of the chill her words struck in his soul, she had tugged at the tumbled bedclothes to cover them both. "I suppose the similarity lies in the extreme of experience," she had murmured as she snuggled into the curve of his body. "Extreme pain and despair, extreme pleasure and elation."

"I need not ask what you think of your father's speech," Matthew suddenly growled in his ear. "It's all too obvious that you're thinking of something altogether different."

"Hush, Turtle. Where have you got your eyes?"

But he had missed most of the speech; his father was already outlining the evening's programme. It would be a topsy-turvy sort of ball. Since there was no knowing when the triumphal procession surrounding Louis XVIII and the Prince Regent would arrive in London, let alone Piccadilly, the streets might be expected to fill early in the day, as indeed they had. Entertainments had to start equally early to enable the guests to get there at all, and so the ball at Hawksfield House would begin with the light repast that was usually served around midnight. This would be followed (rather than preceded) by dancing, although the music would stop as soon as the procession was sighted, when the French windows were to be thrown open to allow the guests a good view of the spectacle. Supper would follow at the usual time. In one particular respect, however, the ball would comply with conventional patterns: a beautiful debutante would open the dancing.

Lord Hawksfield flourished a bow towards Alba. There was a murmur of appreciative laughter when she gave a demure curtsy in reply. "She's not as silly as she often behaves," Justin said to his cousin. "Go on, this is your cue."

"Will you take me in?" Claire reappeared at his side. "Did you see Matthew bear Alba off? I do love your cousin," she added.

How easily the words came to her now! "Had you not rather be grateful to him, and love me instead?"

"Certainly," she said lightly. But when he set her chair for her, pausing with his hands on the armrests, she twisted her neck to look up at him and added, "The two are not mutually exclusive, you know. I am grateful to be seated, but the feeling it gives me to be thus sheltered between your arms

220

is not gratitude." She must have sensed that he was about to do something mad, for in a dry voice she continued, "Nor is the awareness that your eyes are straying quite scandalously, Justin."

"My apologies." He straightened his back. But it was impossible to keep his eyes from straying – to all the entrancing details of her physiognomy when she was close, at table or while dancing, to her person when she was out of reach, dancing with some other gentleman or running up the stairs to fetch her younger sisters when the procession was sighted at last.

~ ~ ~

Dusk was falling. The narrow balconies provided a precarious foothold above the crowds thronging the streets below. Their excited buzz rose and mingled with the expectant chatter filling the drawing room, while outside a mounting roar came closer and closer, erupting into huzzahs as the procession of royal carriages turned the corner of Albemarle Street. The sound crashed like waves against the houses, ricocheting from the walls, climbing up to the balcony. Claire put a restraining hand on Percy's shoulder. The little one clung to the railings, hopping up and down with excitement. At her side, Stella maintained a ladylike composure. Although Lucy had been back on her feet for several days, Justin had lifted her up on his arm, carrying her safely above the press of guests clustered into the windows. Her eager questions, uttered in an audible childish treble, made him the centre of a group who also wanted to know which regiment was escorting the royal carriages ("The Horse Guards; no, the fellows in gold lace are merely trumpeters."), which was the Prince Regent ("He's wearing a field-marshal's uniform. Yes, that's him."), and why Louis XVIII was so fat. ("Eighteen in French is *dix-huit*, but they call him *dix huîtres*, ten oysters.")

He spoke in the clear, carrying voice he used so rarely, although this would be the voice in which he had commanded his troops, a part of that army which had finally defeated Bonaparte, Emperor of France. His matter-of-factness kept the children's excitement in check despite the surrounding fury of colour and noise.

"You can't get fat on oysters," Percy reasoned, her eyes fixed on the carriages receding up the street. "Besides, how would he get oysters on the battlefield? Unless it's on the coast, like the place where you said the army crossed into France."

"Saint-Jean-de-Luz. I suppose it's a metaphor, or is it metonymy, Miss Quinnault? To stand for everything else he's going to eat."

"You are thinking of synecdoche, Captain," Miss Quinnault said. "And Percy, you forget that Louis has been in exile all through the war; he never fought any battles."

"No, but Justin did." Lucilla put her arms around his neck.

He had been in battle, exposing to lead and steel the warm limbs that were so delightful to the touch. Lord Hawksfield seemed moved by a similar vision, for turning suddenly, he shook Justin by the hand. There was a surge of movement among the guests, but before it could gather momentum, Justin said, "Come, children, it is time for you to go. Come along, Percy."

"May we watch the dancing a little longer?" Lucy piped up. The upstairs gallery was an ideal vantage point.

"You looked so beautiful, Claire, dancing with Justin," Percy added. "As if you were alone in the world, although it was a country dance."

And now, instead of mounting barbèd steeds . . . But that was exactly how it had felt. "Flattery will get you nowhere," Claire said. "You may watch until after the first waltz."

"I'll come upstairs with you and tell you who everyone is," Alba volunteered.

A young gentleman next to Claire groaned. "Isn't Miss Lammond joining the waltz?"

"Of course not! What are you thinking?"

He grinned. "I wasn't thinking, I was hoping. I would ask you to do me the honour, ma'am, but I have a feeling that I'm too late."

~ ~ ~

It was very late, or early, rather, by the time the last guests departed. "That went off very well," Lady Boughton remarked. "But there's no need for you to look pleased about it, Hawksfield, although your speech was very fine. So fine that I expect that pushy young man wrote it, didn't he? Forgive me, I keep forgetting that he's your brother, Mrs Sumners. He'll do, however. There's a lot to be said for new blood. You've done wonders for the house, dear, an excellent supper, and have you had the curtains changed? Just washed? Goodness!" She inspected her long gloves. "This is the first time I haven't come away covered in dust from ornaments and side tables."

"You do have an odd habit of picking things up, Mama. Come along now, let Miss Lammond get some rest. Mrs Sumners, I mean."

This lapse was the only sign of Matthew's inebriation, and the way he scrutinized her hands, then her face, before making his bow.

"Poor Dallington," Lord Hawksfield said when the door had closed on his relatives. "He's jealous, I suppose. Has Justin gone up to bed? Very wise."

Sketching a vague gesture, he moved towards the steps but stopped in mid-motion, turned, and took both her hands. "You know, my plan was for him to marry and go north, safely out of the way but with money to spare for Hawksfield Manor, the enclosing in particular. And now I don't know how I would manage without him, or you; things have fallen out very differently from what I imagined, but I could not do without you." His eyes were hazy from drink and sleep. She murmured thanks, but he shook his head, not listening. "This is one of those insights one has at four o'clock in the morning; by tomorrow, it will seem quite silly, if I can remember it at all. Well, never mind, my dear. Good night, and thank you . . ." He gave a puzzled look at his hands, which were still holding hers, then with a flourish kissed her fingers and trod up the stairs. Sometimes he was very like his son.

But where was Justin? At Hawksfield Manor he would be found in the garden, smoking a cigar. A light frisson ran down her spine. But here, in town? There were things to see to, however. In the front rooms, two footmen were loading trays with crystal and crockery. She acknowledged their bows, commended their assiduity, alerted them to a crushed cream tart under the table. "That will need to be cleared away immediately. Rats, you know."

In the back drawing room, lamps had been lit; the old butler looked wrinkled and strained in their unforgiving light. "Carry on," she said as everyone froze, stared, bowed. "That went off very well, Bootle," she added before the silence abated. The debris was nearly cleared. They must have been busy while Lady Boughton made her lengthy farewells, but then the entire staff was at work. "I can see you have everything well in hand. His lordship wishes me to say that he is very pleased."

Pepe came in from the landing and addressed her in Spanish, Doña Clara, and said something about Don Justín. He beamed at her, combining gesture with bow, and seemed to take it for granted that she would understand him. For Bootle, he switched into a throaty form of English: "*El capitán* is in the library."

Where else? "That's alright," Claire told the butler. "Captain Sumners will close up there before we retire."

"Very good, ma'am." The butler held the door for her. "If you please, ma'am." Clearly he was not reconciled with the Spanish form of address.

"Thank you, Bootle. Good night, Pepe."

The library lay in semi-darkness. A candelabrum was burning by the hearth, its light obscured by the wing chairs in front of the fireplace, but the curtains were open and the night outside was bright, the façades across the street glowing yellow. On the mild air came music, huzzahs, sounds of merriment – and a faint smell of tobacco. She thought she had seen a man's silhouette against the open window, a red point of light and swift movement, but now it was gone.

She paused, disoriented, half across the room. "Justin?"

"Claire, *cariño*." He was next to her. "Did I startle you? Sorry about that. Tobacco is such a visible vice. And a smelly one, too, I'm afraid."

The swift movement must have been the flick of his wrist when he pitched his cigar into the street. "I like the scent," she said. "It's so much part of you."

"What beautiful things you say." Yet his smile did not quite reach his eyes; he seemed distracted, not knowing whether he was coming or going. It was unusual for him, but the reason became clear when a man suddenly unfolded himself from one of the wing chairs.

"You have the right instincts, Captain Sumners," he said in a creaky voice. "I've seen the results of your work; it's interesting to see some of your method. But it's alright, you don't need to hide me. I'm here quite officially, bearing official papers. How d'ye do, ma'am?"

She almost expected him to creak, too, when he bowed from the middle, but he performed this courtesy smoothly, almost elegantly. "How do you do?"

"This is Mr Russ, Claire." With a grave look Justin added, "From Whitehall."

"Oh." She felt the blood drain from her face, then recollected herself. "Do sit down, gentlemen. May we offer you – but I see you have been fed, Mr Russ." Stepping towards the fireplace, she had spotted the low table with the remains of supper upon it.

"And very glad I was to be fed, and fed so well." Mr Russ bowed again. "Now, I will leave you to give the news to Mrs Sumners. I beg your pardon for intruding upon you at this ungodly hour, ma'am, but I knew his lordship was entertaining, and so took the liberty."

"And it is official?" Justin's voice was husky.

"Signed and sealed." Mr Russ gestured towards a sheaf of papers lying next to the soiled plates. "Took them long enough, and that's partly why I came despite the lateness of the hour. Sir Joseph and I were afraid that they'd change their minds yet again if we left them to sleep things over." His laugh was like a rusty hinge. "All it needs now is your consent. Unfortunately, we cannot give you orders until you have rejoined, for I can see there is a charming obstacle in our way. You'll let me know tomorrow? I mean today. Then I will bid you goodnight. And – congratulations."

226

Her heart was beating too fast. She barely managed to incline her head when Justin saw his strange visitor out. Unable to keep still, she walked to the window, intending to shut it, but was distracted by a handsome folio lying open in the window-seat. Sitting down to inspect it, she recognized the old Drayton edition she had noticed when first a guest in the house.

"Like an adventurous seafarer am I, who hath some long and dang'rous voyage been," she read softly to herself, repeating the lines when Justin came back. She met his eyes across the room. "Is it Spain, Justin?"

He nodded. "It is."

She had known it, of course she had, but all the same she had to turn away her face to hide her sudden distress.

Then his arms were around her, gentle, comforting. "And I wish you could come with me, but it's not safe. The situation at present is so volatile that only a fool would risk it."

She made room for him on the upholstered bench and he hooked one leg around her, holding her in the familiar three-limbed embrace, her head on his shoulder. "And you're no fool, more's the pity."

His simple, affectionate way was deceptive. Beneath it lay depths of experience unfathomable to her. Perhaps this was what made him so extraordinary and lovable. She thought of those three or four other women he had loved, and who presumably had loved him, and what might have become of them in Spain, which was no place for women. A chill crept up her spine. Terrible things he had seen, and yet he retained his capacity for loving. And he loved her. She drew a shaky breath. "Some long and dangerous voyage. When must you go?"

"Don't look like that, Claire. There's no danger for me! That's not why I took down the Drayton. No, as another poet once said, the most dangerous voyage we undertake in our lives is sailing up the Amazon of love."

She snorted. "You made that up."

"I did not. One of our modern authors; a fellow called Barnes, although he really did say it and never put it to paper, not to my knowledge."

It was impossible not to smile, not to put up her face for more when he kissed her swiftly on the corner of her mouth.

"Claire." He gave a low, almost exultant laugh. "How strange it all is. Do you remember? This is where you stood on the night I came back. I saw the pale shimmer of your dress. A different world."

The street had been dark and deserted except for the two horsemen riding through the snow. Now flambeaux and lanterns carried by an astonishing number of pedestrians, chairs, cabs lit the fronts of the houses; the street was alive with footsteps, shouts, hoofbeat, and the roll of carriage wheels.

"The wind rattled the windowpanes, and there was snow on your shoulders. Yet I was comforted to know that you were not alone and were going somewhere." She turned her head. In the flicker of candles, only the lighter sections were visible in the portrait above the mantelpiece – a flash of eye, a gleam of neckcloth, or the frogging on Justin's uniform. "I went and talked to your portrait."

"And did it reply?"

Thinking back, she said slowly, "I suppose it did, in a way. It told me that it wasn't real, it was a work of art; and no matter how lifelike, you would have changed."

"So I have." There was a long pause. "I got rid of the moustache." Profiting by her position, she dug an elbow into his ribs. He tightened his hold on her.

"That young cockerel had a lot to learn, and although I did learn to do my duty as an officer, I was rather doubtful about my duties in civilian life. That glimpse of you here in the window was the first inkling, the intimation of a possibility, that on returning to the world you stood for I might find someone like you."

"And here we are." She kissed him on the chin, this being the nearest part of his features accessible to her. "But not for long, it seems." With a sigh she added, "Tell me about your visitor."

So he told her about Mr Russ and the power he held at Whitehall; about Sir Henry Wellesley's request for an aide-de-camp; about the great honour it would mean to be attached to the British ambassador at the Spanish court; and about the consensus among the people who mattered that this honour was to be conferred upon him.

"For various reasons," he added. "Sir Henry wants a handsome sprig of nobility to bedazzle the Castilian grandees, Russ is determined to learn more about the situation in Madrid, so I'm afraid with my rank and record I'm the obvious choice."

"If that is so, then of course you must go." Pride and regret mixed heavily in her breast, as though her blood had turned into salad dressing. "King and Country and all that."

"'I could not love thee, love, so much?' I do love you, Claire, d'ye know that?" When she murmured that she did, rather, he shifted his position to look her full in the face. A worried crease had sprung up between his brows.

"You're not angry – or disappointed – that I did not turn him down out of hand?"

"How could I be?" She frowned, puzzled. "He did mention an obstacle, but I didn't understand what he meant."

"I don't know if I'm relieved or disappointed." He gave her a lopsided grin. "Mind you, I haven't consented yet. I was making a case against my going, arguing that a mere captain would not serve their purpose. But Russ had got there before me, and I've been promoted."

"Major Sumners?" She tried out his new title. "But that's marvellous, Justin. Except –" She did not quite know how to phrase her objection without offending him.

He grinned. "They're not quite so blatant, Claire. The promotion holds whether I go or not; it's been backdated to the time when . . . well, to a service for which a majority could be seen as a just reward for an ambitious officer."

"I'm glad of that." But she still did not understand. She regarded him anxiously. "Isn't it your duty to go? How could I be angry?" Nor did she understand the trace of bitterness in his voice when he replied.

"From a military point of view, no, it is not my duty. I sold out, didn't I? From a moral one – well! Has it not occurred to you that you might reasonably expect me to reject any position that takes me away from you, my love, my wife? That Mr Russ meant you when he spoke of an obstacle – a charming obstacle?"

She raised one hand to smooth away the cloud upon his brow. "Doesn't he know," she said, "that our love is simple? That between you and me there are no expectations, no sacrifices, no debts, no rewards?"

He caught her hand and held it against his chest. At her mild tease, his troubled look had deepened. "Don't mock, Claire. I know you have no faith in love, and I don't blame you, but don't mock mine."

"I'm not mocking you, Justin. But I cannot talk seriously about something as serious and great and frightening as your love." She cast down her eyes. "Or mine, for that matter."

She was in his arms, his lips on hers, breathless, crushed, tingling all over. Time and place fell away until loud whistling and some raucous comments from the street brought them apart. But Justin only laughed, and with a wave to the interested onlookers, assured them that love was indeed sweet. More whistling and some booing erupted when he closed the shutters and the window. "Sweet and simple," he repeated, adding with a grin, "and absorbing. Look at us, it's a good thing we were interrupted." He kissed her naked shoulder.

It might be a good thing, and not just in that moment. Surely it was tempting fate to admit, declare, assert, and make love so unrestrainedly? Yet whatever fate might be preparing, she would have loved and known happiness. "I don't care," she heard herself say, rather fiercely.

"What's that?" He did not look up; he was absorbed in her collarbone, his hands wreaking unspeakable havoc in the folds of her dress.

"I don't care," she repeated. "Whatever happens, I will have loved you and been happy."

"*Mi amor.*" He pressed his lips to a piece of skin he had just bared, and she felt the warmth of his breath when he added, "Nothing will happen."

Author's Note

Damn the motto!
Scott, *Letters*

While the epigraphs in this book have been sourced to the best of my abilities, there is one quotation in the text that requires a proper reference.

The "modern author [...] Barnes" is Julian Barnes, who said the memorable words cited in Chapter 18 in an interview he gave on the radio some years ago. Not realizing how they would stick in my memory, I failed to note down the time and date of the broadcast, but I hope he will forgive this rather sloppy reference.

The friends and family who encouraged and supported me while writing this book have all, I believe, received my thanks at various times and in different ways. There is, however, one gratuitous act of kindness I should like to acknowledge specially. Many years ago, I wrote to the British Met Office to inquire about the weather in early 1814. While I do not recall the name of the officer who replied, I still have the pages he photocopied for me from Ian Currie's *Frosts, Freezes and Fairs*, along with tables of average mean temperature and precipitation. It was the information he supplied that set the stage for Claire and Justin's first meeting in Chapter 3 and really got the story going. Thank you.

Reader, allow me to thank you, too! I hope you have enjoyed this book. If you have, please consider rating or reviewing it on the usual channels.

About the Author

Elizabeth (Elsie) Grant grew up in Germany, Yugoslavia, and the United States. After studying languages in Glasgow and Berlin, she went on to work as a translator and proofreader, specializing in contemporary architecture and mediaeval art. She lives in France and Germany with her husband and too many books.

If you would like to know more about the background to *An Independent Heart*, please check out Elsie's blog at www.elsiegrant.blogspot.com. A companion to the book, it provides pictures, music, sources, and historical detail to enjoy alongside.

Lightning Source UK Ltd.
Milton Keynes UK
UKHW010628010322
399389UK00001B/217